Acclaim For Novels
by Roy French

"A creditable and contemporary Canadian terrorist thriller."

- John North, Toronto Star

"The fast-paced action is backed up by painstaking accuracy."

- Mike Beggs, Toronto Star

"201 pages of Damn-the-torpedoes adventure."

- Jim Wilson, Brampton Guardian

"A stunning twist at the end of this gripping novel."

- Des Blackadder, Ballymena Observer

"A compelling narrative."

- L. McGuire, Saskatoon Times

*"Enjoy reading
this book, Richard."
your Dad.
and Aaron.*

Also by Roy French

The Raven Series:
Raven's Honor
Raven's Return
Raven's Revenge (Fall 2004)

The Patrick Kelly Series:
Whispers on the Wind
The Black Rose

For more information please visit:
www.blackrosepublishing.com

DEDICATION

To Joe, Rick, Dave, Andy, Julian, and Les, aka the 'lads.'

"Think where man's glory most begins and ends, and say my glory was I had such friends."

William Butler Yeats

CHAPTER 1

Floater

The girl floated on the tide, bobbing up and down in the detritus from the beach. Tiny fishes darted about in front of her face but although her eyes were open, she did not see them.

Part of the chain wrapped tightly around her legs to hold her at the bottom of the bay had broken away and now, her body bloated with the gasses from decomposition, she floated at the surface like a fisherman's bob. Her long dark hair spread out in a circle on the water, covering her head like an umbrella. Her hands were tied behind her back with a plastic cuff.

She was naked.

At the end of the pier, feet up on a rock, a cup of hot chocolate in one hand and his fishing rod in the other, sat Michael Ryan. It was Saturday afternoon and he was spending it the way he always did, fishing for rock bass off the end of the pier. He had been coming here for as long as he could remember, first as a toddler with his father, then reluctantly as a rebellious teenager, and finally as an adult, delighting in sharing the companionship of his father.

His father had died only a few months earlier, creating a huge void in his life. For several weeks after his father's death he had not come, the memories being too painful to bear, but then he returned, finding a strange solace in sitting in their usual spot. It was as if his father was still there, watching him and laughing at his excitement when he felt a tug on his line.

Over the years they had pulled some strange looking creatures from the bay, and some even stranger objects, some of which still adorned his apartment. Over the years he had watched the ecology of the bay deteriorate due to pollution caused by numerous factories spilling virtually untreated sewage and effluent into the ocean. And still their destruction continued unabated, even though the government watchdogs issued warning after warning to the corporations. And then Greenpeace stepped in and showed that the government was by far a worse offender than private industry. But still nothing was done and the bay suffered.

Ryan had pulled some fish out of the bay recently with the most horrible tumours growing from their bodies. From that moment on he stopped eating what he caught, preferring now to release his catch. He set down his mug of hot chocolate and took a bite from his sandwich. Already the gulls were swooping around, shrieking as they looked for scraps of dead fish or pieces of used bait. Pulling off a piece of bread, he tossed it into the air to see one of the gulls intercept it like a fighter pilot as it arced towards the water.

He felt a tug on his line. A tiny valve opened and spilled adrenaline into his bloodstream, causing his heart to race as it always did on that first hit. He felt another tug and yanked back the rod, hoping to set the hook in whatever was taking his bait. Instantly he felt the familiar jerk as the fish tried to get away, the glass-fiber rod bending in a semi-circle. The strain on the line caused it to hum in the air as winds from the ocean blew against it, causing the thin filament to vibrate.

Whatever it was, it was big. He was experienced enough to tell what size of fish was taking his bait for a merry dance. He loosened the drag on the reel, afraid the line would snap, and instantly the reel buzzed as the line played out. He watched excitedly as the line cut a great arc through the water, droplets of water rippling off it like a thin curtain. And then the line stopped dead in the water.

Ryan cursed under his breath. He was snagged on something. He yanked back on the rod and at the point where the line met the water, something black and hairy broke through the surface.

"Aww fuck," he groaned. "Not another fucking dog!" He had snagged several dead dogs floating in the bay. The first time he had brought the damned thing in to shore so as not to lose his hook, but the stench from the decomposing carcass had made him throw up. From then on he sacrificed the tackle rather than risk another episode like that.

Taking a filleting knife from his tackle box, he was about to cut the line when a wave rolled in from a passing boat and caused the black thing to bob up out of the waves. He shivered when he saw the white face, the black hair hanging down over it like a piece of seaweed.

"Oh Jesus, no," he cried, tossing the knife to one side and pulling gently on the line as he reeled it in. He looked around and could see a teenager coming down the pier on rollerblades.

"Hey, you. Over here," he cried, waving wildly as the young man skated over to where he was standing.

"What's up man?" said the youth, pulling a set of earphones from his ears.

"There's a body in the water," said Ryan. "I'm snagged on it. Go and call the police and I'll try to bring it into shore."

"Cool man," said the youth, looking out into the waves.

"Quickly," hissed Ryan, "I may not be able to hold it with this light line."

"No problem, man," said the youth casually and took off his backpack. He put his hand inside and pulled out a cell-phone. He dialed 911, asked to speak to the police, and gave directions to the pier before slipping the phone back inside the backpack.

"They'll be here in a few minutes," he said, and hunkered down on the pier beside Ryan to watch. It took only a few moments before the piercing wail of sirens filled the air and three squad cars screeched to a halt at the end of the pier.

A few miles to the north of the pier, Daniel Riordan strapped a paramotor unit to his back and fastened the velcro straps around his chest and legs, ensuring the unit had no room to move. Looking over to where his friend, Allan Brown, was tightening his unit, he grinned and grasped the lines leading to his drive chute.

With a gentle tug, air flowed into the brightly coloured silk rectangle making it billow and float into the air with a soft fluttering sound. The wind was strong enough that Riordan had to lean back against the heavy drag. He reached to his side and pressed the starter motor for the propulsion unit. He felt the kick in his shoulders as the tiny gas engine turned over and then the thrust as the propeller started to push him forward. Running across the open ground he was soon airborne, gunning the engine to push him up into the clear blue sky.

It was a beautiful clear day in the tiny village and people stopped to watch as Riordan and Brown glided quietly across the sky, their engines making no more sound than that of an angry bee.

Behind them, Riordan's wife Nancy put her hand across her brow to shield the sun from her eyes and watched the two men soar out over the ocean.

"They're like two overgrown children," she commented to the woman sitting on the grass, struggling with a wine opener. Allan Brown's girlfriend of six months, a Homicide Detective named Susan Delgado and a big hit with the Riordan's, cursed as the opener slipped out with only half the cork.

"Fuck," she snorted, and then grimaced, realizing what she had said. "Oops!"

"Quite alright," said Nancy. "I do it all the time. You might have to push the cork into the bottle with a knife. Oh, and just half a glass for me please, and top it up with soda water. I have to watch my intake." Nancy watched the lady detective fiddle with the bottle, taking time to look at the high cheekbones, the proud heritage of her Spanish father and the dark shining hair she allegedly took from her mother's side of the family. Susan was a truly beautiful woman, and could easily have graced the pages of a fashion magazine instead of chasing murderers and rapists. Nancy knew that she constantly struggled with the fact that people, especially in the police business, could not get past the looks.

Susan managed to get the cork into the bottle and poured two glasses, one of which she topped up with Perrier and gave it to Nancy, who had seated herself awkwardly on one corner of the blanket.

"How long have you known Allan?" asked Susan, who seemed anxious to get some more information on her prospective beau. Nancy smiled.

"About five years now," she replied. "He and Daniel apparently knew each other before they moved to Vancouver, met up again here, and have been inseparable since. Daniel always says that a friend is someone who will help you move, and a true friend is someone who will help you move a body. Allan fits the latter case."

Susan nodded. "I heard all about Daniel the first time Allan and I went out on a date. I learned more about Daniel than I did about Allan."

"That surprises me," said Nancy, sipping her wine. She picked a small piece of cork off her tongue and tossed it away. "Daniel is pretty close-mouthed about his past, so there's a lot I don't know. It comes out in dribs and drabs but he's a guarded character. He's like a puzzle with several of the pieces missing, and I don't think I will ever find them."

"How are things going with the baby?" asked Susan, when she saw Nancy unconsciously rubbing her swollen stomach.

"Great. I'm seven months now and the twins are doing as well as the doctor expected. Everything is going perfectly at the moment."

"I don't know how you can stand the suspense; not knowing the sexes I mean," said Susan, raising her glass to her lips.

Nancy laughed aloud. "That's all Daniel's doing. He wants to wait and see for himself, right there in the delivery room. Honest to God, the way he acts sometimes you'd think he was the first person on this earth ever to have a child."

"That's nice," commented Susan.

"To be perfectly honest, it's a bit of a pain," snorted Nancy half-heartedly. "I don't know what colours to decorate the nursery, or what sort of clothes to buy, or any of that stuff. But we've been buying two of everything. I..." A loud beeping noise interrupted the conversation. Susan turned to her handbag and took out a pager which was beeping wildly, a tiny red light on the side flashing on and off like a strobe. She pressed the button and looked at the number on the LED screen, a frown crossing her face as she recognized the digits.

A long sigh escaped her lips as she reached into her handbag and took out a cell-phone. She keyed the number in and said "Hi, it's Susan. What's up?"

Nancy watched as she nodded her head a few times and then said, "Give me the address." Susan rummaged in her bag again and took out a tiny notebook and a pen. She stuck the pen in her mouth and pulled off the top, then spat it out on the ground. "Go ahead," she said, and proceeded to scribble notes on the page. "It'll take me about twenty minutes to get there," she said, and closed the phone.

She looked over to Nancy, a sorrowful expression on her face. "I've got to go," she said. "My partner said he wouldn't bother me unless it was an emergency, and it appears we have an emergency, another floater. I'll take Allan's car and perhaps he can get a ride back with you. Tell him I'll call as soon as possible.

"I'm really sorry about this."

Nancy said, "It's alright. I'm an ER nurse–I know what it's like being on call all the time. You go on and I'll talk to you soon."

Susan smiled and said, "Thanks." She threw all the stuff back in her handbag, leaned across and kissed Nancy on the cheek, and ran off to the car.

Brian Dymond, Susan's partner, was standing talking to two uniformed patrolmen when Susan pulled up at the end of the pier in Allan Brown's green Porsche 944. Yellow warning tape, strung across the entrance to the pier, flapped in the wind as more and more people congregated there to see what was going on. In the distance she could see a news truck making its way slowly along the street, hampered by heavy traffic as motorists driving past slowed and tried to see what was going on.

As she stepped out he whistled and said, "Going up in the world, are we?" and received her index finger in reply. "I'm sorry to interrupt your day off," he said, shaking his head sadly, "but we found another one."

Her shoulders slumped as he spoke, knowing that there was yet another young girl lying dead at the end of the pier. If the pattern was true to form, she would be about fourteen or fifteen years old, possibly a runaway, and killed in some sadistic fashion.

There had been three of them prior to this one, all around the same age, all as yet unidentified despite exhaustive attempts to do so. That was the link, the fragile bond that tied them together. The method of death, however, was different in each case. One had been pummeled to death, another had had her throat cut, and the third had been bludgeoned by a blunt instrument, possibly a baseball bat as some wooden splinters had been found in what remained of the girl's teeth and gums. There was another victim, a headless corpse found in another county, and they were trying to determine if she fit the profile as well.

All had been sexually assaulted; traces of semen had been found in all orifices. DNA testing on the samples was still in progress so it was not yet possible to ascertain if the same person was responsible for the killings.

"Where is she?" she asked.

Dymond turned and looked out across the bay. "The marine unit are bringing her body in to the end of the pier because they felt they might cause more damage if they tried to get her out across the rocks. Let's go down." She nodded.

"Are you okay?" he asked, his voice full of concern. They had been partners in homicide for almost five years, and had developed a bond stronger than that of most marriages. At thirty-six years of age, he was in great shape and extremely handsome, an absolute rogue with the ladies. With his chiseled jaw, the blue eyes, longish, brown hair and that mischievous twinkle, there was no shortage of women eager to drag him off to bed. At one point she had almost considered it, but put those feelings away as they would only have jeopardized both careers and a wonderful working relationship.

He touched her elbow as they walked. "I'm alright," she replied. "It's just that we don't seem to be making any progress on catching this guy, and you and I know he's going to do this again and again until we get him."

Dymond shrugged his shoulders, a gesture of helplessness. "I know, I know. But we'll get him. Sooner or later, preferably sooner, he'll make a mistake and we'll have him. The odds are in our favour."

"You're right," she admitted. "I know that too, but the emotional side of me is having a hard time with this. They're so young! We were out with Daniel and Nancy this afternoon, and she's about seven months pregnant with twins. These poor kids have been abandoned for whatever reason. It makes me sad when I think about that."

"Is that the Daniel I met in the bar with you and Allan one night; the guy with the Irish accent and all those stories?"

She smiled. "That's Daniel all right. Never lost for a story."

"And how are you and Allan getting on? Correct me if I'm wrong but it seems like you two have been together for more than six months. That's something of a record."

"We're getting along famously," she replied. "We've actually talked about..."

"No, no, don't say it," he gasped, putting his hands to his face in mock horror. "I don't want to hear those words."

"Fuck off," she replied testily. "Yes, we've been talking about moving in together. He's the only man I've ever met who can accept what I do for a living and not feel threatened by it. You've met him so you know what he's like."

"I was only joking," he replied. "And I'm delighted for you. I wish I could find someone as understanding as that."

"If you could keep your dick in your pants for long enough you just might."

"Ouch," he grimaced. "That hurt. Never mind that it's true, it still hurt."

"Boo hoo," she laughed, the dark mood evaporating as the professional investigator's instincts took over.

The marine unit's Gemini inflatable was pulling into the pier when they reached the end. Two divers, in full scuba gear, were sitting beside a black tarpaulin. Two bare feet wrapped in a length of heavy, black chain protruded from under the tarp.

"Who are those two at the end of the pier beside the guys from the coroner's office?" she asked.

"That's the fisherman who snagged the body, and the roller-blader who made the 911 call. The uniforms should have taken their statements by now."

"Did you speak to them?" she asked.

"Just briefly. They didn't have much to say. We've got their names and addresses if we need to talk to them again."

"Good. Get rid of them then and encourage them not to speak to the media. They've no need to see the body." Dymond walked over to speak to the witnesses as Susan, gritting her teeth, made her way over to where the divers were lifting the body. The men raised the body gently and laid it on the gurney from the coroner's wagon. A body bag had been opened and laid flat on the gurney so that when the forensics photographer had finished the bag could be zipped up to preserve some dignity for the dead girl. At the moment, however, she lay exposed for all the world to see.

Both detectives pulled on rubber gloves, snapping them in place and began a careful, inch by inch examination of the body. When they finished, the photographer stepped in to do his piece. The man knew his stuff, but Susan directed him to take specific shots of unusual marks on the body, marks an untrained eye might have missed. She knew they might be irrelevant to the case, but anything at all could be a clue, and clues were sadly lacking so far. It took only a few minutes and then she instructed the coroner's assistants to take the girl to the morgue. The forensic pathologist had already been called, as this autopsy was to take priority over any of his existing cases.

"I'll go with her," offered Dymond, knowing that protocol demanded someone accompany the body to preserve the chain of evidence.

"Thanks," she said, peeling off the gloves and tossing them in a trash can. "I'll meet you at the morgue." As the gurney was being wheeled down the wooden boardwalk, she caught up with him. "Can you have one of the guys take some video of the people at the end of the pier? I know it's a long shot but it might be useful. We can compare it to the others."

"Teaching your grandmother to suck eggs, are we? Already thought of it," he said, smiling to take the sting out of the rebuke.

Dymond was sitting waiting for her on a bench outside the morgue, coffee in hand and another styrofoam cup beside him. Dymond said, "He's just started the prelim. I told him to go ahead and we'd join him. Are you sure you're up to this? I can do it on my own if you like."

She took a long sip of the coffee, a deep breath and said, "No, I'm not alright, but I want to see this through." She pulled on a pair of green cloth shoe-covers and a facemask before pushing open the doors of the autopsy room and walking through into the harsh, artificial light. Immediately, the strong, cloying antiseptic scent of the place filled her nostrils until she could hardly breathe. And there was something else. The smell of death was heavy in the air, despite the overwhelming odour of the cleansing agent.

The haunting strains of classical music filled the room. There were five stainless steel trays in the room, all with tiny microphones suspended above them. Only one of the trays was in use. A tall, cadaverous man hovered over the body like a vulture about to feast on a carcass. It was Doctor Michael Graham, better known as the ghoul.

Periodically he would lift his head up from his inspection and speak into the voice-activated microphone.

Despite his macabre appearance, he was recognized as the best forensic pathologist in the province and had performed the autopsies on the other girls. At the sound of footfalls he turned around and raised his nose into the air as if he had just smelled something horrible. He was looking to see who it was through the tiny specs perched on the end of his nose.

"Ah, detectives. Glad you could join me. I take it you think this victim is connected to the others."

Susan nodded. "The age and the marks on the body would lead me to think that. Do you have any idea how she died?"

"There's no water in her lungs so she was dead when she went in the water. And given the temperature of the water and the state of decomposition she was only there a couple of days at my estimate. I'd say there were two separate coils of chain keeping her submerged, and one of them for whatever reason broke away or fell away allowing her to float to the surface. It's a bit of a fluke that she's here at all.

"Her neck is broken and I think that's what killed her. I'd say someone took her head in his hands and gave it a quick twist, like they do in the movies. She died quickly, if that's the case. However, what she must have suffered up until that point is beyond anything I have ever seen.

"I won't know the cause of death for sure until I get the tox report back. I've taken swabs from her mouth,

vagina, and anus and I'll have them tested for the presence
of semen. However, she was badly beaten prior to death.
Two ribs are cracked, on the right side; third and fourth.
From the lividity marks, she was lying on her back after
death for a while, and there are extensive burns all over her
body, especially around her nipples and labia. She was
tortured, looks like... or you're dealing with one very sick
person." He paused to let the details sink in. Dymond was
scribbling furiously in his notebook.

The coroner continued, "However, there doesn't seem
to be a pattern compared to the other girls, which sort of
refutes the serial killer premise. Given what I have read,
and from the FBI people I talked to, these serial killers
follow a very rigid pattern, often using the same weapon
over and over again until they are caught. None of the other
victims had a broken neck."

"Fuck," Susan snorted. "I don't care what it looks like.
My gut tells me these are all linked somehow. So maybe
we're not looking for one guy; maybe there's more than
one serial killer out there."

The doctor had turned back to the body and continued
his examination. "There's one other thing you should
know," he said, peering into the girl's insides that he had
exposed earlier. "From the marks on her uterus, this kid
had an abortion recently. Within say a month or so. That
might help you determine who she is."

Brian Dymond leaned over and looked at the burn
marks down the inside of her legs. "Are those bruises on

the inside of her thighs?" he asked, pointing to some greenish black discolorations.

The doctor nodded. "Probably. It's hard to tell for sure, but they probably are."

"Any idea of how she might have got them, Doctor?" asked Susan. The man hesitated for a moment, thinking how to frame his response.

"From the position of the bruises I'd say the person who did this was holding up her legs while he had intercourse with her."

A frown crossed Susan's brow. "But..." A shiver ran down her spine and she felt the bile rise in her throat. The doctor nodded, seeing she had come to the same conclusion as him.

She said, her voice no more than a whisper, "He had sex with her after she was dead. That's why he was holding up her legs. My sweet Jesus," she gasped, one hand coming up to cover her eyes. She shook her head slowly from side to side. It took a long moment before she raised her head again, but when she did the mask was back in place. "We've got to get this guy, and quickly," she said. "Please fax me over the tox reports as soon as you get them. And if you find anything else..."

"You'll be the first to know," interrupted the doctor, and went back to his gruesome task.

CHAPTER 2

Virus

Daniel Riordan swept the paramotor low in across the ocean, shrieking like a banshee and barely skimming the waves as Allan Brown followed at a more prudent altitude, shaking his head at the cavalier attitude of his friend. But that was Daniel for you, thought Brown, always pushing the limits with a zest for life unmatched in anyone else he had ever known.

"It's me Celtic soul, you understand," Riordan would say in that soft Irish accent which never failed to have a profound effect on the ladies. The fact that Riordan was handsome in a rugged kind of way, so Susan had commented, didn't hurt either.

Nearing the shore, Riordan pulled back on the guide ropes and the chute billowed and climbed again into the clear blue sky. Allan Brown was already making his descent into the clearing where Nancy was waiting for them, their food spread out on a picnic table with bottles of red wine opened and breathing the fresh summer air.

Riordan noticed the Porsche was missing as he landed and assumed that Susan had gone to fetch something that Allan had forgotten to pack, as usual. He landed gently on the soft green grass, turned off the engine and unstrapped the motor unit before beginning to fold up his parachute. When he had finished, he stretched the ache out of his arms and carried the unit over to the back of his Range Rover and stowed it away.

When Brown carried over his unit to put it away, Riordan said, "So what did you forget this time, you useless bastard?"

Brown glared at him, his expression serious, and Riordan immediately knew something was wrong. "What's up?" Riordan asked.

Brown replied, "Susan got called away on an emergency. You remember this case she's been working on?"

"The dead girls?"

"Yes, that one. Seems like they've found another body floating in the bay."

"Dear God," said Riordan, grimacing. "What a fucking job. It must be pretty hard on her, dealing with this sort of case." Brown stowed his parachute and leaned on the back of the tailgate.

"It certainly is taking its toll on all the detectives involved, especially Sue. They just don't have any clues or leads to go on at the moment, and the pressure on them is intense. You know what things are like in our business with deadlines and such, but it pales in comparison to what they have to deal with." Riordan reached out and grasped his friend's arm.

"Come on," Riordan said. "There's a ton of food over there and plenty of wine. Nancy can only have one glass, so as we don't have to drive we might as well make a serious dent in it."

"Now there's a thought," grinned Brown. "Not an original one, but a thought none the less!"

"Fuck off," replied Riordan, heading over to the picnic table.

In the tiny room the man shivered, not so much from the chill of the air-conditioned computer room as from the action he'd just taken. However, there was no way to retract the e-mail message he had just sent off into the ether. Peter Dickson was a computer genius, a hacker by choice, a pedophile by nature, or so he claimed, and a total recluse. In his early teens he had had a devastating case of acne that made him the laughing stock of his classmates, who cruelly nicknamed him 'black-head.' The girls in his class shunned him like the plague, and so he refused to mix with any of his classmates, preferring instead to skulk away to the library and lose himself in a good book.

At twenty-two years of age, he had already spent five in prison for sodomising young boys whom he was supposed to be baby-sitting. He had manipulated his wards with money and gifts, and then threats of violence and exposure of the Polaroid's he had taken of their sex acts. In jail, he had been assigned to work in the prison library and had spent all his free time on the library's computer, learning how to hack into highly secure areas, and establishing his reputation among the hacker sub-culture on the net. The internet also provided an escape for him during his incarceration, as he could talk to young people on the web, connecting to newsgroups for pedophiles or chickenhawks, as they were commonly known.

When he got out of prison, reformed, or so the prison psychiatrist thought, he went straight back to his old activities, this time being careful not to get caught. A second conviction he knew would bring a long, long sentence. One day, when he was staking out a video arcade in a shopping center looking for a prospective victim, a huge black man, with a gold earring the size of a hubcap, grabbed him by the arm and ushered him out of the mall and into the back of a waiting limousine.

Sitting facing Dickson was a powerfully built man in his early forties, with a well-trimmed black beard and long, dark hair, slicked back and tied in a ponytail. The man wore a black silk shirt with a round collar, black cotton trousers, and shiny black cowboy boots with silver accents. Both hands rested on the handle of a cane, whose brass head was molded in the shape of a lion. A heavy gold bracelet hung around one wrist, and there was a diamond stud in his left ear lobe. Dickson struggled to remember the significance of the ear. Was it the left ear meant you were gay? Or was it the right?

The impression he got however was exactly the opposite. An invisible aura of menace exuded from the man, who was staring at him like he was a butterfly in one of those collection boxes with the large pins stuck through their bodies. The car moved off smoothly, and Dickson shrank back into the leather seat.

He had a bad feeling about this. "What do you want with me?" he asked, his voice quavering.

"You've been up to your old tricks again, Peter," said the man, his voice deep and resonant, like that of a radio announcer.

"I..." The man raised one hand to cut him off.

"Don't bother denying it, you little worm. I have photographs, video, and taped records of your voice. As I recall, the last little boy's name was Steven. Ten years old and you gave him one hundred dollars to play the video games if he would suck you off in the mall washroom."

"But how?"

"I've been watching you on the internet. The police computer crime unit has as well, so they'll be paying you a visit in the very near future. And if some anonymous citizen was to mail them these tapes and photographs you'll be going away for a very, very long time." Dickson shivered.

"So why am I here?" he asked.

"I need someone with your computer skills to assist me in a little venture I have going. You will be well paid for your services, and I will do what I can to allow you to indulge your particular deviancy. All I ask in return is your loyalty. What you will see and witness will not be a problem for you, as I have carefully scrutinized your final psychological evaluation."

Dickson nodded. "No problem, no problem at all."

Up until a couple of weeks ago it hadn't been a problem. As it transpired, the man called Slade owned a sprawling complex on a tiny island just off the Vancouver coast, perfectly isolated for his purposes. Dickson had his own room and all the computer equipment he had ever dreamed of, money no object, and there was an endless supply of kiddy-porn tapes to keep him occupied. Living on the island was a bit of a drag, but there were enough distractions to keep him occupied. What Slade wanted him to do was create CD-ROM disks from a set of videotapes, taken from cameras positioned at different angles in the rooms in the house.

The videos depicted young teenage girls being raped, beaten, and tortured by a variety of Slade's 'clients'. The master CD-ROM had these men as they appeared in the videos, usually naked, or partially dressed as they acted out their fantasies. This disk was given to the client as a memento. Dickson made another ten copies which Slade then sold on the black market for enormous sums of money, further lining his pockets, but each of these had the face edited out, so there was no way to identify the men.

He had no problem doing the conversion, or dealing with the contents of the videos; they were not his particular type of kink but each to his own, he thought. The men probably paid a fortune to Slade for the opportunity. And often he would see the same girls with different clients.

The equipment he used was top-of-the-line: a Compaq Pentium Four loaded to the gills with RAM; a 100 gigabyte hard disk; assorted video-drivers, and a video-capture board. A 21-inch, flat screen monitor completed the system. A high-speed, color graphics printer sat off to one side, used for processing stills from the videotapes. There was another line to a modem pool which he did not have access to, but knew was located somewhere in Slade's private area.

However, the most recent batch of tapes he got showed a client raping one of the girls, which was pretty much standard fare, but then he tied her to a hook in the ceiling and proceeded to beat her to a pulp with a baseball bat. The ferocity of the attack had left blood and brains scattered all over the room, some even splashed on one of the lenses. The muffled crump of the bat against soft flesh was nauseating, but after the first rib cracked loudly, Dickson turned the sound down.

He sat back in his chair, picking at a large, pus-filled zit on his face, and watched the client, a man of middle-eastern origin, masturbate over the dead girl's face. His heart pounded and he found he could barely breathe; he had just witnessed a murder, and by virtue of what he was doing, he was now an accomplice. Having been in prison and finding himself the 'property' of a large oriental gangster, he had no desire to return, and not for the stretch accorded to someone involved in a murder.

Still, despite his reservations, he knew that Slade wanted the tapes converted, so he produced them as quickly as possible. Slade watched him like a hawk when he handed over the finished product, looking for some hint of a problem, but he managed to get away with it.

The next set of tapes involved an oriental man with a ceremonial sword, a katana. It was not the first time Dickson had seen the man–he had prepared a CD-ROM already for him–but this time the oriental had gone completely berserk, decapitating the girl when he had finished with her. As her head spun off into a corner of the room, her long black tresses whirling like a matador's cape, the man impaled her headless body on the blade as her blood fountained into the air and covered him like a red mantle.

Dickson threw up into his wastebasket at the sight of all the blood, his eyes darting over to the pile of tapes waiting to be processed. God only knew what was on those. When he lifted his head from the reeking bin, the oriental was licking the girl's blood from his lips. Dickson threw up again and again until his stomach was empty. With the thought of life imprisonment hanging over him, he made a quick decision, set the bin to one side and logged on to the Internet, reviewing all the news clippings about the bodies which had been found recently in the area.

Reading quickly, he noted the names of the two detectives whose quotes appeared in most of the articles. He took the first name, Susan Delgado, and looked it up in the telephone directory. There was only one Delgado listed, but that was a doctor–she must have an unlisted number, he thought, which would make sense given her profession. He then dialed into one of the back doors to his Internet service provider to see if she had an account on the internet. There was no entry for Delgado, so he quickly logged off and signed on to another service, logging in as the system administrator, and checked the directory. There were only a few providers in the area, and he had surreptitious access to each of them.

He smiled, his lips pulled back over his yellowing teeth when he saw her name listed in the directory: sdelgado@infomarch.com. He wrote down her address and phone number and signed off the system. Picking up his cell-phone, he quickly dialed her number, surprised when she answered the phone.

Susan Delgado brushed her hair back over her ear, munched on a carrot stick, checked her cookbook and continued stirring the sauce she had just made. Dipping the wooden spoon into the brownish liquid, she extracted some of the sauce and sipped tentatively at the hot liquid. She smacked her lips a few times then said, "Needs some more bite," and took the jar of cumin back down out of the spice rack. Sprinkling some more of the spice into the pot, she stirred it gently and turned up the gas to reduce the sauce. It was perfect now. She let it simmer and quickly diced the cubes of chicken she had pre-cooked in the microwave and scraped them into the pan.

As she stirred, a soft smile crossed her lips as she thought of the evening she had planned for them both. Allan was going to be pleased. He loved curries, especially her home-made variety, and then there was the strawberry-rhubarb pie, clotted Devon cream and the two bottles of Mumm's Cuvee Napa champagne chilling in the freezer.

She loved to cook and had taken several night courses at the local college to enhance her skills. It was one of the ways she could relax after the rigors of her job, especially after a day like today. Cooking was a blessed anathema to the death and violence that were the everyday occurrences she faced in her chosen vocation.

And Allan, bless him, was such a good subject. He loved to eat, even when she experimented on him, and never complained when some of the dishes did not exactly turn out as planned. She was in the process of getting the rice ready when the phone rang. She looked quickly at the display that said 'unknown caller', frowned and picked up the receiver. Hers was an unlisted number, and only a few close friends and co-workers had her number. It was probably one of those sequential dialing units, she thought, wanting to sell her new insurance or wanting to know if she would consider selling her house.

"Hello," she said, tentatively.

"Is this Susan Delgado? Detective Susan Delgado?" She cursed under her breath. She didn't recognize the voice but it was probably some fucking reporter who had gotten her number and wanted information about the cases.

"Who's asking?" she said brusquely, anger rising in her voice. "And how did you get this number?"

"My name isn't important right now, and getting your number wasn't hard either. I don't have much time. You're working on the killings of those girls?" It was a question. She was about to hang up the phone with a curt "fuck off", when some inner sense told her this might be important.

"I am," she replied. "What about it?"

"I have some information for you. I'm in over my head and I'll need protection if I help you; a lot of protection. We'll trade." She detected a glimmer of fear in the voice, a minuscule tremor that came and went in a heartbeat.

"I'll decide on that. Now tell me what you have."

"Check your E-mail. I've extracted a bunch of binaries for you to look at. I'll call back when I get another chance. It may not be for a few days."

Click.

She hung up the phone and immediately ran over to her computer. The system was already on as she had been making some notes, so she activated the internet icon and waited while the system dialed the number and connected to her local service provider. When the 'LOGIN COMPLETE' message appeared she clicked on the icon for e-mail and waited for the password prompt. A window appeared in the middle of the screen prompting for a password. She entered her mother's maiden name and the system went off and logged into the mail server.

A message 'receiving message 1 of 1' appeared on the screen and immediately asked what drive the file should be written to. She selected 'C:' and clicked on the process button. The HDD light on the front of the PC came on as the mail message was downloaded to her hard drive. When it was complete, she logged out of the internet, shut down Windows, and keyed in the file name she had downloaded.

Immediately the screen went black and a detailed graphic image of a young girl, dressed in leather S&M gear, appeared. The image vanished to be replaced with a close-up of the girl's face. Susan scrutinized the face carefully but it was not one of the girls who had been murdered. The screen went blank and another image appeared. It showed a man wearing a hood and nothing else, with a naked teenage girl kneeling in front of him. Her hands were bound, his cock was in her mouth and both his hands were clasped against the side of her head. His head was thrown back as if he were at the point of orgasm.

The next shot showed the girl's face, semen trickling out of her mouth. Susan gasped, not at the image, but at the fact it was the first girl they had found dead. The screen went blank and another image appeared. Her mouth went dry. It was picture of a man dressed as a Samurai, a bloody katana in one hand and a young girl's head in the other. He had a fistful of long dark hair and was grinning at the camera as he held the bloody trophy aloft.

The screen vanished.

A mocking message, "Want to make a deal now?" appeared and then the message started to disintegrate before her eyes. The screen went blank and returned to the C: prompt. Heart beating like a jackhammer, she re-keyed the name of the file again to have a look at the images again but nothing appeared. When she checked the file characteristics it said the file was empty. "Bastard," she hissed. She realized he must have attached a virus to the end to the file to destroy the evidence once she had seen the images. At least now she knew how he had found her number. There were not too many people skilled enough to put a graphics show together like the one she had just witnessed. Furious with herself, she slammed the side of the computer with her fist and leaned back in her chair to think.

At least now they had a lead, a break at last, however tenuous it might be. Now all she had to do was have the guy call back. A burning smell reached her nostrils and she immediately leapt out the chair and ran to the kitchen where the rice was smoking, burned to the bottom of the pot.

"Goddammit," she yelled, grabbing the pot and throwing it in the sink. It hissed for a few seconds when she turned the cold water on and sprayed the pot to take away the smell. Wincing at the pungent odor, she ran through the house throwing open all the windows. To add insult to injury, the smoke detector went off, the high-pitched whine ceasing only when she ripped the unit off the ceiling.

The man called Slade waited for the modems to hiss and squawk at each other, performing their handshake process before clicking on the Eudora icon to get into his e-mail. He watched the bar flash across the screen, indicating the status of each of the three messages he was receiving, then the screen disappeared briefly before returning with contents of his in-box.

The messages were from three of his fifty clients, each requesting a few days at his 'spa', at the usual fee which would be deposited upon acknowledgement of their request in his numbered account in the Cayman Islands. Pulling up the client master files, he looked to see the date of their last visit; he had one rule–only two visits per year. They were all okay so he switched to a different database and checked to see how many girls were currently at the house. There were four, and he quickly matched the clients' requirements for size, age, and ethnic origin against the girls available. He found matches, and so quickly responded to each of the e-mail messages that they should plan their trips for the following week.

That now depleted his stock, as he referred to the runaways, so there was now another set of calls to be made. Picking up his cellular phone, he dialed the first of five numbers he would call; he had one contact in each major city who would supply him with street kids–runaways who were difficult to trace, and who would rarely be missed.

Ten minutes later he had finished. Within the week there would be another five girls at the house, locked away for the fun of his future 'guests'. And also within the week,

his bank account would have been inflated by another three
million dollars, one from each of the clients.

Business now complete, he walked over to his
sideboard, poured himself a large shot of gin and tonic,
skewered an olive, and dipped it into the glass. Sipping at
the glorious liquid, he switched on his hi-fi system and
inserted a CD of the Three Tenors in concert. Immediately
the room was filled with sound, and he went and sat down
on a long black leather couch in front of the entertainment
system. Picking up a control unit from the chrome and
glass coffee-table, he switched on the 40-inch television,
and pressed 'play' for the VCR.

Instantly, the huge screen was filled with multiple
images of a young girl, kneeling on the floor of one of his
rooms, hands bound behind her back, and a black mask
over her eyes. She was naked, and the cameras zoomed in
on the reddish, purple bite marks on her breasts and arms.
There were five cameras positioned in the room, one in
each corner and one directly over the bed.

The music soared in his heart, filling him with a
strange surreal calm and he took a long sip of his drink, his
chest heaving as his breathing came in short pants. This
was his favorite video, and he knew it almost frame by
frame. He moistened his lips and watched as the oriental
came back into the room, dressed in a white Gi and
carrying an unsheathed sword by his side, the black
lacquered handle gleaming in the light. The video now
switched to slow motion. The oriental strode over to one
side of the girl, who trembled at the footsteps, her head

turning towards the sound and her body shaking gently as a tear ran from under the mask.

Her body jerked slightly when the man reached out with the blade and touched the tip of her chin, forcing her head upwards. When her throat was totally exposed, he moved the blade away, took the pommel in both hands and swung the sword in a great arc down and around, the finely-honed steel severing her head in one clean cut. The camera zoomed in on his face, blood lust there in the bright eyes, his teeth bared in a feral growl as the head spun away into the corner of the room.

Slade groaned aloud, rubbing his hands into his groin, touching the tiny nub of flesh he found there, and angrily hurled the glass across the room, tears filling his eyes at the image that flashed through his mind.

He had been stationed in Saigon, just prior to the Tet offensive, as a Lieutenant in the Criminal Investigation Division, one of the most despised outfits in the U.S. Army. The duty was not a problem for him; he was as tough as any of the soldiers he found himself arresting, and besides they were almost always drunk or stoned, which made the collar simple.

While drinking in an off-duty bar one evening, he was approached by the most beautiful oriental girl he had ever seen. Every head in the place turned when she walked across the room and sat beside him, ordering drinks for them both. Her English was excellent, and after a few drinks they went back to her home, a tiny well-kept apartment overlooking the foul-smelling Yankse River. She undressed him by the light of one candle, then disrobed herself slowly, allowing him to savor the contours of her body in the flickering light. By the time she finished, he had created a tent in the thin sheet, his erection so hard that it hurt.

She pushed him back on the bed, took his proud member in her tiny hand and ran her tongue around the tip, licking and sucking on the head. Raising himself on his elbows, he watched for several minutes as she continued the motion, bringing him to the brink of orgasm several times then drawing him back when she sensed he was about to let go. When he could stand it no longer, feeling himself again at the point of release, he grasped the back of her head in both hands and with a mighty thrust erupted into her mouth again and again, his back arching off the bed with the power of his orgasm.

Suddenly, his groin was on fire and he felt a momentary sharp pain, and warmth trickling down his legs. He opened his eyes to see her standing at the bottom of the bed, a wicked looking knife in one hand and his cock dangling out of her mouth like an unlit stogie. Blood pulsed out of his torn body in great gouts and he grabbed at his clothes, padding them quickly between his legs. Spots danced in front of his eyes.

She spat his severed member on to the floor, then hawked up a mouthful of bloody phlegm and spat at him, ranting in rapid-fire Vietnamese as she pulled on her clothes. Feeling himself weaken, he pressed the other hand against the wadding and felt something hard and lumpy. He was losing blood rapidly, his fingers wet and sticky from the thick, viscous liquid. He grasped the end of his service pistol, a Colt P45, which he had slipped under one of the pillows and fired through the sheets. The first round hit her in the arm, spinning her around, but the next two hit her high in the back, erupting through her chest and showering the other side of the room with blood and gore.

Neighbors heard the shots and called the police, who arrived moments later to find him on the verge of death. Sometimes he wished he had died, but the doctors nursed him back to health, apologizing for the fact that they could not re-attach his severed penis.

He received an honorable discharge from the army, but instead of returning home, he remained in the dank and dirty streets of Saigon, acting as bouncer in the clubs which were once his territory. He studied Akido and worked as an enforcer for one of the gangs, then moved into the drug business prior to the fall of Saigon. His reputation for being ruthless was unparalleled, his empire was growing, and so he headed for Japan, falling easily into the underworld because of his extensive connections. It was there, where life was cheap, that he discovered the clubs frequented by men from all parts of the globe, who would pay enormous sums of money to physically and sexually abuse young girls and boys.

He tired of the Tokyo scene, and decided to make the move back to America to set up his own operation using the contacts he had established. The scheme turned out to be more profitable than he could ever have imagined, the operation grossing at least fifty million dollars a year, sometimes more depending on the appetites of his clients.

Then there was the market for the ten CD-ROM's he produced from each client visit. These he sold on the black market, to dealers whom he trusted. They had been personally vetted by him, and usually the initial visit by Slade and his two Yakusa bodyguards was sufficient to make any dealers think twice about crossing him. Besides, being greedy men, they each received an enormous cut of the profits, which they would be reluctant to lose.

Slade turned off the screen, rubbed his eyes and got up. He was about to switch off his computer when the image of a burning flame appeared in the middle of the screen. A frown crossed his brow. He moved the mouse arrow to the flame and clicked the button, wondering what could possibly have activated the warning image as the hourglass appeared on the middle of the screen.

The screen went blank for a moment, and reappeared with a copy of a message which had been sent out through the internet. As a precaution, Slade had had a copy of every message leaving or arriving the island loaded into a database which only he could access. Periodically a special program he had created would scan for messages, looking for specific keywords or phrases. He looked at the destination name, sdelgado, which meant nothing to him, then clicked on the Icon to view the contents. He saw there was a file attached to the message, and immediately loaded it on to his hard drive, went into the file manager and clicked on the file name. The screen blanked for a moment and then the images of the girls appeared. He watched the slide show all the way through, and when the final message 'Want to make a deal now?' appeared, Slade slammed his fist against the side of the terminal. "Bastard, fucking little weasel."

He jammed his finger on the speed dial for his phone and when the bodyguard answered, he said, "My office. Now!" The bodyguard, a well-built oriental with long black hair tied in a ponytail, arrived a few moments later, his breathing slightly labored.

"What's up?" the man asked, his English only slightly accented.

Slade spat, "That bastard Dickson has contacted the authorities about our operation. Seems he might have developed a scruple or two. Bring him to the dojo."

The guard bowed slightly and left the room.

Using the back stairs, Slade went down two flights to the basement level where he had built an accurate representation of a dojo, with bamboo walls, rice-paper screens adorned with colorful, elegant murals, and a tiny shrine at one end. He went quickly to the dressing room, undressed and donned his outfit, attached a gauze facemask to his head and selected one of the bamboo swords from the rack.

He was a Kendo expert, and both his bodyguards had been selected because of their expertise in the art. Neither had managed to defeat him, but they ensured a long and tiring workout each day for him. Sometimes, he would take them both on at once, reveling in the fight.

He knelt before the tiny shrine and prayed, hearing the door open as he finished. The bodyguard pushed Dickson into the middle of the room where he cowered in fright. His face was ashen save for a great reddish lump on one cheek. Slade smiled, climbed to his feet, and strode across the dojo to where Dickson stood wringing his hands, his piggish little eyes looking everywhere but at him.

"Ahh, Mister Dickson. We seem to have a little problem," Slade said.

"P..p..problem," stuttered Dickson.

"Yes. One of my security procedures is to mirror all information leaving or entering the building, and guess what? I found a message from you there this afternoon. Who is sdelgado?" Dickson's eyes widened immediately when he realized he had been discovered, and the hand wringing intensified.

"She's a c.c..cop," he stammered. "Homicide, 22 division!"

"How many times did you contact her?" asked Slade, pacing back and forth in front of Dickson.

"Just once. I w..w..wanted to get away before we get caught. I didn't have anything to do with killing the girls, so I wanted to make a deal."

"You were going to shop us, weren't you?" said Slade, walking in a circle around the frightened man. Dickson's head, covered in lank, greasy hair, shook vigorously–"No".

"And what do you think I should do with you now?" asked Slade.

"P..p..please give me another chance. I was just frightened. I'm sorry, honest. I won't do it again."

Slade stood behind Dickson. He pointed to the array of swords on the back wall and the bodyguard lifted one down quietly, took the bamboo sword from Slade and stepped back.

"I'll tell you what I'll do, Mister Dickson. You'll get a second chance, but you have to have a reminder of this incident. Hold your arms at shoulder height, extended at your side." Dickson held out his arms and Slade moved, the motion a blur as the sword came down and lopped off the man's hand cleanly at the wrist. The severed hand bounced on the floor. Dickson wobbled at the blow, then screamed aloud, blood pumping from the stump. The bodyguard went in the changing room and returned with a towel which he wrapped around the shattered limb. The bleeding temporarily stanched, he took a thin piece of rope to use as a tourniquet and wrapped it tightly around Dickson's elbow, cutting off the flow of blood.

Dickson dropped to his knees, his lips quavering. The floor of the dojo around him was covered in splashes of blood. He cried when he saw his hand, and he nestled the damaged arm close to his body. Already his t-shirt was sopping with blood. Slade walked in front of him, touching the tip of the blade to Dickson's chin. "Next time it will be your head." To the guard he said, "Take him over to the mainland and have the doctor seal the stump. And have our friend here feed his hand to the dogs on your way out; it will be a nice snack for them."

Slade returned to his office, still dressed in the Gi and picked up his phone, pressing the digits of a number he knew by heart. It was answered on the first ring.

"Slade here. I need some damage control. The target is Susan Delgado, a homicide detective with 22 division. You get double your fee if you can do it tonight, and it has to look like an accident."

"Consider it done," came the reply.

"Is that dinner I smell?" asked Allan Brown, wandering into Susan's kitchen, dressed in faded jeans and her favorite, his white denim shirt, the first few buttons opened to expose his well-tanned chest. In his hand was a magnum of Cuvee Napa Champagne, a whitened layer of frost clinging to the neck of the bottle like candle drippings.

Traces of the odor of burned rice still hung in the air despite her frantic attempts to air out the room. She scrunched her face up. "I burned the first batch," she admitted, "but the next one is nearly ready." She came out of the kitchen and threw her arms around his neck, kissing him hungrily. She felt his huge arms come around her, hugging her closely to him, and his aftershave awakened her senses.

His hands caressed her back, and she felt the heat of them through her thin silk blouse. Her nipples, now erect and firm, rubbed against the rough material of his shirt, making them tingle. She felt the heat building between her thighs, juices flowing as she kissed him fiercely, enjoying the feel of his tongue dueling with hers, her body reacting to him as always.

"Dear God," he said, pulling away, breathless. "I must go away more often." She released him, poking him playfully in the ribs as she ran her hand over the front of his jeans, feeling the hard bulge in the crotch.

"We could skip dinner," he said, his eyes twinkling.

"Not a chance," she replied, taking his hand and dragging him over towards the kitchen.

"You're in a good mood," he said, sliding on to one of the bar stools lined up against the island in the kitchen. She took the bottle of Champagne and placed it in the freezer, beside the others.

"Some wine?" she asked.

"Grand. A chardonnay, if you've got it."

"Grand, is it now?" she laughed, imitating an Irish accent. "You're starting to sound like your friend Daniel. Ohhh, that Irish accent he has..." She sighed deeply. She poured two glasses, replaced the stopper and took a long sip. "I've just had a break in the case, at long last, so Brian and I can stop beating our heads against the wall."

"That's great news," Brown replied cheerfully. "I could see how much it was eating at you. You've been a bit distracted for the past few months."

"I'm sorry," she said, and leaned over and kissed him on the cheek. "You've been really good about it, Allan. But it's good you've been here to see it because that's what I get like during an investigation. The intensity frightens most people off, and the hours ... it makes it difficult to maintain a relationship under such circumstances, but I'm glad you decided to stick around, especially since I've fallen madly in love with you."

Brown grinned. "Ah, you're just like all the others. It's my body you want, and my great talents at home renovations."

"Well I hope you won't mind me using it for a little while after dinner. All that tension of the last few days needs to be relieved and I think you might have one or two good ideas on how to do just that." Her eyes twinkled.

Dinner was over quickly, and Brown was soon pouring two glasses of the chilled champagne into Waterford crystal flutes. They had gone through one bottle over dinner, and he had just cracked open the second. This time, however, he poured a small amount of cassis, a blackcurrant liqueur, into the bottom of the glasses before topping them up with champagne–a Kir Royale. Susan was curled up on the couch in front of the fire, and soft Latin music wafted through the room.

He handed her a glass, said, "To us," and they clinked glasses gently. At one hundred and fifty dollars per stem, he treated the Waterford crystal with respect.

"So when are you leaving?" she asked.

Brown looked at his watch and said, "Daniel's picking me up here at five o'clock. It's going to take a few hours to get up to the lodge so I can sleep on the way."

"Maybe we should take these to bed with us?" Susan suggested. "It's getting late and you might want to get a little sleep."

"Oh?"

She downed the remains of the champagne, handed him the glass and said, "I'll have a refill, please. I'm going to change for bed. Come on in when you're ready."

He felt a stirring in his groin when she said the word 'change'. Susan liked to dress up from time to time when they made love, especially in a black leather outfit, with chains and a leather riding crop. The first time she had done it, he had had the most intense orgasm he could ever remember. She liked to dress like a dominatrix, but she was the one who liked being dominated, especially when she put the dog's choke chain around her neck and made him fuck her doggy-style, getting him to pull on the chain while strapping her buttocks gently with the riding crop.

The champagne bottle rattled against the glasses as he attempted to pour them another drink. "Dear Lord, don't let me get the brewer's droop," he said aloud, carrying the two glasses down the hallway towards her bedroom.

She was lying across the bed when he walked into the room, supporting her head in one black-gloved hand, her lips done with the bright red lipstick he liked. She was wearing a black leather bra and pants, open at the crotch, and was rubbing the end of the riding crop provocatively through the black curls protruding through the gap. The stainless-steel choke chain hung around her neck, and pooled on the bed under her head. Knee-high, spiked boots completed the erotic ensemble. "Thank you Lord," said Brown, and walked over to the bed, still holding the glasses.

When he reached the side of the bed she crawled over, unbuckled his belt and unzipped his fly, pulling his trousers to the floor. She then pulled down his underwear, allowing his cock to spring free from its confinement and, grasping him in her gloved hand, she gently stroked his hardness while reaching for her champagne glass with the other. She took a long sip, then poured some of the effervescent liquid over the head. The icy shower made him gasp, his legs trembling, and then her warm mouth was around him, sucking, teasing, licking. He took a swig of his champagne, one hand coming around to cup the back of her head as she moved back and forth, taking him all the way into her mouth and then out, her tongue twirling like a propeller.

"Ooh, Susan, that's soooo good," he groaned, watching her every movement. Her fingers cupped his balls, squeezing gently as she sucked him hard, the movement becoming more urgent. He started to thrust into her mouth now, meeting her motions. He felt the onset of that sweet release, about to streak past the point of no return, and immediately slowed his movement, eager to savor every second. She knew he was ready and sucked him in slow, languid strokes, taking him more fully into her throat with each thrust, feeling his taut hardness signaling his imminent eruption.

"Oh no you don't," she said, pulling away, "not that quickly. I want that inside me." She drained her champagne, eyes glazed with want while Brown set his glass carefully on the night table and stepped out of the clothes pooled at his feet. When he had finished, she turned around on the bed, still kneeling and handed him the choke chain. He grasped it tightly, hearing a little gurgle, then climbed on the bed behind her, guiding himself with one hand into her velvety warmth.

It was a long while before they both collapsed, spent on to the sheets.

Outside on the street, Riordan looked at his watch for the third time, cursed under his breath and picked up his cell phone. Behind his car a dark figure ran across the street, the door creaked open and Allan Brown climbed into the passenger seat. Riordan took in the unkempt clothes, the uncombed hair standing up like a rooster tail, and replaced the phone, smiling to himself.

"Oh my poor fucking head," groaned Allan Brown, wriggling around in the seat to try to get a comfortable position. He fastened the seatbelt and immediately eased back the chair, clasping his hands across his chest and closing his eyes.

"Wake me when we get there, James," he ordered, his words a little slurred and a huge yawn escaping his lips.

Riordan laughed. "Had a good night, did we?"

"Champagne and Cassis, that's all I'm saying," replied Brown, squirming around in the seat some more to get into a comfortable sleeping position.

"Been there, done that!" Riordan said. The mention of the lethal combination triggered a memory of the worst hangover he had ever experienced, and as usual Allan had been involved, along with two bottles of Champagne and a bottle of cassis. That hangover lasted several days, but several apologies were due the following morning, a Sunday, as he had promised to videotape the christening of a friend's son. Needless to say the day was a complete and utter fiasco. He sighed. That was a lifetime ago, and a lot of water had flowed under the proverbial bridge since then.

"Anyway, what did you do with your car?" asked Riordan, looking down the line of cars parked at the side of the street for Brown's Porsche.

"I left it at home. Most of these places have street parking permits and I was always getting a fucking ticket when I stayed here overnight."

"And you couldn't get a cop to put the fix in for you? Jesus, mate, you're losing your touch. But all right," replied Riordan, smiling good-naturedly at his friend. "I'll let you sleep for a while. And here's some nice music for you to listen to on the way. It'll take about four hours to get there, so we should be arriving about eight thirty if the roads are okay." He pushed in a CD and immediately the haunting sounds of the Chieftains, playing a mournful lament on the ulliean pipes, filled the air. Riordan checked over his shoulder and then pulled away from the curb, heading out on to the main highway towards the Vancouver bypass. Allan Brown was already snoring softly.

"Don't ever change, mate," Riordan said quietly to the sleeping figure.

Hearing the car pull away from the curb, the man raised himself from where he had been lying across the front seat of the rental car. His information had been correct so far, and he had no reason to believe that this hit would be a problem. As a professional 'mechanic' he had killed numerous times with a variety of weapons, but his specialty, if you could call it that, was eliminating targets in a manner that made it look like an accident. He wore a dark turtleneck sweater, dark pants and leather gloves. On his feet he wore a brand new pair of running shoes. All would be discarded later.

He had removed the interior light of the car, so there would not be a flash of white light when he opened the door. He got out, closed the door of the car, locked it, and walked across the street. He briefly scanned the other houses and was pleased to see that there were no other lights on. It was a residential community, so he would have been surprised to see anyone up and around at four o'clock in the morning.

Blending with the shadows, he crept down the side of Delgado's house and climbed up the steps to the deck where the hot tub gurgled merrily in the darkness. Placing his feet carefully on the wooden boards, he moved quietly across the deck to the patio doors, put his hand in the handle and pulled, expecting to feel resistance from the lock, but to his surprise the door opened. He shook his head; people were so stupid. No wonder burglars got away with so much.

He opened the door wide enough to slip through, then stood quietly in the room, allowing his hearing to become accustomed to the sounds of the house. The odor of curry hung in the air from the kitchen. When he was comfortable, he slipped off his shoes, crossed the living room and crept down the hallway to where the bedrooms were located. The door to the master bedroom was open, and he could see the sleeping form of Delgado silhouetted in the faint light from streetlamps.

The sheet had slipped down from her shoulders, and he could see she was still wearing the leather gear from earlier on, when he had been spying in the window. He admired the curve of her breast pushed against the mattress, and he sniffed the air like a jungle predator searching for prey, recognized the stale scent of sex, and immediately became aroused.

On the bedside table beside her sat the empty bottle of champagne and two glasses that she and her boyfriend had been drinking from during the bout of wild sex he had witnessed. He slid a leather-gloved hand down over the crotch of his trousers and found himself stiff as a board.

He stood at the edge of the bed for a moment, rubbing himself and watching the sleeping figure, knowing she had only minutes to live. The idea had come to him while watching the pair's frenetic coupling, and the 'toys' they had been using during their games. He climbed gently on to the bed and she stirred with the motion, but did not wake. His breath came in small pants now as he reached out and took the loose end of the choke chain, wrapping it several times around his hands until it was tight.

She stirred now, feeling the insistent pressure on her throat from the leash. As her eyes fluttered open, he pressed her face into the pillow and yanked back as hard as he could on the leash, pulling it tightly against her throat. She started to thrash about under the sheets, arms flailing wildly, but he knelt on top of her, one knee on each side of her back using the sheets to pin her to the bed.

It took only a couple of minutes for the thrashing to subside and her body to go limp. He maintained the pressure for a few more minutes to ensure she was dead, then climbed off the bed and opened his trousers. He slipped on a condom and masturbated quickly to relieve the pent-up tension, then went into the washroom and flushed the condom, the wrapper, and several tissues down the toilet.

With one last look at the body, he ran down the corridor, crossed the living room and put on his shoes and went out on to the deck, closing the patio door behind him. When he made it back to his car, he noticed a yellow ticket stuck under the windscreen of the rental car. He tore it off, crumpled it up and threw it away. That was one ticket that was not going to be paid.

CHAPTER 3

Slade

Later that morning, Brian Dymond looked across at Susan Delgado's empty desk, glanced again at his watch and frowned. It was unlike her to be late, but then again they rarely kept regular hours, and she had said that Allan was going away for the weekend on a fishing trip. Perhaps she was giving him a memorable send-off. He made a mental note to razz her about it when she eventually appeared.

He wrote her a brief message and left it on her desk, then pulled on his jacket and headed out of the station. Opening his car and climbing inside, he allowed the air-conditioning to get the interior under control and spent a few moments organizing the clinics by area so that he would not be driving back and forth across the city. He would get a head start on the abortion clinics in the city, at least the legal ones to begin with, to see if anyone recognized the photograph of the most recent victim. It was certainly a long shot but it was one of the few solid leads they had come across.

Allan Brown sat on the bank of the river, sipping a can of beer and watching Riordan cast his line back and forth across the river in long, graceful arcs before letting it settle to the surface. Brown really did not have much interest in fishing, but came anyway because his friend was a fanatic, and it felt good to get away to the peace and tranquility of the woods for a few days.

The day had passed slowly, and Brown was content to sit and read his book on the bank while Riordan fished. Periodically Riordan would take a break and they would have a beer together, and sometimes Brown would discover some other little nugget of information about his friend that he would file away in the part of his mind in which he was creating a picture of a whole person. That was one thing about Daniel, there was always a story on his lips, related in that soft Irish brogue that seemed to attract women like a magnet.

Like himself, Riordan was just over six feet tall and carrying a little extra weight now that the years were climbing on and the demands from work left little time for a strict exercise regime. He rapidly discovered that Riordan, whom he had known in another existence as David Spence, and who probably had other personas as well, was by nature a kind, caring person. It embarrassed him sometimes the way Daniel doted on Nancy, but then he had known Riordan's first wife and young daughter.

He had seen the darkness behind the calm exterior exposed one layer at a time, like peeling an onion, when Riordan's family had been killed, allegedly by a terrorist bomb. Riordan, unsatisfied with the responses from the authorities, did some investigating on his own and unraveled a plot which lead all the way back to the Prime Minister's office. As a result he had gone on a killing spree to force the man to confess to what he had done. When his plan was successful, Riordan simply vanished, assumed to be the victim of a tragic boating incident when he was throwing the ashes of his wife and daughter into a lake.

Brown, surprisingly, found himself the beneficiary of all Riordan/Spence's insurance policies, an amount well in excess of three million dollars. He had left Toronto shortly thereafter and had traveled west in search of a more relaxed climate and better job prospects. He had found both, and lived a peaceful existence for five years until Spence had surprised him one day in Stanley Park and the two had resumed their friendship. At that time Riordan's close friend and his family had been murdered by a gang of emerald smugglers, and Brown came close to losing his own life after being sucked into that quagmire.

He knew what Riordan was, having seen him efficiently and ruthlessly dispose of five of the Yakusa who had mistaken him for Riordan. He knew a little about Riordan's past and the mysterious brass, winged dagger that hung around his neck. And he had met Riordan's adopted father once, that experience being quite sufficient to scare the hell out of him. Riordan hadn't mentioned his father since that meeting and Brown did not want to press the issue. But he still fingered the tiny brass dagger from time to time, a faraway look in his eyes and Brown just knew he was thinking of his father.

The reverie was interrupted by a sloshing sound and he looked up to see Riordan wading back towards the bank, making slow progress in the strong current.

"No good?" Brown said.

"Nah, not this spot," said Riordan , shaking his head sadly. "They're not feeding for some reason. I've seen plenty of salmon, but they're ignoring the fly. I think it's beer time." He clambered out on to the bank, set down the rod and fished a beer out of the cooler. Putting the can to his mouth, he drank thirstily, crushing the can when he had finished. "Ahh, mother's milk," he sighed, and burped loudly. "Tis a shame Guinness doesn't travel well, though."

"So what now?" asked Brown, watching his friend dangling his feet in the river, staring off into space. There was silence for a moment, then Riordan replied, "What was that?"

Brown smiled and said, "You were somewhere else there, weren't you."

"Ach, sure I was. Where I used to live in Ireland, there was a river across the road from our house. It sort of split over a waterfall that we called the Carry, and the other part of the river was called the dead river; it really didn't go anywhere. We fished there all the time and caught beautiful trout: rainbows, browns, and brookies, they were all there. It seems a lifetime ago." He shook his head sadly.

"Maybe if you have a boy, we can bring him up here with us," said Brown.

Riordan's face lit up, like he had just been given a precious gift. "Wouldn't that be something?" he said, a wide grin creasing his face. "That would be grand! Anyway, maybe we should head back now and set up the tent. I'm getting hungry."

"That sounds like a plan," said Brown, rubbing his stomach thoughtfully. "Those sandwiches we had earlier didn't really fill me."

"Jesus, Allan, a load of effin' cement wouldn't fill you," Riordan replied. "I don't know where you put it all; you must have a pet tapeworm hiding somewhere in your body. I don't know anybody who eats as much as you do and manages to stay reasonably in shape."

"Nah," said Brown, climbing to his feet and stretching. "I just have a very active sex life; wears it all off, you see."

Riordan picked up his rod and the cooler. "From the sight of your neck she must bite some of it off as well."

"Fuck off!" Brown replied, swatting a mosquito that had just landed on his arm.

Brian Dymond tossed his coat on his desk and slumped into his chair, dragging out the bottom drawer of his desk. Kicking off his shoes, he rested them in the drawer. "Ooh, that feels better," he groaned, leaning back and twisting his neck slowly from side to side. One of the other detectives laughed. They all knew what it was like to pound the pavement looking for information.

"Bad day Brian?" asked one of the other detectives, a heavy Scot's burr in his accent. Dymond looked over to see Jock Patterson re-filling his teacup from a huge red thermos. He carried the flask to work each day along with the brown bag of sandwiches his wife prepared religiously for his lunch. On occasion there would be a loud curse from Patterson's desk when he discovered that his wife had bravely tried to experiment with something new. Patterson, one of two veteran homicide bulls in the department was the butt of jokes consistently, given that he was a tea-totaller, totally opposite the stereotypical Scotsman. But what he lacked, Billy MacGregor, his partner of many years, made up.

MacGregor, a mane of fiery red hair attesting to his Celtic heritage, would gladly fight with his shadow, was known to be 'fond of the bottle', and had a passion for fried food. MacGregor's approach to cuisine was "If it's not fried, it's not food!" Dymond often commented that the two had their own version of the 'Good cop, bad cop routine', called 'Bad cop, demented cop', which everyone thought was an apt description.

Their clearance rate in solving homicides was in the top three percentile for comparable cities in North America, and each had been nominated for bravery on several occasions. Over a beer MacGregor would delight in showing his catalog of scars depicting his career in the department. Dymond felt like he knew the story by heart: the scar on the lower forearm from a drug dealer while he worked in narcotics, the puckered scar on his wrist from trying to arrest a stoned hooker while in vice, the bullet in the shoulder... Any unwitting rookie who happened to be in the bar at the time was usually cornered and had to endure the saga, almost like a rite of passage for the department. However, the two were a legend in the force in their own lifetimes.

Dymond said, "I feel like I've walked all over the fuckin' city. I've canvassed at least fifteen abortion clinics, and there's no easy access to any of them. Talk about a suspicious bunch; getting in to talk to people is another chore in itself."

"It's from all the crap they get from these pro-life people," Patterson said. "They get in under false pretenses and then spray all the wee girls in there with red paint that's supposed to look like blood. No wonder they're suspicious. But did you have any luck?"

"None, nada, nyet, fucking nein," grunted Dymond. "Another dead end. But there's still the illegal scrape clinics, and I have to find them first, so tomorrow's going to be another gem of a day."

"You might want to talk to Sheila De Gasperis over in Vice," offered Patterson. "She's usually well up in where these places are."

Dymond rubbed his face in his hands. When he lifted his head again, Billy MacGregor was walking into the squad room, a brown paper bag in his hand, and the mouthwatering aroma of french fries filled the air. He eased himself into his seat, opened the top of the bag and chewed merrily on a handful of fries.

"Hello, Brian. What about ye?" MacGregor said, bits of french fries protruding from the corners of his mouth.

"Been a long day, Billy. You know the score." MacGregor nodded knowingly.

Dymond asked, "Anyone seen Susan?"

Patterson shook his head, as did MacGregor, and said, "Not today. But I've been out and about as well. She may have come in, but I've no seen her."

Dymond sat up, checked the pile of pink slips on his desk, but there was no message. And his note was still on her desk where he had left it. Picking up his phone, he punched in the digits for her home number and waited. After three rings the answering machine came on and he heard her cheery message, with Aerosmith's 'Walks like a lady' blasting out in the background.

He said, "Hi Sue, it's Brian. Just wanted to know if everything was okay. I'm off home now, so give me a call if you get a chance. The clinics were a bust so I'm going to try to find some of the illegal ones tomorrow. Perhaps you'd like to help. Bye now."

He hung up the phone, checked the messages again to see if there were any that needed immediate attention, decided that they could all be left until tomorrow, and grabbed his coat and left. Pizza hut and two cold, dark beers constituted dinner, followed by a couple of hours surfing through the channels, watching but not really seeing, and it was off to bed. There were messages from a couple of ladies who would have been glad of a call from him, but he wasn't really in the mood. Something was nagging at him but he couldn't put his finger on it. It was a fitful night of sleep, dark images twisting him back and forth in the sheets until the onset of dawn, when he woke, bleary-eyed and exhausted.

He showered, shaved, and dressed quickly, then set off for the office, stopping at a drive-thru donut shop for a tall, double double and a cruller. Breakfast of champions, he thought to himself, steering the car with his knee. He went to take the Gore Parkway directly to the office but turned off at Blecker on a whim, deciding to call by Susan's house. He was puzzled that he hadn't heard from her.

The porch light was still on when he arrived, an empty, crumpled cup and donut wrapper in his hand. He tossed the refuse in her recycle bin, grinning at the expected rebuke, then strode up to the front door and rang the bell. Chimes echoed in the house. There was no answer.

He looked over at the mailbox and saw the rolled up newspaper protruding from the lip. Then on the ground beside the box he saw another paper. He felt a frown cross his brow–cop instincts. He picked up the paper and looked at the date. It was Sunday's Vancouver Sun. He lifted the one out of the box and looked at the date on it. It was Saturday's, one day old. A shiver trickled down his back like a drop of ice water.

He walked over to the window and peered inside, trying to see beyond the white lace curtains. There was no movement, but then something at the periphery of his vision pulled his head in that direction. It was a large blowfly. There were several large blowflies now buzzing against the window. Calm down, he reminded himself. The fact that blowflies appear in masses around a decomposing body was purely a coincidence here in this situation. Nevertheless he drew his pistol, and returned to the front door where he pounded loudly enough to attract the attention of several neighbors.

Kneeling down, he opened the letterbox to yell inside but had to jump back from several escaping flies. And then there was a vague odor of something unpleasant, a scent all too familiar to his nostrils. He pointed the gun at the lock, fired one shot, which shattered the mechanism, and kicked it in. Sprinting through the doorway, he ran quickly from room to room, looking, hoping. He knew where the bedroom was and went there next.

The door was closed. He prayed he was wrong, that she would be asleep and he would be embarrassed and everything would be all right, but his hand was trembling as he turned the handle and pushed it open. Flies buzzed past his ear, and he saw the rumpled sheets and Susan's bloated face and staring eyes and the stench of her decomposing body filled his nostrils before he had time to react. He turned back and retched violently.

There were voices now at the front door and he ran outside, frightening the neighbors who had gathered,

attracted by the racket and the gunshot. Filling his lungs
with fresh, cold, air, he dragged out his detective's shield
and told them all to clear the area, then ran over to his car
and called the emergency services. He made one more
quick call to the chief of detectives, then sat back for a
moment, trying to absorb it all, hearing the wail of a siren
approaching rapidly, too rapidly in response to his call.
Must have been one of the neighbors, he thought to
himself, and he got out and went back to the house.

Two cruisers arrived within seconds of each other. The
officers checked with him briefly, then sealed off the area,
and a few minutes later an unmarked Ford sedan pulled up
to the yellow crime-scene tape. Two men got out, flashed
their ID's at the officer guarding the area, clambered under
the tape, and made their way over to where Dymond stood.

"Jock, Billy," said Dymond, relieved that the Chief
had been so prompt in assigning the two men he had
requested to the case. "She's in the bedroom. I was the first
officer on the scene. No one else has been inside."

Jock Patterson was dressed as always in his Highland
tweed jacket with the black leather elbow patches, white
shirt and conservative tie, and a pair of black trousers. His
white wavy hair was brushed back in tight curls, not one
out of place. He looked for all the world as if he had just
come from Church. Which he had.

MacGregor, face lined and eyes bloodshot with the
excesses of a Saturday night, looked like he had slept in his
clothes, which, given his track record, was a high
probability. The strong scent of mint was on his breath.

Patterson grasped Dymond by the arm, genuine concern written in the creases on his face. "How are you holding up son?" he asked.

Dymond blinked back tears. "She's gone Jock, she's gone."

Patterson looked over at MacGregor and said, "Billy, you go on in and have a look around. I'll stay with the lad here for a few minutes." MacGregor nodded, pulled on a pair of surgical gloves and extracted a notebook from his pocket. He went to go into the house but Dymond grabbed him by the arm.

"Billy," Dymond said, the strain unmistakable in his voice. "It's a bit delicate. Please..." His voice broke. "...Please be careful how you handle it." MacGregor's brow furrowed, a dark look crossing his face and a curse forming on his lips, but his partner simply nodded towards the house and shook his head behind Dymond's back.

Another car drew up, followed by a dark blue mini-van with the words 'IDENT' stenciled across the back. A dark, sharply dressed oriental man got out of the car, pulled a black leather case out of the back seat, and walked over to where Patterson and Dymond stood. It was Alfred Chang, the chief coroner for the region, who would not normally attend a crime scene, preferring to delegate those to his staff. He did not exhibit the normally ebullient demeanor they were accustomed to seeing, but Patterson realized that the Chief must have fore-warned him about the circumstances of the crime scene. He did not stop, but went directly into the house, followed by the forensic specialist, carrying an evidence-gathering equipment box and a silver, metallic camera case.

"Okay lad," said Patterson, extracting his spiral bound notebook. "I need to get some information from you." Dymond nodded. He knew how important it was to get on the trail of Susan's killer, but from his initial glimpse of the scene, a picture flashing into his mind every few moments like an unwanted guest, he already knew, or suspected what had happened. Dymond knew the questions; they were the same ones he would have been asking had their roles been reversed, and answered them as fully as possible. But he had his suspicions about Susan's death from the very preliminary look he had had at the scene. As if to corroborate his unspoken theory, MacGregor came out of the house, stripped off the surgical gloves and stuck them in the pocket of his jacket. "She have a boyfriend?" he asked, looking directly at Dymond.

"Yes," Dymond replied. "His name's Allan Brown. Lives over on the island." MacGregor took a clear envelope, containing a photograph, from his pocket and held it up. Dymond recognized it as Allan Brown, lying back over a hotel bed with his fly open and holding his penis erect with two fingers, as if demonstrating its length.

"Hung like ..." started MacGregor, the sentence dying stillborn on his lips at a stern glance from Patterson. "Sorry, lad, I didn't mean anything," said a flustered MacGregor, a characteristic Dymond had not seen before. But then he had never lost a partner before either.

"I think I'll go and have a word with him," said MacGregor, putting the photograph away in his pocket.

"There's no point in making the trek over there," offered Dymond. "Brown went away for the weekend on a fishing trip. Susan was seeing him for dinner on Friday night, then he was leaving early on Saturday morning. He'll be back later tonight, I should imagine, and he'll probably come here, or at least call."

"Alright, lad. I'll keep this under wraps until he gets back, but I'll send a couple of uniforms over to the Island to watch for him."

"Why the attention?"

MacGregor took out his notebook and scrutinized the neat, handwritten notes. "The coroner puts the time of death between three and six o'clock on Saturday morning. She was choked to death by the chain around her neck. There is one deep ligature mark, and from what I can see there was a lot of alcohol involved. Looks like our lad got a bit carried away with all the bondage stuff." Dymond winced, and bit his upper lip. MacGregor continued. "But no matter; he goes down for this. We play it by the book." MacGregor closed the notebook and looked at them defiantly, obviously expecting an argument, but Dymond merely shook his head.

"What a waste of life," he said. "What a fucking waste."

CHAPTER 4

Suspect

Feeling a trifle sad that the fishing trip was over, Riordan leaned back against the car's headrest, rubbed the last vestiges of sleep from his eyes and took a sip of coffee from the mug on the dashboard. God, he thought, there's nothing like Starbucks coffee. A lifesaver, especially with a hangover. Beside him, Allan Brown snored softly, exhausted by the aftermath of the previous evening's drinking session, having polished off a new bottle of Bushmills whisky between them. It was almost noon, and as the first view of the city came into view, still over a hundred kilometers away, Riordan picked up the car phone and dialed his home. It was picked up after the first two rings.

"Hello darlin'," he said, "how are you feeling today?"

"Much the same," came the reply. Riordan could hear the exhaustion in his wife's voice. "I've no energy to do anything. I've switched my shift tonight with one of the other girls, so we can have an early night. How did the fishing go, or should I say how did the drinking go?" Riordan laughed.

"Ach, sure don't you know me too well, love," he said, picturing his wife standing by the phone, shaking her head. "We did do a wee bit–sleeping beauty beside me here might come round in an hour or two."

"How far away are you?" Nancy asked. "I haven't eaten yet so I can hold off for a little bit. I've got a craving for bacon and eggs, for some reason."

Riordan said, "Bless you, darlin'. We'll be there in about an hour. Allan will need something to soak up the booze. See you in a bit." He hung up the phone, smiling when he felt his stomach growl at the thought of a big fry–an Ulster special, as he called it–and leaned over and turned the radio on low. The dash clock said 11:29 a.m., almost time for the news.

The lead story, about the suspicious death of a female police officer in Whiterock, grabbed his attention, and he immediately cranked the volume, rousing Brown from sleep. "What, who..."

"Ssssh, Allan, and listen," Riordan said.

The announcer stated that the woman's body had been discovered by her partner, and that the police were treating it as a suspicious death, not coming outright and saying it was murder. The next of kin had not been yet notified, so they were withholding the woman's name. The interviewer then played a tape of a statement made by the woman's partner. When the partner was identified as Brian Dymond,

Riordan turned his head to look at Brown, whose face had gone completely white.

"No, no, it couldn't be," said Brown, shaking his head in disbelief, "it couldn't be Susan." But Riordan heard the rising panic in his friend's voice. He knew about such things.

"Why don't you call her number?" suggested Riordan, lifting the phone and handing it to his friend. Brown fumbled with the luminescent keypad, rubbing his fingers back and forth across his brow, trying desperately to remember the number. He pressed the digits, cursed, and cleared the screen. Twice he tried, his trembling fingers touching against adjacent numbers to the one he was trying to dial. "Wait a minute," Riordan said, and pulled the Range Rover over to the side of the road.

Taking the phone from his friend's shaking hand, Riordan punched the digits one at a time while Brown repeated them from memory. Riordan listened to the phone ring three times, expecting it to go to voice mail next, but it was picked up. A voice said " Hello" and Riordan handed the phone to Brown.

Brown said, "This is Allan Brown speaking. I'm a friend of Susan's and I just heard the announcement on the radio. Is Susan..." His voice cracked, his eyes welling up with tears. Riordan heard him say, "Yes" a number of times, and then he hung the phone back in its cradle.

Brown buried his face in his hands, his broad shoulders shaking, huge sobs racking his body. "Fuck it," Brown spat, between the tears. "That was the police. They want me to come downtown as soon as possible. The detectives in charge of the case want to interview me. Daniel, she's dead."

Riordan sat, his face expressionless, staring through the windscreen, a chill creeping into his bones. Many times he had been in Allan's position. First his wife and young daughter were murdered in a terrorist explosion, then a close friend and his wife and daughter were murdered by the Yakusa, and now his friend Allan had lost the woman he loved. It seemed like everything he touched turned to ashes.

Yet there was Nancy, the woman who had dragged him from the depths of despair over his friend's death, and married him, despite his past, and was now several months pregnant with his children. But he had a sense that something was not right here, a strange undercurrent. From what he had heard on the radio, it seemed that Allan would have been the last person to have seen Susan alive. But surely the police didn't suspect Allan.

Riordan said, "Allan, I'm sorry. What do you want me to do?" He reached out and touched his friend's shoulder gently. Brown sat up, wiping the tears away with the back of his hand.

"What a fucking way to find out," Brown spat in anger. "Let's head into town and maybe you could drop me at the police station. I'll deal with it from there on."

Riordan said, "Thanks mate. I don't want to get any closer to them than I have to. But they'll have to talk to me at some point, to corroborate your story." Brown spun around in his seat, a dark look crossing his face.

"What do you mean, corroborate my story. You sound like I'm covering something up."

"No, Allan, listen to me," Riordan said gently, touching his friend's shoulder in a gesture of affection. "I know how these things work. The police will want to know your movements for the last few days, and given that you were likely the last person to see her..." He paused, wincing as he forced the words out. "... to see her alive, apart from whoever or whatever killed her, they will ask if anyone can corroborate your statement. And that someone is me. So give them my number and they can come and see me. At this moment you are probably the prime suspect and we have to eliminate you from the list." Brown nodded, took a deep breath and seemed to deflate into his seat.

Riordan started driving towards the city. Without turning he said, "When I was nineteen, I was sitting in a bar in Dublin having a quick pint after work. The news was on, and there were several pieces about the troubles in the North, there always were, so you watch but don't really register much. Until they said that a reserve policeman had been ambushed on his way home from work in Ballymena, and they flashed his face on the screen. He was a friend of mine–we had gone to school together–and I knew he was dead. You see, for security reasons, if a policeman was wounded, there would be a report but no photograph. But if the officer was dead, there was no point in keeping his identity a secret. So I knew, and I sat in silence while the bastards in the bar cheered the fact that the IRA had gotten another 'Proddy'."

Brown said, "But what were you doing in an IRA bar?"

"I was just explaining that I know how it is to have news sprung on you like that," said Riordan. "What I was doing in a Republican bar is another story entirely, and not for now."

The drive finished in silence and Riordan dropped Brown off at the police station and headed home. The mouth-watering aroma of frying bacon fill the air as he walked into the house, slipped off his coat and shoes and padded toward the kitchen. Nancy stood, still in her nightdress, sipping a cup of coffee beside the island and poring over the newspaper.

She smiled, but it was wiped quickly away when she saw the look on Riordan's face. "Daniel, what's the matter? Where's Allan?"

"In a moment, love," he said softly, kissing her brow and holding her close for a few moments. He poured himself a cup of coffee. The strong, Kona brew tasted wonderful, and he took a couple of sips before sitting down on one of the high-back chairs. "Have you heard the news this morning?" he asked.

"Yes, but what has it got to do with Allan?"

"Did you hear about the policewoman who was found dead in Whiterock?" Riordan asked, and saw the realization cross her face when she made the link between the death and Allan Brown being missing. Her hand flew to her mouth, stifling a gasp.

"No Daniel, no. Not Susan." She burst into tears and came into his arms and he held her close, savoring her warmth and the smell of her and feeling like he was holding the most precious person in the world.

When his friend Jamie Laverty and his wife and daughter had been killed in a fire, the police investigators ruled it an accidental death. But based on earlier conversations with Jamie, Riordan knew otherwise, and had returned to the persona of the Raven, one of the most dreaded paramilitary enforcers of the 'Troubles' in the North of Ireland. Using the arcane skills of his past, he uncovered the truth behind the deaths.

He had tracked down and executed all the men responsible, almost getting Allan Brown and himself killed in the process. When he returned from the hunt, Nancy had stood by him, refusing to be judgmental and telling him simply that she loved him, and would help him share the burden he carried. He had told her many things about his past life, but there were many secrets he could not divulge for fear of making her a potential witness. Still, she accepted him and they married soon after, and now she was carrying his children. It should be their time to rejoice, but as fate had done many times in the past, there was to be no peace.

The paroxysm passed, and she stepped back and tore away a piece of kitchen paper and dried her eyes. Riordan sighed deeply, and took another mouthful of coffee. Nancy said, "Do you want something stronger for that?"

Riordan smiled and shook his head. "No love," he said. "I better stay sober until we hear from Allan. I have a bad feeling about this."

At the same time, Allan Brown was being ushered into one of the homicide interviewing rooms. When he had identified himself at the front desk, there was an unmistakable air of hostility followed by a flurry of activity. A detective, who identified himself as DS MacGregor, came downstairs and escorted him to the interview room. The man seemed civil enough, but there was a hardness behind the blue eyes that made Brown uncomfortable. He was relieved when the detective went out to get a coffee, staring into the two-way, mirrored glass on the wall in front of him, wondering who was out there looking in. He was starting to feel like a caged animal. The door opened again and the detective came back in, followed by another man. MacGregor set a styrofoam cup of coffee on the table and sat down. The other man sat down also, staring at Brown all the while, his body language denoting suppressed fury.

MacGregor said, "This is my partner DS Patterson. We'd like to ask you a few questions about Susan Delgado. Some of them will be of an extremely personal nature, but

they are relevant to our inquiry into her death, so I hope
you will cooperate fully."

"Of course," said Brown, his nostrils twitching. Was
that peppermint candy on the detective's breath, a sure sign
of a heavy drinker trying to conceal his vice? "I can hardly
believe she's gone. Have her parents been told? I have their
address and phone number at my house. I can..."

"We'd like to tape this interview, if that's okay by you,
Mr. Brown," interrupted MacGregor, his tone hard. "Susan
was a colleague of ours and we are very anxious to get to
the bottom of what caused her death. If you don't mind I
would like to ask the questions here."

Brown hesitated, a second from blasting the man about
being insensitive, but realized that they too were fond of
Susan and wanted to do right by her. "Sorry," he said. "Go
ahead with your questions."

MacGregor pressed the 'RECORD' button on a tiny
tape recorder, identified himself and DS Patterson, and
gave some details about the time and the purpose of the
interview. When he was finished, he opened a manila file,
took out a black and white autopsy photograph, and tossed
it across the table in front of Brown.

It was Susan.

Brown's eyes widened when he saw the deep ligature
marks around Susan's neck and her eyes closed as if in
sleep. There was no way he could control it. Turning to one
side, he retched violently, spewing the contents of his
stomach across the interview room floor. He heard a door

slam and a pair of hands grabbed him and pulled him upright.

"Drink this," said another voice with a deep Scottish accent, and he drank greedily from the mug of cold water.

"We'll go in the other room," said MacGregor, gathering up his notes and the photograph.

Brown stared at the man, fighting back the desire to reach across the table and punch him right in the face. "You're a bastard, a cold callous bastard," he said. "I loved her and you throw this crap in my face. You'll hear no more from me until I get my lawyer."

"Suit yourself," replied MacGregor. "We're going nowhere tonight, and neither are you."

Riordan sat watching television, Nancy sleeping against his arm as he found himself checking his watch more and more frequently. It had been seven hours since he dropped Allan Brown off at the police station, there was no answer from Allan's home phone and he had not called. Riordan had a sinking feeling in his stomach that there was something bad about to happen, that Susan's death was not the end of this mess. As if in agreement, Nancy stirred, wiped her mouth and yawned.

"Finished drooling on me?" said Riordan, and she punched him on the arm.

"Anything from Allan?" she asked, rubbing sleep from her eyes. "I didn't hear the phone but I was in a deep sleep."

Riordan laughed. "Darlin', you wouldn't have heard a bomb going off. No, I haven't heard anything from Allan yet. But I'm sure he'll call me as soon as he can. You go on back to sleep. I'll cook supper for us in a little while."

Supper was created by a call to Pizza Hut, and the two ate in silence, Nancy knowing when to leave her husband to his thoughts. Riordan opened a bottle of wine, a husky Australian Chardonnay he had seen recommended in the local paper, poured himself a glass, poured a little for Nancy and topped it up with soda water. She had been very conscientious about alcohol since discovering she was pregnant, much to her chagrin, as Riordan would get to finish the bottle.

However, tonight the wine had no appeal, even though Chardonnay was one of his favorites. Riordan chewed his pizza, brow furrowed, wondering why in hell Allan had not gotten in touch. A fleeting thought crossed his mind, like the shutter opening and closing on a camera, and he tried to ignore what he had just seen. Maybe Allan Brown couldn't contact him because he was unable to. Maybe Allan had made his one phone call, and used it to call his lawyer. Maybe... But then that would mean Allan was being charged. No, stop it, for God's sake, Riordan admonished himself, you're letting your imagination get the better of you.

"What's on your mind, love?" Nancy asked, interrupting his internal debate. Riordan took a sip of wine.

"Sorry about that," he replied. "My mind's conjuring up all sorts of weird possibilities as to why Allan hasn't called." Nancy smiled and touched the back of his hand gently, a quiet gesture of affection.

"He'll be fine," she said, but her tone betrayed the fact that she too had been wondering. "Now give me another piece of that delicious pizza–I am eating for three you know." As Riordan was scooping two slices on to her plate, the front doorbell rang.

"Go and get it," Nancy said. "That's probably him now." Riordan kissed her on the forehead and ran down the hallway to the door. It was dark outside. Dragging it open, he was surprised to see two men standing on the porch. A quick scan of the two set alarm bells ringing in the back of his head–these were cops. His first impression was quickly corroborated by the more well-dressed of the two.

"Good evening, Sir," said the man. "Would you be Daniel Riordan?" Cops always said "Sir," just before they kicked the living shit out of you, at least that was Riordan's experience from growing up hard in the hinterlands of Belfast.

"That's me," Riordan replied, his eyes absorbing every feature of the two men like a sponge soaking up water. The tiny network of broken veins on MacGregor's nose told their sad tale, and Riordan recognized the Scottish accent immediately. "What can I do for you?"

"I'm Detective-Sergeant MacGregor and this is my partner DS Patterson. We got your name from Brian Dymond. I'm told you are acquainted with Allan Brown." The man paused, a question on his face.

"What's this about?" said Riordan, making no attempt to allow the men into his house.

MacGregor said, "We're making inquiries into the death of Susan Delgado. We think Allan Brown was one of the last people to see her alive and we have some questions we'd like to ask you." The man took a fraction of a step forward, but Riordan did not budge.

"Ask away," said Riordan.

"It might be better if we do it inside," MacGregor said. Riordan stared into the man's eyes. He had met such men before, career policemen, who thought that with a tough stare and a menacing attitude they could get anyone to confess. These were the dinosaurs who would have vehemently opposed the use of videotape in the interrogation rooms; they could no longer beat a confession out of a suspect.

"My wife is inside," replied Riordan tersely, blocking their way. "She's pregnant, has only a few weeks to go, and is very, very fond of Allan Brown. She was also very fond of Susan Delgado. I don't want to upset her in any way, so it might be better if we do it out here."

"We could always do this down at the station, if that would be more convenient for you," said the other detective. Riordan heard the implied threat in the detective's voice, another Scottish accent. This was

obviously the bad half of the 'good cop, bad cop routine.'
Riordan allowed a tiny grin to cross his lips. These guys
wouldn't have lasted twenty minutes in Belfast.

"All right, inside it is," Riordan said. "But I warn you.
Upset her and you're out."

"We've done this before, Mister Riordan," said
MacGregor and stepped past Riordan into the house. Nancy
was wiping her mouth with a piece of tissue and two crusts
lay on her plate. Riordan made the introductions, explained
the circumstances of their visit and the two men sat down.
MacGregor said, "We understand you were fishing with
Allan Brown this past weekend."

"That's right," Riordan replied. "I picked him up at
Susan's house at four a.m. on Saturday morning and we
drove up north. We fished all day, camped out overnight,
and came back this morning. We heard the news on the
radio and I dropped Allan off at the station."

MacGregor said, "Did you see anyone suspicious
when you picked Brown up?"

"Nope."

"And what time was it again?"

Riordan leaned over and pressed down the top of the
detective's notebook, pointed to the scribbled text and said,
"You wrote it down correctly. I did say four a.m. Now how
about you answering a few questions? Where is Allan?"

"Mister Brown is helping us with our inquiries at the
moment. We're trying to locate his lawyer at the moment
as he has decided not to talk to us any more without legal
representation."

Riordan sucked air through his teeth. It was like being kicked in the stomach. Legal representation? He said, "Is Allan really a suspect? Have you charged him with anything?"

"No," replied MacGregor, folding up his notebook and putting it away in his inside pocket. "But we're keeping him overnight for questioning."

Riordan spat, "You can't possibly think he did it, do you? Allan loved Susan. They were talking about moving in together." Patterson shrugged his shoulders.

"We've seen all sorts in this job, so nothing surprises me any more," Patterson said with the authority of a man who has seen and done everything. "The autopsy report will be finalized by the morning so we will know more by then."

"Can I speak to Allan?" Riordan asked, knowing well what the answer would be.

"No," came the firm reply from MacGregor. "Not until we've completed our inquiries."

"You're both wrong," said Nancy, speaking up for the first time. Color rose in her cheeks and her Celtic temper flared. "You think he's guilty, I can see it in your eyes. But I knew Susan, and I know Allan. He wouldn't hurt a fly, let alone someone he loved. You're looking in the wrong place."

"We'll see," said Patterson, and they both stood up. MacGregor produced a card and said, " If there's anything else you remember, please give us a call. Mister Brown's lawyer will probably call you in the morning, and you should be able to see him after that. Goodnight."

Riordan saw them to the door and slammed it behind them. Then, with his back against the door, he growled, "Morons, fucking morons." He wanted to yell at them, tell them that they had the wrong man, but he knew it would be to no avail. They were cops, and had already formed their opinions about who had killed Susan. He had seen it in their faces, so his references for Allan were for naught.

CHAPTER 5

Raven

Riordan slept fitfully, his dreams full of dark images. At around 6:00 a.m. he slipped out of bed, went downstairs to the basement and showered there so as not to wake Nancy. Sleep was hard to come by for her these days. After dressing quickly he ground some fresh beans, put on a pot of coffee, and sat at his desk, staring out the window at English Bay. The sea was calm and fresh, boats plying their trade in the early hours. In a few moments the tantalizing aroma of coffee filled the room and he sniffed the air hungrily like a dog picking up a scent.

He returned to the desk with a full mug and sat, deep in thought, reflecting on times past and the oppressive feeling that his life was about to change; a paradigm shift was the term, a phrase much abused by the current spate of computer gurus. A right bunch of wankers, Riordan thought. In his former life as the Raven, a hardened paramilitary enforcer at the ripe age of seventeen, death meant little to him. A victim of his youthful naiveté, he rationalized that his targets were 'bad' men who carried out barbaric acts of terrorism and therefore deserved to die. Many men had died at his hands, his anonymity protected by the fact that no one, save for his adopted father, knew his identity. And none of his victims survived their encounter with the Raven.

Unknown to him, however, the killings were taking their toll on his psyche, and eventually he put the violence behind him, fleeing to a new country under an assumed identity, that of David Spence, with his new wife.

Here he had started a new life, and had tried desperately to put the past behind him. A little daughter had been born, and for the first time in many years he had felt as if the burden of his early years had been relieved, that there was hope of a normal life, normal friends, a loving family. But the tranquility was to be short-lived. His family had been killed in an explosion aboard a jet, hijacked by terrorists demanding the release of their comrades languishing in a Toronto jail, pending extradition to Israel.

Riordan, then living under the identity of David Spence, did not believe the official explanation, and did some investigating of his own. Twice in a matter of days he had almost been killed, but then he uncovered a link which led all the way back to the Prime Minister's office. In order for him to expose the people behind the conspiracy, he needed to revert to the arcane skills of his former days as the Raven, a transformation that had extracted a severe toll on his psyche, and cost him the life of his adopted father.

But he exposed the men behind the explosion, providing some grim satisfaction that those responsible were punished for their actions.

The veneer of respectability, carefully constructed over several years, had been ripped away in a heartbeat by that shameless act. And then he disappeared again, living a peaceful existence, building a new, delicate veneer until another friend was killed under suspicious circumstances and he arose once more as the Raven, punishing those responsible for his friend's death. That selfless act again exacted a terrible toll, both physically and mentally, but through it all Nancy had stood by him, refusing to let him be sucked into the quagmire when it threatened to overwhelm him. And now, as he was about to have another chance at a normal life, his friend Allan was languishing in jail, accused of murder. Riordan sipped his coffee.

I'm a fucking pariah, he thought to himself.

Easing out the desk's middle drawer, his searching fingers touched the tiny set of keys secreted on the back like a believer reaching for a religious icon. It had been over two years since he had handled them, but it was an omen of things to come. The keys opened pre-paid airport luggage lockers in several major Canadian cities, each with a cache of weapons: ammunition, guns, explosives and detonators, rolls of currency, and several sets of well-forged papers. His soul felt heavy and he rested his head in his hands, like a priest in prayer, his fingertips touching gently against his eyelids. He stayed that way for a long time, the reverie broken only by the gentle chirping of the phone. He had turned down the tone.

"Daniel Riordan speaking," he said.

"Good morning Daniel," came a rich, aristocratic voice, "this is Oliver Wentworth." Riordan recognized the name as that of Allan Brown's lawyer. Riordan sipped his coffee and waited. He did not like lawyers.

Wentworth said, "I'm sorry you couldn't get in to see Allan yesterday, but the Crown wants to move quickly on this one–it is an election year after all. You can get in to see Allan this morning at nine-thirty a.m. and I will meet you at the station and take you through to him. He was formally charged first thing this morning with second-degree murder. I am trying to plea-bargain the charge down to involuntary manslaughter, which has a mandatory jail sentence, but with good behavior it may only be a year, two at the most."

Riordan's insides froze at the thought of his friend going to jail. "Is he guilty?" he asked, finding great difficulty in pronouncing the words.

"His recollection is rather fuzzy, and is corroborated by your statement to the police that he was intoxicated at the time, but the DNA evidence and other physical evidence is overwhelming. I believe he killed her accidentally during a bout of wild sex, in which the choke chain was pulled too tightly about her neck. I have dealt with other such cases."

"Auto-erotic asphyxiation?" said Riordan. An endless curiosity about forensics sated by reading and watching documentaries had provided him with a detailed knowledge of the subject.

"That is the technical term for it, yes," said Wentworth after a brief pause. "Allan believes he killed her, but his show of remorse is not going very far with the police officers in charge of the case. They want to throw the book at him–the 'blue wall' and all those types of emotions are running high. They want to make an example of him. I'll be lucky if I can get the Crown Attorney to bargain with me, but given the backlog of cases, a guilty verdict in what they see as an 'open and shut case', would probably have a lot of appeal to them."

I can't believe Allan killed her, thought Riordan, but maybe it truly was an accident. It was not the first time that Allan had been involved in wild, kinky sex. He was reminded of the time that Allan had brought a lady home and, after much champagne, she suggested that Allan tie her to the bed. Allan, always open to such suggestions, had complied, using the thick cords from his drapes. Apparently the effort had been too much for him, for he passed out on top of the woman. As Allan, always the master of understatement, had put it, "she was not terribly impressed with me when I came around." So it was not out of the realms of possibility that Allan had actually killed Susan. Riordan hung his head like a penitent. "Do what you can," he said, his heart heavy. "I'll see you at the jail."

Oliver Wentworth was waiting on the steps of the station, looking at his watch when Riordan pulled the Range Rover over to the curb. Grabbing his leather jacket, Riordan climbed out and locked the vehicle, scrutinizing Wentworth as he walked over towards the doors of the police station to meet him.

Wentworth was about six feet six inches tall, a thin, cadaverous, gangly creature with thinning hair and a narrow, hawk-like face. There was feral cunning hiding there in the dark eyes, and Riordan disliked the man instantly. One of his natural talents was the ability to size up people quickly and it had saved his life many times and later in life had proven to be a tremendous asset in business.

Wentworth, exquisitely dressed in a greenish, two-piece, Armani silk suit and a flamboyant, brightly patterned tie, reeked of money. His reputation as a criminal defense attorney however, was unequalled in the city, the best of the best, depending on your point of view. Allan must have paid a fair penny to get him, thought Riordan.

Wentworth looked up, making eye contact as Riordan approached, and held out his hand immediately. Riordan took the limp rag in his hand and gave it his best bone-crushing grip, grinning at the expression in Wentworth's eyes. "Daniel Riordan," he said, pumping the man's hand furiously.

"Oliver Wentworth," came the pained reply. "I went in already and had the officers bring Allan up to one of the interview rooms. We can have a little bit of privacy there.

They're talking of moving him to the correctional facility on the west side this evening."

Riordan asked, "What about bail?" and received a withering look from Wentworth, as if to say 'let me do my job, you moron'.

"A snowball's chance in hell," said Wentworth sternly, and the two men went up the stairs and into the station. Riordan was mildly bemused by the situation. All the days in Belfast, in that cauldron of violence where he had been the most feared enforcer in the Protestant paramilitary movement, and he had never been inside a police station.

The hackles on the back of his neck rose, a reflex reaction to the surroundings. He followed Wentworth up a flight of stairs to a room where several desks sat abandoned, their occupants either on their way to work or out on a call. Steam rose from a cup of coffee on one of the desks, and presently another door opened and one of the detectives from the previous evening came into the room. He glanced in surprise at Riordan, then addressed Wentworth. "I've put him in interview room three. Take as much time as you need."

Wentworth wound his way through the desks and out through the door by which the detective had entered the room. Riordan followed, and immediately his nostrils were assailed by the pungent odor of ammonia and another, more familiar smell. It was the scent of fear, a long time resident of the holding area. Don't like this much, thought Riordan. If I put a foot wrong on this I could be languishing here instead of Allan.

The door to room three was partially open, and as Wentworth opened it and strode in, Riordan could see his friend's back. The room was painted in a shiny yellow color, with gray concrete floors and a tiny, chipped Formica table and four chairs in the center. A single bulb, recessed in the ceiling and protected by a strong wire mesh, cast an eerie pall over the room. Wentworth set his briefcase on the table and sat down. Allan Brown started in surprise when Riordan sat down also, his eyes widening.

"Daniel, what...."

Riordan almost choked at the sight of Brown's pallid complexion, his greasy unwashed hair and the sour smell emanating from his friend's clothes. Even worse was the eye almost puffed shut and a long gouge down one cheek. Riordan's eyes went immediately to Brown's knuckles, the bloody ridges telling their story. "Jesus Allan, what happened?" Riordan exclaimed.

Brown shrugged his shoulders. "I had a couple of visitors from the local chapter of Satan's Riders last night. Apparently there was nowhere else to put them so I got to play host for the evening. The first few minutes were okay but then they wanted to play 'hide the weenie' so that's where I drew the line. It wasn't much of a fight, as there were only two of them, but the guards were a bit over enthusiastic in getting me off them."

Riordan smiled and touched his friend's arm. He knew that Allan was a top-ranked kick boxer who practiced Tai Chi almost daily. He worked and worked on the same kata like all the other students at the dojo, preparing for the day it would have to be used, and like them, never expecting to have to use it at all. Riordan asked, "Did you use it?"

A wisp of a smile crossed Brown's face and he nodded. Brown's eyes were red-rimmed, like he had not slept, and his knuckles constantly returned to his eyes to rub away the sleep. A worm of anger crept into Riordan's stomach.

It was not the first time he had seen a victim of sensory deprivation, a favorite technique of the Royal Ulster Constabulary in trying to wear down the resistance of their suspects. The victims were literally not allowed to sleep for days, and then they were forced to stand against a wall draped in a hood while a loud, mechanized roar was generated around them. The sensation of drowning was almost universally acclaimed by the victims. There were not many who could resist, but Riordan knew how. His father had prepared him for such a session by exposing him to the technique on several occasions to toughen his resistance. It was one of many lessons Riordan would never forget.

Riordan turned to Wentworth. "Can't you do something about this?" he asked.

"I'll have a word with the Captain and make sure it does not happen again," Wentworth snorted indignantly, then opened his briefcase and took out several green manila folders, each with a neatly typed label across the top. Brown turned his head away immediately. "I don't want to look at that shit," he hissed. "I killed her by accident. I loved her and I fucking well killed her. And not one of these bastards believes me."

Riordan reached out to pick up the top folder but Wentworth snatched it away like a petulant child. "You can't look at that," he said in a tone which made Riordan want to grab him by the throat and give him a good shake.

"He can look at it if I say so," interrupted Brown. "Not that it'll do any good. Any word on the plea bargain?"

Wentworth handed Riordan the file without looking at him, and addressed Brown directly, talking for several minutes. Riordan ignored them, concentrating on the series of black and white crime-scene photos in the folder. He was no stranger to death, especially violent death, as he had meted it out on many an occasion, but the photographs of Susan Delgado, a woman whom he considered a friend, unnerved him. He went through each in turn, the wide angle shots of the bed through to the detailed close-ups of the ugly ligature marks and the deep impressions of the stainless steel dog-collar on her neck. She had a tiny tattoo of a red rose on her left shoulder and Riordan was surprised by it–he had never seen it before, but then again he had never seen Susan naked. And Allan had never mentioned it. He looked at the close-up of the rose, then went back to the wide angle photo where it was barely visible.

Closing the folder, he set it back on the pile and waited while Wentworth made copious notes from his chat with Brown.

Brown said, "So how's Nancy?"

"Bigger by the day," replied Riordan. "She's been asking for you, and as soon as we get through this delivery business she'll be down to see you."

Brown ran his fingers through his beard and scratched. "I'm not going anywhere," he laughed, a forced ironic sound, "not for a long time by the looks of things. I may even have to get a prison tattoo to fit in with my new surroundings."

It was out before he realized it, and Riordan winced as he heard himself say, "I'm surprised you didn't get a tattoo to match Susan's. It looks fairly recent." He continued, "I'm sorry Allan, that was thoughtless of me. I didn't mean anything..."

"It's okay Daniel, no offense taken." His brow furrowing, Brown said, "But where did you see the tattoo?"

Riordan pointed toward the stack of folders. "It was in the crime scene photos I just looked at. The first one where they do a wide-angle shot of the area to try to capture as much detail as possible."

"But that's not possible," said Brown, suddenly animated, his countenance transformed in an instant. "You couldn't see the tattoo. She was lying on her left side when I left her, so the tattoo would be hidden. I remember kissing her right shoulder just before I left. Let me see that."

Riordan's hand slammed on to the folder a fraction of a second before that of Wentworth. "It's not a good idea, Allan," Riordan said. "They're pretty hard to stomach."

Brown said, "You're preaching to the converted, mate. Those two detectives showed me the autopsy photos the first night I was here and I threw up all over the place. But I won't do it again. Let me see the photograph." His tone said this was not a matter for discussion.

Opening the folder, Riordan extracted the first crime-scene photograph and laid it on the table between them. "That's it," exclaimed Brown, his voice full of incredulity. Susan Delgado lay face down on the bed, the blanket modestly draped across her waist and her face turned to the left side of the bed. A pained expression crossed Brown's features, the man torn between the image of the woman he loved lying dead and the realization that something was wrong.

Riordan saw the inner struggle mirrored on his friend's face and said, "What's wrong Allan, what's the matter?"

Brown stabbed at the photograph with his finger. "This can't be the first crime scene photograph. This is not the way I left her." Riordan allowed the enormity of what his friend was saying to sink in, then turned to Wentworth and saw the look of disbelief in his eyes. "You do believe me, don't you," snorted Brown. "If this is the first crime scene photograph and she was not moved, I didn't kill her. Daniel?"

Riordan looked into his friend's eyes, looked beyond the tears deep into his soul and believed him. He nodded. Wentworth, on the other hand, exploded.

"Allan," Wentworth spat, "do you honestly expect me to go out there and tell the detectives that you've changed your mind? Think about it for a moment. You already admitted to killing her, and that you were intoxicated at the time. Daniel here even corroborates the fact that you had been drinking and passed out in his car."

Wentworth paused to let his words sink in. Taking a deep breath, he stretched across the table and placed his hand on top that of Brown's. "If you really want me to I will do it, but as your lawyer I strongly recommend that you think seriously about it before you ask me to proceed. The plea bargain will go out the window and they will throw the proverbial book at you. That means serious jail time for you if convicted, and the evidence they have against you is overwhelming. Please give yourself a little time to think about it."

Brown sagged back in his chair like a deflated balloon, wiping away a tear with the back of his hand. "Whatever you say Oliver, whatever you say." Riordan felt his breath catch in his throat.

"That's a sensible decision," replied Wentworth, replacing the files in his expensive Louis Vuitton briefcase and shutting it with a loud click. "I will come back tomorrow morning and discuss this with you further. I have to go now to a plea-bargain meeting with the crown attorney."

"I'll see you tomorrow, Allan," said Riordan, his stomach in knots at the plight of his friend, and got up and followed Wentworth out of the interview room. Outside in the corridor, out of earshot of Allan, Wentworth said, "The only mitigating circumstance is the fact that Susan liked it rough, so this can't be the first time she has done this. If I dig hard enough I'm sure I can find others to testify that she was really into this bondage, and if I can find someone who has used the choke chain on her before that would assist Allan."

Riordan shook his head furiously. "Don't," he growled, fire in his eyes. "Allan would never stoop to such things. Let her rest in peace – her family doesn't need any more grief."

CHAPTER 6

Judas

The following morning, Riordan, dressed in shorts and a t-shirt, opened his front door to find yet another ugly surprise awaiting on his doorstep. The front page of the newspaper carried a photograph of Allan Brown, under the heading 'Sex Killer Charged.' Closing his eyes for a moment, he took several deep breaths, fighting back the rage at the unfairness of the newspapers, the ugly side of the media who sensationalized every tragedy, searching for the grail of market share.

He remembered when his first wife and daughter had been killed in the explosion on the jet, that at the airport a reporter had stuck a microphone and a camera into his face to ask him how he felt. Despite Riordan's protestations the man had doggedly persisted, intruding into his grief and despair and frustration, and when nothing else could convince the man to leave him alone, Riordan had left him writhing on the terminal floor in agony, clutching badly bruised testicles.

Sipping his coffee, he quickly scanned the article but there was nothing he didn't already know so he crumpled the rag and tossed it in the garbage–no point in upsetting Nancy further. There had been numerous questions the night before, and then the question of 'what are you going to do to help him?' That set off a further long discussion about identities and how strong his new veneer was and how much scrutiny it could take.

Riordan held her hand, full of love for this woman who had given him another chance, who looked beyond the violence and pain, as she said simply to him, "I know you're a good man, Daniel. What's done is done–there's no need to dwell on the past."

She was about to deliver his children, and yet she was prepared to give it all up to help Allan Brown. She knew, as he did, that if he got involved in anything to do with Allan's situation, there was always a chance that someone, especially the police, would pry too closely into his past. That would force him to go on the run again, this time with another person in tow. It was a huge burden and it weighed heavily on his mind.

He put the empty coffee cup in the dishwasher, pulled on his jacket and headed down to the police station for his meeting with Allan and Oliver Wentworth. He stopped at the corner of the street and ran into Starbucks for a quick coffee. The young man at the counter reminded him of the solemn vow he made the last time never to come in the store again. When the youth, with all sorts of hoops and studs in various parts of his body, asked what flavour,

Riordan smiled, remembering Dennis Leary's rant about ordering coffee at Starbucks. "Coffee flavoured coffee," he asked, and saw the indecision on the youth's face. He ended up settling for an African blend, shaking his head at the state of the youth's dress, especially the baggy pants with the crotch at the knees and a couple of inches of underwear showing.

He drove downtown, sipping tentatively at the scalding hot brew. Construction on the main drag slowed traffic to a crawl, a fortunate circumstance for him. Turning the corner on to the main drag he cursed under his breath, seeing a group of photographers and media types clustered around the steps of the station like tame sparrows waiting for crumbs. Cruising slowly past he saw Wentworth in the center of them, flapping his gums like there was no tomorrow, further reinforcing Riordan's original dislike of the man. Riordan drove on for another block, turning down behind the station to see if there was a back entrance, away from prying eyes–he did not want to get caught in the media frenzy. He saw uniformed officers coming out a back door, so he pulled in quickly, locked the car and was soon in the lobby. Wentworth was just making his way through the front doors and came directly across to Riordan.

Riordan grinned, noticing that Wentworth did not offer his hand this morning. He knew he was being petty, but where Wentworth was concerned, that was okay.

"Daniel," said Wentworth, "good of you to come. As you can see the media are about to have a field day with this, so I'm doing what I can to keep the situation under control. I actually managed to negotiate a plea-bargain with the Crown so I need to discuss it with Allan. I hope he's put that foolish notion out of his head about changing his plea." Wentworth tapped his upper lip with his index finger, as if an idea had just struck him. "Maybe you could have a word with him, Daniel, without me being there, to convince him how foolish it would be to alter the plea. As I told you the evidence is overwhelming and the Crown will go for the maximum sentence if he decides to change it. Would you do that for me, Daniel?"

Riordan thought about the request for a moment, and for the space of a heartbeat he was about to refuse– there was something in Wentworth's voice... The thought of playing a Judas did not sit well with him, but if it was in Allan's best interests then perhaps it could be tolerated. Riordan nodded, and Wentworth led the way up to the interview rooms. It was a different room from the previous evening. Wentworth paused at the door and said, "You go on in. Take a few minutes on your own with him. I'll join you shortly."

Riordan opened the door and almost gagged, the harsh odor of ammonia from the previous evening's cleaning assailing his nostrils. Allan Brown was sitting at the table, dressed in a light-colored boiler suit when Riordan entered. The windowless room was again dark and oppressive, faint light spilling from a single wire-encased bulb recessed into the ceiling. Other lights in the room were deliberately switched off, adding to the intimidating ambiance. Brown managed a weak smile, but the multi-hued bruises on his face removed all semblance of hope from the gesture. Riordan grasped his friend's shoulder, and sat down across the table. "Real fashion statement you are," he said. "Joined the village people, have we?"

"Fuck off," muttered Brown, looking back towards the door. "Where's the mouthpiece?"

Riordan grinned. "He's gone back downstairs to preen some more for the media. He wants me to convince you to keep the guilty plea."

"And?" said Brown.

"You told me yesterday you didn't kill her, and you've had all night to think about it. Have you changed your mind?"

Brown spat, "No!" Riordan was surprised by the force of the reply, and saw the fire in his friend's eyes.

Riordan nodded. "All right then. The police are not going to be too enthusiastic about investigating this as they already think you killed her. They've done enough due diligence to satisfy themselves, and a jury, that you're the one. And they have a formidable stack of evidence, not to mention the fact that you've already confessed."

"So what do you think I should do?" asked Brown, clasping his hands together on the table. Riordan noticed the fresh cuts on Brown's knuckles immediately and pointed towards them. Brown looked down and said, "I needed a bit of help to get out of my clothes it seems, and for some strange reason I decided to resist. Funny thing that–I said 'okay' and suddenly I'm supposedly resisting, so there was a tiny bit of police brutality. I'd show you my scrotum but I might get a reputation."

Riordan thought for a moment, then said, "I'll do what I can for you, Allan, but I can only go so far, as you well know. The veneer's a bit thin, especially given the circumstances with Nancy, but she says I'm to do whatever it takes, no matter the cost."

"She's a great lady, Daniel," said Brown, a wistful look on his face. "What about a private detective? There's a guy I read about in the paper a couple of weeks ago. His name is..."

"...Brian Featherstone," laughed Riordan, knowing exactly where Allan was heading. "I read the article too. All right, I'll contact him and explain your circumstances."

Brown looked relieved. The tension seemed to evaporate from his body. "You do believe me, Daniel. I honestly didn't kill her." The look on his face said he desperately needed someone to believe him.

Riordan rubbed his face in his hands. This was one of those times in life where there could be no doubts, no half-truths, just hope for a friend adrift in turbulent waters. His voice never wavered, his eyes met those of his friend, and he said, "I believe you, my friend, and I will get you out of this mess, one way or another. You've been put in a frame, and a very, very good one. But whoever did it is going to be sorry. I know about these things. Somebody wanted Susan dead, and you provided that person with a convenient patsy. Talk about Lee Harvey Oswald." There was a loud rap on the door and Wentworth entered, briefcase in hand.

He sat down across the table from Brown, looked at them both for dramatic effect, then opened the case and extracted some papers, and set the case on the floor. Shuffling the papers into alignment like a newscaster, Wentworth said, "The Crown wants to bring this case to court soon for sentencing, and given the hoopla that's appearing about the case in the news, it is not a bad thing. We don't want to give anyone time to reconsider the plea-bargain, so we go to court in one week."

Brown said, "Oliver, I didn't do it. I want to change my plea." For the briefest moment, a look of annoyance appeared on Wentworth's face, then it was gone, leaving Riordan to wonder if it was only his imagination. Wentworth swiveled his hawkish face towards Riordan for a moment, a sneer on his face. "I take it you weren't able to convince him."

Riordan shrugged, resisting the urge to wipe the sneer off the bastard's face and said, in a heavily exaggerated Irish accent, "He's a thick bastard he is, not the sense God gave him. But he is my friend, and I believe him."

Wentworth leaned back in his chair and threw his hands in the air in resignation. "All right, Allan, if that is what you want me to do." Picking up the briefcase, he tossed the papers into it, obviously displeased with the turn of events, and got up, waiting for Riordan to do the same.

Brown said, "Daniel, you'll need some money to pay Featherstone's retainer, if he decides to help me."

"What's this?" interrupted Wentworth. "You're surely not talking about Brian Featherstone, the private detective. The man's a thug."

Riordan's estimation of Featherstone leapt up several notches, and he said, "And that's a bad thing? I thought we might need some extra help on the case, as the detectives have pretty much made up their minds."

"You thought..." spluttered Wentworth, color rising in his cheeks and his voice raising an octave. "You thought! Leave the details of this to me. You are way out of your league." He jabbed his bony index finger into Riordan's chest, emphasizing each of his words.

Riordan, once the most feared of all Protestant paramilitary enforcers, allowed a smile to play along his lips. Allan Brown actually cracked a smile – he knew what was coming. If only Wentworth knew how much danger he had just placed himself in. Riordan's hand was a blur, arcing up to grasp Wentworth's wrist and twist it harmlessly out of the way. Wentworth cried out in pain, his wrist almost shattering in Riordan's fierce grip. "Don't ever do that again," said Riordan, winking at Brown. He released his grip and left the room.

Outside, Riordan drove around to the front of the station and parked a few yards away from Wentworth's Red Porsche. For some reason he remembered the joke about what's the difference between a Porsche and a hedgehog—the prick's on the inside. His eyes twinkled at the thought. It was certainly true in this case. A few minutes later Wentworth appeared, pushing his way through the reporters, looking somewhat harried, and climbed into the Porsche. As the Porsche screamed away from the curb, Riordan could see the car phone cradled against Wentworth's ear, the man obviously agitated about something.

Riordan called directory inquiries, got the number for Featherstone and Associates, and called. A pleasant lady with an English accent answered and waited patiently while Riordan explained the reason for his call. The lady had obviously been reading the newspapers, as she scheduled a luncheon appointment for him without question.

At the same time, a few miles to the south of Vancouver, the private line on Slade's phone console chirped, distracting him from his terminal. He had been going over the bookings for the next few weeks–he only planned for eight weeks in advance, a necessary precaution, as it was sometimes difficult to get 'merchandise' for the clients. As it stood at the moment, he had more demand than supply and needed to get some more runaways, which was the most dangerous part of his operation. Dealing with pimps in various parts of the country, who would sell their own mother if the price was high enough, was the weak link. But as long as they were paid well and on time by his bodyguards, who brought their own menace to the transaction, he was fairly well protected.

"Slade here," he said.

"Oliver Wentworth speaking," came the reply. A wry smile crossed Slade's face. Wentworth, a fairly regular customer for the past three years, was booked for two weeks hence, requesting a dark-haired oriental girl between twelve and fourteen years old and the younger the better. Wentworth had never killed any of his 'girls', but knew he could go as far as he wanted and was becoming increasingly more violent during his sessions. Slade had him on tape, saw the bloodlust growing in his eyes, and knew Wentworth would kill soon. It was just a matter of time.

"What can I do for you Oliver?" Slade asked, examining his nails.

Wentworth said, "We have a bit of a problem," and immediately Slade sat bolt upright in his chair.

"What kind of problem, Oliver? " asked Slade, keeping his voice even, his mind racing with all sorts of possibilities. He didn't like problems.

"Brown has decided that he didn't kill the girl and wants to change his plea to "not guilty." He has also decided to hire a private detective to look into the matter. I tried to get to him through his friend Daniel Riordan, but Riordan's a smug bastard, and sided with Brown."

"That's not good, Oliver," said Slade, an edge creeping into his voice. "Which private detective is he going to use?"

"Someone called Featherstone."

Slade tsked tsked through his teeth. "Ah yes, Featherstone, I've heard of him. Seems to be getting a lot of publicity these days. All right Oliver," he said, "this is what I want you to do. Get me as much information as you can on this person Featherstone and this Daniel Riordan, and I want it today. You do what you have to do regarding Allan Brown changing his plea-bargain. Perhaps mister Brown could have an accident, a fatal accident in the holding cells. After all, he is depressed over his circumstances and you heard him saying that he doesn't think he could face a long sentence in jail. You did hear him say that, didn't you Oliver?"

"Yes, yes, I did," replied Wentworth, and Slade knew the man was thinking about the hold Slade had over him.

Slade said, "Thank you for warning me, Oliver," and hung up. It was always good to get information on possible threats, because you could always find a weak spot and exploit it if necessary. Everyone had a weak spot: wives, girlfriends, parents, children, all could be used. Slade was good at using people.

Riordan parked in the underground carpark at the address which Featherstone's secretary had given him. He was making his way towards the parking elevator when he passed a green Jaguar XJ8 with the vanity license plate of 'FEATHR'. He smiled. Must be a lucrative profession, he thought to himself.

The offices covered one end of the eighth floor of the building, and Riordan found himself standing before a pair of very solid looking metal doors, with two video-cameras peering down at him from the corners. He pushed and pulled but neither would budge, so he pressed the tiny doorbell and smiled up at one of the cameras. There was a soft metallic 'clunk' and the doors swung open. Electro-magnetic locks–Riordan was impressed. Directly ahead of him sat a matronly English lady, who smiled sweetly but whose demeanor spoke volumes–she would brook no nonsense from visitors.

"You must be Daniel Riordan," she said. "Mister Featherstone will see you in a moment. Would you care for a cup of tea, or coffee perhaps?"

"I'd love a cup of tea, darlin'," Riordan said, smiling at the woman, who instantly warmed to him. "Milk and sugar love?" Riordan nodded. She pressed a button on the console in front of her, spoke quietly into her discreet telephone headset, and a few minutes later a young secretary brought out a tray with his tea and a plate of cookies. Riordan recognized the Spode china immediately, and commented on it.

"Oh that's Mister Featherstone for you. He likes the best of everything. How did you know it was Spode?" asked the receptionist.

Riordan sipped at his tea. "My wife, who unfortunately is of Scottish heritage, is educating me on fine china, and I'm educating her on the merits of Waterford crystal. A fair exchange, wouldn't you say?" He bit into the chocolate digestive and was savouring the taste when the door opened again and the young secretary came out. Riordan drained the tea and set the cup and saucer on the receptionist's credenza.

The secretary wore a short black mini-skirt, complemented by a black silk blouse, and Riordan was entranced by the swing of her hips under the fabric. She led the way down past a row of offices, some of which were open. Each of the offices had a narrow floor-to-ceiling window beside the door. Riordan peered inside as he passed, getting a sense of the individuals inside. They were mostly male, in their thirties and dressed casually for the most part.

He was surprised to see some female operatives, but then remembered the article saying that Featherstone had hired some people from the 14th Intelligence Group in Northern Ireland. The 14th were a special intelligence-gathering unit who worked side by side with the Special Air Service and the police force in the hot spots of the province. Their selection process was grueling, the failure rate extremely high, yet women were an integral part of the group. To all and sundry they were known as the 'Det', short for detachment, just as MI5 were affectionately known as the 'Box', as their favoured method of communicating with their agents was via a PO box number.

The door to the office at the end of the corridor was open and Featherstone stood looking out the window, sipping a cup of tea when Riordan entered. There were no curtains on the windows. The office faced English Bay, providing a breathtaking panoramic view of the harbor and the many boats scuttling back and forth. Featherstone, well dressed in white chinos, brown penny-loafers, and a chambray shirt, turned around. Riordan took in the short sandy hair, the piercing gray eyes and the wry smile, seemingly fixed in place as if Featherstone was constantly amused at the world. He moved across the room with a sinewy movement, and Riordan knew immediately that Featherstone had been some form of special forces operative in a previous life. In Belfast he had spent many an hour watching SAS undercover soldiers from a distance as they came and went from what they thought was a safe-house.

Riordan extended his hand and Featherstone shook it warmly. In a cultured British accent he said, "Mister Riordan, I'm Brian Featherstone. Come tell me your tale. We can sit over here." Looking over Riordan's shoulder he said, "Jenny, could you bring us some more tea, and another digestive for Daniel here." Riordan knew then that Featherstone had been watching him in the lobby, which was a sensible precaution, given his occupation.

Featherstone led the way to a corner of the office where a couch and two leather, high-backed armchairs flanked a marble gas fireplace. A glass coffee table sat between them, and a copy of the most recent Mars & Minerva magazine lay on top. There were several plaques on the wall, with campaign medals, and Riordan recognized the famous winged dagger immediately. Featherstone was ex-SAS.

Riordan sighed and sank into one of the armchairs. He could never get away from the bastards. Beside the magazine sat a tiny box, recently unwrapped, with a tiny model of a Ford WW II jeep lying on the green velvet. He peered at it and Featherstone said, "It's a commemorative emblem for Colonel Paddy Mayne, one of the founders of the Special Air Service regiment." Riordan nodded, "I know. I've been to his grave many times."

Featherstone shifted almost imperceptibly in his seat, like a rattler about to strike, and Riordan grinned. "Relax," Riordan said, but it was blatantly obvious that Featherstone was far from comfortable. "If I was going to harm you I'd put a mercury-tilt detonator on a couple of pounds of Semtex and stuff it under your car, the jag with the vanity plates."

"Touché," Featherstone said. "I'm curious now. I get a sense of your accent, Ballymena isn't it, but you've been away for a while. Just the odd word or two gives you away."

Riordan said, "Let's get the shit out of the way and then you can focus on my problem. My adopted father served with David Stirling during the war, and was good friends with Paddy Mayne." Opening his shirt, Riordan showed Featherstone the tiny brass emblem he wore on a chain around his neck. "It belonged to my father. He was killed a few years ago." Featherstone's right eye raised in a question at the sight of the SAS cap badge, but Riordan shook his head.

Riordan asked, "When did you serve with the regiment?" Featherstone was about to answer when the secretary entered with a pot of tea, and a fresh cup for

Riordan. Featherstone graciously poured a cup, added milk and sugar, and handed the cup to Riordan. Sitting back in his chair Featherstone said, "I left the regiment shortly after the Gulf war. I had done my time, all twenty-two years of it, and figured it was time to do something else. So here I am."

"Did you do any time in the North of Ireland?" Riordan asked.

"Oh yes, that was one fucking evil place. From the bastards I met there, I'm hardly surprised the peace process has broken down." Riordan heard anger creep into Featherstone's voice.

Riordan said, "I know the extensive network the SAS maintains throughout the world, so to save you time worrying about me, I was known in Belfast as the Raven. Probably around the time you were there, given we're about the same age. One of your guys saved my life a couple of years ago when the provos found out where I was living, and tried to kill me."

Featherstone almost choked on his tea and Riordan laughed aloud. Featherstone spluttered, "Jesus, you have a way of surprising people, haven't you?"

In a thick Belfast accent, Riordan replied, "All part of me charm!"

"What do you need me for?" asked Featherstone. "I should think you're pretty capable of doing any investigating you need."

Riordan replied, "I'm tired of all the shit. I had a family once and they were killed, and now I have a new wife and twins on the way and I don't want to run any more. I've got to stay in the shadows, but I will help you in any way I can."

Featherstone filled his teacup, added some milk and sugar, and leaned back in the armchair. "Tell me what you want me to do."

So Riordan did.

CHAPTER 7

hamlet

Featherstone sat quietly, listening intently during Riordan's recollection of the events of the evening Brown was supposed to have killed Susan Delgado, and his recounting of the evidence Riordan had seen at the station. Featherstone moved only to refill his cup from the teapot. When Riordan had finished, Featherstone rose and crossed the room to his desk where he picked up a notepad and pen.

"How long have you known Allan Brown?" Featherstone asked, when he had returned to his seat

"Several years now," replied Riordan, watching Featherstone make some notes, intrigued by the large antique Mont-Blanc fountain pen which he used. Such things were a rarity and spoke volumes about the man.

"Do you think he killed the woman?" Featherstone asked, his eyes closely studying Riordan's features as he replied. Riordan did not hesitate.

"No," he replied firmly.

Featherstone said, in a very matter-of-fact tone, "He originally confessed to the killing, though. Did you believe him then?" Riordan felt his anger grow at the question like a tiny bud bursting through the soil, even though he knew well Featherstone was only playing the devil's advocate with him.

The anger flared and his knuckles turned white on the arms of the chair. Forcing down the anger Riordan said, "I was with him right after he was supposed to have killed her, and if he did it was truly an accident. However, drunk and all as he was, I think he was framed for the killing."

"Or he could be a drowning man clutching at straws," interrupted Featherstone. "He seems to have convinced you!" The spark of anger flared again, and Riordan felt his body tense, but Featherstone diffused the situation quickly by saying, "but that would not make any sense. Giving up a plea bargain to take the chance he might get the full sentence for manslaughter if found guilty is the move of a man who believes in his innocence. He is lucky to have you as a friend–such things are rare these days." Featherstone laid down the pen and sat staring off into space for a moment, obviously mulling over the facts Riordan had given him.

"If Allan Brown is innocent, as he claims," said Featherstone, holding his hands together in front of his face as if in prayer, "then Susan Delgado was obviously the target. And to put someone in a frame in such a way was pure opportunism, given the fact that your fishing trip was planned only a few days prior. Whoever meant to kill her had to make it look like an accident, and your friend Allan Brown provided a convenient means to an end." Featherstone paused for a moment, his brow creased as he strove to recall something. "There are people who specialize in this sort of thing, but they don't come cheap, and they don't work for just anyone. They're usually ex-spooks and the like who have been involved in black ops. A few names pop to mind, and I'll pursue that lead with some of my contacts to see where it leads."

A cold finger traced a path slowly down Riordan's spine. "That means whoever killed her had to have been watching them, and saw a chance."

Featherstone nodded. "I agree."

Riordan leaned back in his seat and shook his head. "Fuck me," he snorted. "I might even have seen the guy."

"All right," Featherstone said, abruptly rising to his feet. "I'll take the case. I presume you know my services don't come cheap, but I'll need to move quickly since your friend has changed his plea. Give me a number where I can reach you and I'll be in touch as soon as I can. I will take this on personally, and I'd also like to talk to you about your time in Belfast, when we're done. If you'd like to, that is."

Riordan smiled, in spite of himself, having a good sense of the man before him, and nodded. "That's fair," he said, shaking hands with Featherstone. "When we're done. I'll see myself out."

"You're going the wrong way," Featherstone said, "there's another elevator here outside my office. Some of my clients like to be discreet, so I don't have them hanging about in the waiting room if they are that way inclined. This elevator that I had installed goes directly to the ground floor. Cost me a bloody bomb, it did."

Riordan laughed aloud, and Featherstone, realizing he had used the Irish slang for expensive, did so as well. Riordan said, "I can make one of those for you!" and followed Featherstone's lead out into the corridor.

Four hours later Riordan stood in his kitchen, or more correctly Nancy's kitchen, since it was she who had completed gutted and remodeled the room. Discovering his love of cooking was matched only by her own, Nancy had created a gourmet kitchen where both of them could work independently without crowding one another.

He munched contentedly on a slice of apple while slicing red and green peppers and some cloves of garlic on a heavy wooden cutting board. In front of him sat a knife block with an expensive set of German knives, honed and oiled to perfection: he believed in owning the best utensils available. Downstairs, in the recreation room, were mounted several presentation cases containing his collection of knives from all over the world.

He had to admit that it was a strange hobby, collecting knives, but he was fascinated by them, and by the workmanship from the many different countries where they had originated. He had his favorites; the Kukri bought from a former Ghurka, a knife which had to taste blood if removed from its sheath, a fine Moroccan curved dagger elaborately inlaid with precious stones, a limited edition, fantasy creation by Gil Hibon of the United States, and then the exquisite Japanese Katanas, their edges honed to an edge sharper than the finest scalpel, and mounted in a special case.

He reflected often, and only to himself–though he was certain that Nancy had formed her own opinion–that the fascination for knives must have come from his time in Ireland. As the Raven, he most often used a gun as a means of dispatching his enemies, but there were times when a knife was the only weapon available. Guns killed from afar, using a knife you had to be up close and personal.

Beside him on the stove, several chopped onions simmered in butter, spiced with a heavy helping of coriander, ginger, cumin and turmeric, filling the air with a heady aroma. Behind the pan, a pot of water gurgled as it reached boiling point, and Riordan poured in the pre-measured container of Basmati rice. Nancy loved Indian food, and she was feeling tired so he gladly took on the task of cooking supper. The pregnancy was taking its toll, and with each passing day she grew more and more weary, and now the additional burden of Susan's death and Allan's imprisonment weighed heavily on her mind.

On the stereo the Three Tenors blasted out 'O Sole Mio', one of Riordan's favorite pieces, and he sang along, glad to have the distraction. He sensed her come into the room, there was no noise, but he knew she was there, and he soon felt a hand slide around his waist.

He looked down to see Nancy, pillowcase creases still on her cheeks, puckering her lips for a kiss. "Hi there big boy, fancy a quickie?" she said, and he smiled and kissed her gently.

"My God, aren't you the wanton woman?" he said, adding the diced vegetables to the mixture and stirring it slowly. "I thought I'd let you sleep for a while, and it has been a while since we've had a curry. They say it brings on labor."

"So does a quickie," she laughed. "But I guess you'd rather have some food, so I'll have to take a rain check this time. Oh, by the way, what happened with the private detective? Or should I say 'dick'?"

Riordan shrugged. "Oh you know I love it when you talk dirty. The guy's name is Featherstone. He's a good head and he says he'll take the case personally."

She stole a piece of his apple from the counter and took a bite. "Are you going to help him, you know..."

Riordan continued stirring the curry. "I'll do what I have to, but I have too much at stake to do anything overt. As you well know the Raven was a part of my life that I am not proud of, but I have managed to reconcile what I did to some degree. That's a world I don't want to go back to. Featherstone has the necessary legitimate contacts to help the investigation, so we should be okay."

Nancy stroked his face gently. "You'll be fine love," she said. "You won't lose your way again." Riordan lifted out some of the sauce on a wooden spoon and held it for her to taste. "Wonderful, as always," she said, as the doorbell rang. "I'll get it," she said, "you keep cooking."

Straining his ears when he heard the door creak open, Riordan heard her say, "Not you two again," and immediately lifted the pan off the heat and strode down the hall, alarm rising. The two detectives from the night before were being led into the dining room, and he went in the other door and confronted them.

"Well, if it isn't Laurel and Hardy," he said, his voice heavy with sarcasm. "What are you two doing here?"

McGregor said, "Your mate changed his plea this afternoon, so we want to ask you a few more questions."

Riordan did not offer them a seat. "We're in the middle of supper, so make it quick," he said. "But there's not much I can add to what I already told you." Nancy went off into the kitchen and Riordan answered their questions as best he could, but he could tell that it was a half-hearted exercise. The detectives already believed that Allan Brown was guilty. McGregor folded up his notebook and put it in his jacket.

As they turned to leave, Riordan could barely contain his contempt for the pair. He spat, "You guys are just going through the motions, aren't you. You don't believe Allan's story at all."

Patterson, whom Riordan thought was playing the bad cop role, and who was trying hard to keep his emotions in check said, "I've seen lots of guys change their pleas for all sorts of reasons, but I tell you not one of them was ever successful in getting a 'not guilty' vote from the jury. Once they hear that you've already confessed to the crime, you might as well give up."

"And to think I actually contribute to your salaries," snorted Riordan. "Makes me sick."

When they had gone, Riordan returned to the kitchen to see Nancy setting two plates of steaming curry on the table, along with papadums and Naan bread. A bottle of German wine sat uncorked in the middle of the table. Droplets of condensation ran down the neck of the bottle and pooled on the table. "Thought you might need a drink," she said and sat down. Riordan joined her.

Riordan said, "I hope Featherstone is successful in getting somewhere with this, 'cos those two don't give a shit."

Featherstone phoned early the next morning, just as Riordan was sitting down to his morning coffee. It was another night of fitful sleep, and after waking for a second time in the wee hours he got up and went down to the living room couch. Sleep was a precious commodity for Nancy, and with him tossing and turning in their bed he threatened to deprive her of what she needed most.

Without any preamble Featherstone said, "I did some checking. The only thing I can surmise from what you told me is that the killing may have something to do with the case she was working on with this Detective Brian

Dymond. Allan Brown said she had had a break in the case, but Dymond was not aware of anything like that. In fact, he states that up to the day before her death they had not made any progress. If she had a break it must have happened shortly before she was killed. Dymond says he checked her place thoroughly, even her computer system and could find no trace of notes or clues. As you may imagine, he's not being terribly cooperative about this. And as for a conspiracy theory... the detective doesn't put much credence in that.

"I also talked to this Oliver Wentworth the second or third or whatever fucking number he is, and didn't get much farther with him. He's a complete and utter asshole in my opinion." Riordan grinned. Sometimes it was nice to have your opinion corroborated.

Featherstone continued, "I also checked with the parking infractions department and there were five parking tickets issued in Delgado's street between four and five o'clock in the morning, which is shortly after you and Brown left for the mountains. I'm getting the license plate numbers run down at the moment. That's as far as I've gotten. When I get more information I'll be in touch. Can I still reach you at this number?"

Riordan replied, "I'll be here. I'm a freelance computer consultant so I've taken a few weeks off to help my wife with the babies, if she ever manages to deliver, that is."

"Computers eh?" snorted Featherstone. "Fucking bane of my existence, they are. Maybe you can help me out, whenever you are ready to go back to work?"

"No problem," said Riordan and hung up. He was impressed with the speed at which Featherstone had acted, and felt somewhat assured that if anyone could turn up some sort of clue it would be him.

The clue, or somewhat tenuous clue, came later in the day. Featherstone called again to inform him that one of the parking tickets had been issued to a rental car from a company out in Whiterock, and that he was on his way to talk to the lady who issued the rental agreement. "I'm coming with you," said Riordan. "Nancy has had a cleaning fit and wants me out of the house."

Featherstone arrived ten minutes later in his Jaguar and they were soon heading out towards Whiterock, a southern suburb of Vancouver not far from the Washington border. Dressed in a gray workout sweater and faded denims, he was a far cry from Riordan's stereotype of a private detective.

"Don't get your hopes up," said Featherstone, when Riordan climbed into the car. "It may just be a dead end. But it needs checking."

"Did you pass this on to the police?" asked Riordan, and Featherstone shook his head.

"They haven't checked with parking infractions yet, and I doubt they will. I'd rather check out the lead before I get them involved. After all, I do have a reputation to protect." The rest of the drive was spent in silence, Featherstone selecting some CD's from a portable case and inserting them in the player. Riordan was surprised to hear the haunting strains of the Chieftains and commented as such.

Featherstone laughed. "From all the time I spent doing undercover in and around the bandit country of South Armagh, I developed a liking for traditional music. It's all you ever hear in the drinking clubs–the shebeens, you know."

They were soon pulling up to the rental car office in the wilds of Whiterock. The narrow road on the way out of the city, lined with majestic pine trees, reminded Riordan of the forests in the Glens of Antrim, only a few miles from where he had been raised, and for a brief moment he was homesick, whatever that meant. Home was here with Nancy and their soon-to-be family, but still, from time to time there was a longing for the sights and sounds of the places he had known as a youth, places to which he could never return. A momentary sadness tugged at his heartstrings.

The young lady at the counter, with a badge on her shirt that said 'Debbie', was very helpful, especially when Featherstone turned on the charm, and they were soon reviewing a copy of the rental agreement she had printed off for them.

"The guy has a California driver's license. Probably thought he wouldn't have to pay the ticket," commented Featherstone.

"Oh, we get a lot of those," interrupted the clerk. "Americans just throw away the tickets but we mail the ticket to them directly. The province deals directly with them after that."

Riordan pointed at the agreement. "It says here he was dropping the car back at the airport, instead of here, on Monday. Can you find out if he did so?" The girl smiled and picked up the phone, then set it back in its cradle. "Oh, I don't have to," she said, and pointed out the window. Featherstone and Riordan both turned to see a black Mustang drive into the lot. "That's Michelle with the car," she said, by way of explanation. "She must have picked it up at the airport."

Michelle, a young fresh-faced blonde girl in her early twenties by Riordan's estimation, was built like a model and well-endowed, a fact enhanced by the tight-fitting lycra top she wore. She was totally enchanted by Featherstone, and the fact that he was a private detective. By the way he acted, Riordan also believed that Featherstone had more than his fair share of the ladies, which would account for the absence of a wedding ring.

Michelle said, "The car was returned at the airport on Monday morning by Mister Fleming. It was just a coincidence that I was over there picking up another drop-off rental and I saw him. He was getting another rental car – said he didn't like the one he had. He didn't recognize me but I remember him. The guy gave me the creeps when he came in here to get his car the first time. You know, one of those lecherous types who likes to look at your tits." She blushed, realizing what she had said.

"You'd never catch us doing that," whispered Riordan.

"Do you remember how he got here to pick up the Mustang?" Featherstone asked. "It is a bit of a remote location."

The lady behind the counter answered. "I took his booking," she said. "It was a quiet time and that's why Michelle and I were having a chat when he came in. He was dropped off at the door by some oriental guy driving a black Toyota Pathfinder–I know cars, you see." Featherstone made some notes on his notepad. He frowned. "I know this is a long shot," he said, "but by any chance did you see the license plate on the Oriental's truck?" The lady shook her head.

"No problem," replied Featherstone. "Now, about the other car he rented. Do you happen to know who took the order at the airport?"

Michelle smiled, and blushed a little. "It was Bob, and he's sweet on me. I can find out for you."

Featherstone said, "I can understand why he's sweet on you, and if you could that would be a great help for me." Riordan turned away and rolled his eyes towards heaven. Not enough O's in smooth, he thought to himself.

A few minutes later they were sitting in the Jaguar with Featherstone going over the notes Michelle had made for them. "He's rented a blue Toyota Pathfinder for a week and he's given his place of residence as a hunting lodge about three hours north of here. I can't fucking believe it– we've actually got a break. Something stinks about this, of that I'm certain. Something is rotten in the state of Denmark." The last statement was made in a very cultured English accent, a reasonable impression of Laurence Olivier performing Hamlet.

Riordan said, "Very impressive, Laurence, now what's the number at the bottom of the page?"

Featherstone looked a bit sheepish. "That's Michelle's phone number–totally unsolicited, I promise you, but she certainly is a looker."

"Pervert, she's young enough to be your daughter!" snorted Riordan. Featherstone thought about that for a moment, and then leaned over towards Riordan in a conspiratorial manner.

"You know," he said, "sometimes I like it when they call me daddy."

Riordan almost choked. "Jeez, Featherstone, that's just too much information. Now getting back to reality, what do we do now?"

"We follow the old principle of striking while the iron's hot, mate. We better get on up to this lodge and have a word with Mister Fleming. If he is involved, and he hears that Allan Brown changed his plea, he may do a runner."

Riordan looked at his watch. "It's going to be getting dark by the time we get up there so I'd better phone Nancy and let her know what we're doing. I don't like leaving her on her own, so she can have a friend come and stay over."

Featherstone said, "You told me Nancy was a nurse. I'll bet she has lots of single friends, and I've always had a thing for nurses!"

Riordan felt his eyes widen in amazement. "Featherstone, I don't believe you. Is there nothing you won't shag?"

Featherstone shrugged his shoulders with the demeanour of a naughty schoolboy and handed him the car phone, then pulled the car out on to the highway and set off towards the mountains. When Riordan had finished, he replaced the phone and asked, "What's the plan once we get up there?" Featherstone nodded towards the back seat.

"Lift over that case," Featherstone said. "There's one or two things we might need in there."

The case, constructed of rugged plastic and resembling a cooler was extremely heavy and Riordan had trouble lugging it into the front seat. "Jesus, Murphy," he said. "Have you got a few bricks in here?" Featherstone grinned. "In this business we always follow the motto of the boy scouts–Be Prepared! Each one of my lads has a similar case in his car. There's a tiny transmitter inside should any of the cases ever get stolen. And there is an explosive gas dye canister built into the lid. If you try to pry the lid open without the correct combination, you get a nasty surprise."

Riordan's fingers leapt away from the case at that revelation. "What's the combination?"

"Seven-two-seven-eight," Featherstone said.

Riordan started to move the dials, following the combination numbers carefully, then opened the case slowly and peered inside. A low whistle escaped his lips as he viewed the contents. It contained a miniature arsenal. Recessed in a foam insert were two 9-millimeter Browning automatics–the infamous SAS 9-millys–each with a laser aiming device attached to the underside of the barrel. Beside the guns were four magazines filled with hollow-point ammunition. In addition to the weapons, there were two Fairbairn-Sykes commando knives–Riordan had two like them in his own collection–two sets of PNV's (Personal Night Vision goggles), and a large surgical kit. On the bottom of the case lay several sets of metal handcuffs, some of the more-disposable plasticuffs, and a small, hand-held Magellan ground position system.

Riordan said sarcastically, "What, no explosives?"

"Nah," replied Featherstone. "We only use that stuff in emergencies. It's totally illegal to have the stuff in your possession, you know."

Closing the lid over, Riordan laughed aloud. "Oh, like the SAS ever followed the rules. Don't make me laugh."

Dusk was falling as they reached the lodge, a majestic orange sunset settling behind the mountains and draping the hills in a reddish-brown mantle. The lodge, an enormous construction of wooden beams and glass, perched precariously on a rock ledge overlooking a lake. A huge glass conservatory ran the entire length of the back of the hotel, and it was filled with patrons dining by candlelight. Waiters in black tuxedos ran back and forth between tables like ants. The parking lot held numerous high-priced automobiles, a testament to the type of clientele who habituated the place.

The setting sun cast a golden path across the lake. It never ceased to fill Riordan with awe, and he stood quietly for a few moments, remembering another time when he had seen such a magnificent sunset. That was the night he had tossed the ashes of his wife and young daughter in the waters of a lake in the northern highlands of Ontario, and the night that David Spence disappeared, resurfacing again as Daniel Riordan. A lump rose in his throat, but Featherstone dragged him back to reality by tugging on his arm.

"You wait here," Featherstone said. "I've been to this place before. This lodge is a pretty upscale place, so I imagine they may try to maintain their guests' privacy. I'll try to find out if this Fleming is staying at the lodge or if he's out camping in the woods. They have several cabins and campsites set up around here where you can fish or hunt, so hopefully he'll be at one of those. I don't fancy storming into one of the rooms in the lodge."

Riordan waited patiently by the side of the car, watching Featherstone walk up to the reception area of the lodge and engage one of the valets in conversation. The man appeared to know Featherstone, given that they shook hands and stood chatting like old friends for several minutes. There was a bit of finger pointing, money changed hands in a surreptitious manner, and Featherstone returned grinning.

"That was a bit of luck," he said. "That lad was on duty the time a few of my staff and I came up here for a celebration after a huge insurance settlement case. He looked after us well and was paid handsomely for his efforts. He recognized me right away, as these people are wont to do. Mister Fleming is staying at the Buckingham, a cabin on the other side of the lake, and is on his own. He has room service deliver his meals, is a lousy tipper–it's amazing the network these service people have–and is a hunter, not a fisherman, which means he is armed with at least one high-powered rifle.

"Lovely, just fucking lovely," Riordan replied. "What now?"

"Oh come now, my dear Watson. It's elementary," Featherstone said, doing a Basil Rathbone accent, and got into the car.

Riordan sighed. "You don't get out much, do you?" he commented, as Featherstone started the car and drove off into the darkness.

"I love old movies," Featherstone replied, settling himself in the seat. "One of my passions in life."

Riordan nodded towards the rental agreement lying on the dashboard of the car and said, "It's a wonder you have time."

The roads to each of the cabins were well sign-posted, illuminated by the only lights available along the road encircling the lake. They came to a halt a few yards past the sign for Buckingham cottage, and got out. Featherstone opened the case, took out one of the pistols and extracted the magazine. He checked the magazine was full, then replaced it and jacked a round into the chamber. "Want one of these?" he asked, looking across the top of the car at Riordan.

Riordan hesitated for a moment, his stomach roiling slightly at the prospect of perhaps having to pull the trigger again, but in his mind he heard his wife's words, "You won't lose your way," and held out his hand. The cold metal felt comfortable against his skin, like the feel of an old, well-worn pair of slippers. By reflex, he pulled back the slide and chambered a round, then slipped the pistol into the back waistband of his trousers. Featherstone had already donned a pair of the PNV's, giving him the appearance of a large insect. Riordan pulled on a pair, settled the lenses over his eyes and blinked a few times as night became a greenish tinted day. A minor adjustment to the focus and he was following in Featherstone's footsteps, the big man leading the way to the cottage through the trees and undergrowth.

The cottage was well lit up by area-wide halogen spotlights, and the sound of Latin rhythms drifted through the trees. Riordan tilted up the goggles–they were no longer needed. The cottage, facing the lake, was enormous, surrounded on three sides by trees. A tiny jetty ran out into the water and a small aluminum boat rocked gently against its mooring. The mournful cry of a loon echoed across the water as they slipped closer to the cottage. The Pathfinder stood at the back door. Featherstone slipped a tiny pair of binoculars from his pocket, focused on the room at the back of the cottage, and began reciting his observations.

"White male, about 150 pounds, dark hair and a mustache, slight build. He's cleaning his guns at the moment. There's a seven shot Mossberg shotgun lying on the table with an open box of shells. The carry clip on the stock has five shells in it. He's pulling through a... looks like a Remington .308 with a Zeiss scope. There's a handgun lying on the table also–looks like a .44 Blackhawk–probably carries it in case of bears."

Riordan asked, "How do you want to handle this?"

Featherstone said, "I'm a legitimate investigator, so I'm going to ask him a few questions about the case I'm working on. There's no harm in that, and I want to get a sense of the man, see if I can spook him. You stay here and keep an eye on me through the glasses."

Riordan watched Featherstone disappear around to the front of the cottage, then focused the binoculars on the large front window. In a few seconds he saw Fleming's head swivel around sharply, Featherstone's knock or a doorbell's ring surprising their target. Alarm rose within Riordan like a rising tide when he saw Fleming slide a round into the chamber of the rifle, slam the bolt home, and set the weapon within easy reach on the dining table. Not exactly the actions of a man who had nothing to hide, thought Riordan.

The man then disappeared into one of the rooms and came back a few seconds later, shrugging on a blue anorak and fiddling with something at his back. Probably a wallet, thought Riordan, well accustomed to having his wallet tucked in his back pocket. But why would he need his wallet? And why a jacket? Unless he was expecting someone. Riordan felt uneasy, but couldn't put his finger on what exactly was causing the sensation.

The man disappeared again down the corridor and reappeared a few minutes later in the main room with Featherstone in tow. Riordan strained to make out what they were saying by reading their lips, a skill he developed early in life. Featherstone was relaxed and open, smiling widely and using his hands when he was speaking, while the other man's posture suggested aggression–Riordan recognized the subtle body movements, and was certain Featherstone had seen them too. Cleverly, Featherstone had positioned himself beside the table with the weapons, forcing the man to move to the other side of the room. Riordan grinned - the hallmarks of a professional soldier were readily apparent.

Taking the binoculars from his eyes, he blinked once or twice from the strain, then returned to his observation. The room swam into view, and he had just enough time to focus to see the smile on Featherstone's face turn to a grimace. Moving the binoculars a fraction, he saw the man holding a silenced pistol, and then puff after puff of smoke erupt from the end of the barrel. "Fuck me," he yelled, realizing the man had been putting a gun in the waistband of his trousers, not a wallet. Featherstone stumbled backwards across the room, one hand to his chest, then slammed into one of the huge exposed beams at the side of the cabin and collapsed to the floor.

A colossal jolt of adrenaline surged in Riordan's veins, like a massive injection, and he was on his feet and sprinting towards the front of the house. Twigs cracked under his feet and loose branches swept across his face, stinging painfully like someone scraping their nails into his skin. Once or twice he slipped on the soft, spongy ground, but made it to the front door in time to hear the man's footfalls coming down the hallway. On the ground outside the cottage, the front light lay smashed to pieces– Featherstone had obviously been expecting trouble.

Riordan pressed himself hard against the wall beside the door, holding the pistol at the side of his head. His chest heaved with the exertion, and droplets of sweat pebbled his brow despite the cool air. Time to get back in shape, he thought to himself. His breath misted on the cold night air. His heart pounded like a sprinter leaving the blocks. The door opened and the man stepped outside, two large gun cases in his hands. Riordan stepped up behind him and slammed the butt of the pistol into the back of his head, the man dropping to the ground like a stone. He stepped over and kicked him hard in the testicles, to make sure the man was not faking, another lesson hard learned in the dirty Belfast streets. Satisfied, Riordan put away his gun, pulled the man's hands behind his back and attached the plasticuffs.

Inside the house, Featherstone lay face down on the floor, a trickle of blood spilling from his head across the pine planking floors. Riordan shivered and bent down to turn him over. A low moan escaped Featherstone's lips, and Riordan jerked his hand away as if he had just touched a live wire. Featherstone had collapsed over on to his back, and Riordan could see the four holes in the front of his jacket, all centered over the heart. But there was no blood. Riordan pulled back the jacket and saw the puffed up fibers protruding from Featherstone's waistcoat, obviously made from Kevlar, the standard material used to construct body armor. Smart lad, thought Riordan, more and more impressed by the man.

Featherstone gave a huge gasp, like a diver coming up for air, and rolled to his side, his hand grasping for his pistol. "Easy, easy," Riordan yelled, ducking out of the way, afraid that Featherstone would shoot him by mistake.

"Oh fuck that hurts," groaned Featherstone, tearing the waistcoat open and massaging his chest with his free hand. Four large, angry welts, like huge bee stings mottled the left side of his chest. Riordan dragged his hand out of the way and inspected the bruised chest where the skin was already starting to discolour. A soft probe of the ribcage evoked a painful grunt.

"I think the bastard broke a rib," Featherstone said, looking around the room, his breath coming in short, painful gasps. "Where is the bastard? You didn't..."

Riordan replied, "No I didn't kill him. But he's going to have a large bruise on the back of his head, and a pair of very sore bollocks for a while." Featherstone grinned.

Riordan pulled Featherstone up off the floor, helped him over to a chair and then went outside to get the man.

Dragging the man by the feet, Riordan pulled him across the floor and stopped under one of the large beams criss-crossing the ceiling of the cottage. Seeing the look on Featherstone's face, Riordan said, "It's my turn to ask him a few questions. You can stay and watch, or go outside and get some air. It will not be pretty."

"And miss a chance to see the Raven in action," quipped Featherstone. "Not on your bloody life. Besides, I can take a certain amount of satisfaction for the pain he's caused me. What are you planning to do?"

Riordan unwrapped a piece of climber's rope he had found in the man's truck and tossed one end over the beam. He flicked open his knife, cut away the plasticuffs and tied the end of the rope around the man's wrists. "It's called the Savaki meat hook," he explained. "The Shah's police forces used it liberally in their interrogation of prisoners. The pain can literally drive you mad."

"Oh good," said Featherstone, continuing to massage his chest. "I'm glad to hear it's going to hurt."

In the cupboard under the sink in the kitchen, Riordan found a window cleaning spray with a high concentration of ammonia. He sprayed the blue solution on the man's face and as expected the acrid fumes dragged the man back to consciousness quickly. He coughed a few times, spat out some of the liquid that had trickled into his mouth, and moved his head slowly to see who was in the room. His eyes widened in surprise at the sight of Featherstone sitting in an armchair, regarding him like a cat observing a trapped mouse.

"Isn't Kevlar a wonderful thing," Riordan said, and the man turned to the sound of his voice.

"Who are you? You can't be the police," said the man, his voice weak.

"I'm the guy who was waiting outside the door, and my foot is on intimate terms with your genitals as well," Riordan said. "Now, we wanted to ask you a couple of questions and you obviously have something to hide. Shooting my friend here sort of put you in the 'guilty' category. I don't suppose you'd want to talk freely to us."

"You're going to kill me anyway," said the man. "Why should I talk?"

Featherstone interjected, "Actually we're going to hand you over to the authorities, as soon as you tell us what we need to know. Then the legal system can look after you."

"That's a joke," snorted the man. "The man I work for is completely ruthless, and can reach me anywhere, even in prison. So regardless of what you do I'm a dead man either way. I'm not telling you squat."

"Oh, I wouldn't agree with that statement," said Riordan, heaving on the rope. Instantly, the man's arms jerked upright behind him, threatening to dislocate both shoulders. A scream of anguish tore from his lips as the man climbed to his feet to try to ease the pain. Riordan did not hesitate and pulled on the rope as hard as he could. The man was soon standing on tiptoes, his face suffused with blood and contorted in agony.

Riordan said, "I'm going to hold you here for about two minutes, listening to hear if either of your shoulders pop. If nothing happens, my friend is going to shoot you in the kneecap to put more pressure on your arms. Something should happen then. Unless you wish to have a chat with us." Featherstone, a pleased look on his face, immediately raised his pistol and took aim at the man's knee.

"Please, please, let me down," cried the man. "I'll talk."

"Jeez," exclaimed Featherstone. "You're spoiling my fun. After all you did shoot me a few times. Can't I shoot him just once?"

Riordan shook his head in disbelief, let go of the rope and the man collapsed face-first to the floor with a thud. There was a loud crack, like a dry branch snapping as the man's nose shattered, blood pouring freely out across the floor. The man rolled on to his side and spat away a mouthful of blood.

"Talk to me," Riordan said.

The man's eyes were full of tears, the automatic reflex from a shattered nose. Riordan knew it was an old street fighter's trick to smash your opponent in the nose, making his eyes water and blurring his vision. That gave you an edge, one Riordan had used many times in his past.

The man said, "My client's name is Slade, but I don't know if that is his first or last name. He lives on an island off the coast of Victoria and I do odd jobs for him from time to time, eliminating problems which threaten his business."

Riordan sat down on a dining room chair, his hand still holding the end of the rope. "What kind of business?"

"He makes snuff movies. His clients pay to do the girls, or boys, then they get their own copy of the CD. Then he has an expert eliminate their identities and sells a limited number of the CD's on the black market. He has an exclusive clientele who are very rich and very powerful." Riordan shivered, his stomach heaving at the thought. His mind had difficulty conceptualizing what he had just heard. Snuff movies were always supposed to be an urban myth, but in the back of his mind he felt all the pieces fit together.

Riordan said, "That was the case Susan Delgado was working on, and Allan Brown said she'd just had a break. I assume she got too close for Slade's comfort and that's why she was murdered." The man nodded, and spat away another mouthful of blood.

The man said, "Allan Brown was just a convenient patsy. If he hadn't been there it would have been some other domestic accident. That's what I get paid for."

"Get up," Riordan ordered, and the man climbed to his feet. Riordan took a small hand-held dictaphone from his pocket, turned off the recorder and played back the beginning of the tape. The man's voice came through clear and distinct. "Now you get to tell your story to the authorities, one way or the other. And I know two detectives who will have fun with you, especially when they hear the tape."

"Bastard," hissed the man. "You..." He never finished the sentence. The huge, plate glass window at the front of the cottage shattered inward like a stone hitting a car's window. The man's head exploded like a ripe melon, and the rolling report of a high-caliber rifle echoed across the still night. Featherstone quickly shot out the lights and dived to the floor as round after round slammed into the room, shredding furniture and ornaments into a million pieces. The sniper was using explosive tipped rounds.

There was silence for a few moments. All Riordan could hear was his own breathing, and then a motorcycle fired up in the distance, the wail of the engine fading as it sped away from the area.

Brushing pieces of glass carefully off his clothes, Riordan said, "What the fuck do we do now?"

Featherstone, crouched under the window sill, replied, "You need to get out of here as quickly as possible. That tape in your hand isn't worth dick without yer man here to corroborate it. We're pretty much fucked unless we can do something about Slade on our own. We'll have to try that approach."

Riordan backed slowly across the room and out the front door, followed by an ashen-faced Featherstone who was obviously in a lot of pain. Riordan stepped back and put one arm around Featherstone's back to support him in a fireman's carry. "Thanks mate," Featherstone groaned. "There's some morphine syrettes in the first aid kit. When I get one of those I'll be okay. Then drop me at the lodge and I'll call the police."

"What?" Riordan exclaimed. "I can't get involved with the police–there'll be too many questions I can't answer, and I don't want them prying into my background."

"Relax," replied Featherstone. "My footprints are all over this, so I need to contact the authorities. But don't worry, there's no way to connect you to any of this, and I won't mention your name. I'll be dealing with the Provincial Police, and they couldn't find a body if it was buried under their car. As a matter of fact... Anyway, that's another story. You'll have to make your own way back to the city."

"Fine by me," Riordan replied, staggering under their combined weight. "There's plenty of nice cars in the lot at the lodge. It'll be a while before one gets missed."

"Oh, by the way," gasped Featherstone, "my friends call me Feather."

CHAPTER 8

Tears

Stealing a car was a breeze, and Riordan laughed to himself at how many of the skills from his past he had put to use over the last few hours. What troubled him, however, was the fact that he felt so, hell, what was the word... alive. Excitement coursed through him like a stream bursting with the first snow melt of spring and he kept his foot on the accelerator, the speedometer varying between 130 and 150 kilometers an hour. He had tuned into a local rock and roll station, and the raunchy strains of Bob Seger singing "Katmandu" blasted through the speakers. The car, a Red Porsche 911 Targa, handled well on the highway, and could be ditched easily at one of the city's many automated underground car parks. He wore a pair of rubber gloves Featherstone had given him to prevent leaving a trail of fingerprints. Featherstone thought of everything.

He reached the city shortly before 11:00 p.m., ditched the car in one of the higher crime areas of the city where he knew it would be stolen yet again, walked a few blocks and then hailed a cab to take him home. The rubber gloves were ditched in a waste bin along the way. The lights were off when he got to the house, and he let himself in quietly. The scent of garlic was heavy in the air and he sniffed at the tantalizing aroma, his stomach groaning at the lack of food. Going into the kitchen he found a note lying on the island telling him that there were leftovers in the fridge and that Oliver Wentworth had called twice during the evening and had left a number where he was to be contacted no matter what the hour.

Riordan slipped the plate of pasta into the microwave, pressed the re-heat button and picked up the phone. It was answered on the first ring–Wentworth had obviously been waiting by the phone.

"Oliver Wentworth here," came the haughty voice and Riordan felt a scowl crossing his face. He said, "This is Daniel Riordan speaking. I understand you've been trying to reach me."

Wentworth said, "Daniel, good of you to call. I have some bad news, I'm afraid. There's no easy way to tell you this but Allan Brown got into a fight at the jail and was stabbed by one of the inmates. I understand a homemade knife was involved."

Riordan's stomach turned over. He knew about the shivs prisoners made from every material imaginable, then coated with soap so that the ragged wounds they made would not close. He had been stabbed once in his life during a fight and he remembered only too well the feel of the knife slipping into his back, as he lay beaten and helpless on the ground. As the doctor had said, "another half an inch and it would have been fatal!" But it had not been his time, and he recovered and tracked down those thugs who were responsible.

He shivered, remembering Fleming's last words to them at the cottage. "Slade has a long reach, even in prison." The words echoed in his head and his mouth went dry. The next words would not come easily. It couldn't be, not Allan, not another friend. Choked with emotion, he said, "Is he..."

Wentworth replied, "Allan lost a lot of blood from multiple stab wounds, and they rushed him here to the hospital. They lost him once on the way over but the medics managed to resuscitate him and keep him alive until the doctors at Mount Hebron could look after him. He's still alive, but clinging by a thread. I talked to the doctor a few minutes ago for my hourly update. He says Allan will be lucky to make it through the night."

Riordan felt the tears prick at his eyes. Dear God, not again. Please not again. I've lost nearly everyone I've loved to a brutal and violent death. He swallowed hard, fighting back the torrent of sadness that threatened to overwhelm him.

Wentworth said, "Daniel, are you still there?"

Wiping a hand across his eyes Riordan said, "Yeah. I'm going to tell Nancy and then I'm going down to the hospital."

"I talked to Nancy earlier this evening," said Wentworth. "She mentioned that this Featherstone character was following up a lead he had found. Has he made any progress?"

"I don't know," Riordan lied, his mind reeling in confusion. Why would Nancy tell Wentworth about Featherstone? Or maybe it was just an innocent remark. After all, there was no reason for her not to tell him, and Riordan had not warned her to keep quiet. Still, it was disquieting in light of the events of the evening. Riordan said, "Anyway, I must go now. I'll talk to you sometime tomorrow."

Hands trembling, he hung up the phone, shaking like he had walked outside on a chilly evening. There was too much at play here, and he felt like he was looking at a ball made up of many pieces of string. Sighing, he turned towards the stairs, debating whether or not to wake Nancy to tell her the news but the decision was made for him. The microwave beeped loudly, having finished its work, and Riordan heard Nancy's sleepy voice from the bedroom upstairs calling, "Daniel, is that you?"

There was no avoiding the conversation, and for a moment he thought of sneaking back out. But he ran upstairs and sat beside his groggy wife, explaining the conversation he had had with Wentworth. Nancy's eyes brimmed with tears when he told her, and she held him tightly and then pushed him away.

"Go on, get down there. Call me if you want me to come down too!"

"Thanks love," he replied, kissed her quickly and raced off.

Alternating between the emotional extremes of utter helplessness to a black, all-consuming rage, Riordan kept his foot pressed hard on the accelerator, speeding down the highway towards the city. Trees and houses flashed by, and perhaps there were other cars on the highway but he did not see them, his mind singularly focused on one thought–to get to Allan's bedside. Telling Nancy had not been easy, and he felt badly that he had to leave her but she was a strong woman and knew what had to be done. He slipped a CD in the player, skipped to the track he knew well and cranked the volume when the first strains of Horslips playing "Derag Doom" filtered into the car. Instinctively he began slapping the wheel in time to the raucous beat, a sense of calm falling over him like a blanket. Music to calm the savage beast, he thought to himself, or perhaps it's the calm before the storm. Many times in Belfast the newspapers had called him just that–a savage beast–after one of his many executions. What they had failed to take into account was the history of violence of those he had dispatched.

He mused to himself at the strange turns his life had taken since those violent days in that dark and evil place. It was strange to be an outsider looking in, like a scientist observing the behavior of rats in a laboratory. Being born and baptized a Presbyterian in Belfast, he had no choice but to be educated through the British school system, and learned only of the battles and history of that nation while ignoring the rich and lyrical history of Ireland.

An avid reader, when he first escaped the troubles he found himself learning about Celtic mythology, of the Kings and Queens of old Ireland and listening to the wonderful music that was so rich and all at once sorrowful. From there came the strange dichotomy of the understanding of it all, of the love of things Irish to his fierce and proud Protestant heritage. There were those who would call him a turncoat, a traitor for his thoughts and feelings, especially those who thought that the only good Catholic was a dead Catholic. Conversely there were those who thought that the world would be a better place with a few less Orangemen, and burning them to death was a suitable means to achieve that goal.

"Michael Collins" was playing in the rep theaters again to rave reviews, and he had promised Nancy a date to see it when she was able. He was surprised that in all the articles he had read no one had mentioned the fact that Collins, one of the leaders of the uprising, had been a Protestant. Big Liam Neeson was also garnering excellent reviews as well, and there was more talk of an Oscar for his current work and wouldn't he be surprised if he ever discovered that he had once walked the same boards as the Raven, in several of their high school productions.

God, the world is a strange place, he thought to himself, pulling off the highway and heading straight to the hospital three blocks further on. Wentworth's Jaguar was parked outside the hospital in the almost empty carpark and

Riordan pulled up alongside and got out, resisting the juvenile urge to run his keys along the Jag's doors. Most of the cars were parked near the entrance, but in the distance, at the other side of the lot there was a large, dark 4-wheel drive vehicle.

Riordan noticed such things and questioned them, a reflection of old habits dying hard. Shrugging his shoulders, he ran up the steps and into the deserted reception area where Wentworth was waiting. It was the first time Riordan had seen the man not wearing one of his expensive Armani suits, but even his casual clothes spoke of money and pretension. Especially the tennis sweater draped precisely over Wentworth's shoulders with the sleeves tied in a neat bow at the front. Wentworth was a 'Country Club' type.

"Ponce," thought Riordan and walked over to the man. Wentworth did not offer his hand, but Riordan noticed that Wentworth was a lot more at ease than he had been at their last encounter.

"Daniel," Wentworth said, with a pitiful excuse for a smile on his lips, "I've cleared the way for you to get in to see Allan. He's under guard at the moment, but the detectives have given you permission to have access to the room. The police officer on guard will let you in when you provide identification–a driver's license should be sufficient. I'm off home now–there has been no change in his condition, and I've asked the nurses to notify me if there is any improvement at all or if..."

Riordan ignored the last comment and took the elevator to the floor where the intensive care unit was located, the antiseptic scents and smells of the hospital, which he always detested, having an unnerving effect on him. The elevator bumped to a stop and the doors shuddered open. He went straight to the nurse's station, behind which a bank of instruments hummed and beeped and produced funny looking waves on circular scopes. There were two nurses on hand, both monitoring charts and instruments with the intensity that Riordan admired in their profession.

Since meeting Nancy, he had come to understand the constant pressure that nurses had to endure, and the little thanks they received in return. Between fighting government cutbacks and the atrocious treatment they received at the hands of the doctors, they were constantly under stress but the level of care never faltered. Riordan was amazed at the attitude of the doctors towards nurses at Nancy's hospital, and it was probably a good thing he had never witnessed an encounter between one of them and his new wife.

"Evening ladies," he said, and both nurses jumped, startled by his appearance. The rubber soled shoes he wore were completely silent on the marble floors. He laughed at their discomfort and said, "I'm here to see Allan Brown. The police have given me permission to see him."

One of the nurses, an older lady, gave him a stern look, totally unamused by the fright he had given them. She said, "You'll have to wait for a few minutes as the orderly is cleaning up the rooms in the ICU and he's just gone into 308. Mister Brown is in room 310 and an officer is sitting outside. I'll let you know when you can go in." Riordan nodded at the curt dismissal, smiled pleasantly and sat down in the waiting area, flicking through a pile of well-scuffed magazines, which were months old.

He heard the slight squeak of rubber wheels on the floor, and looked up to see the orderly's back disappear into room 309. The orderly, a large, well-built individual wore his dark hair in a ponytail and was pushing a trolley with many different supplies stacked on top and underneath. Both the man's hands were on the bars at the side of the trolley, and the one hand that Riordan could see was heavily callused along the ridge with the end of a multi-hued tattoo just poking out from under the white sleeve of the man's jacket.

Riordan's first thought was that the man was Yakusa, an oriental gangster of which there were many in the city, but laughed at himself for immediately stereo-typing the man. Talk about tolerance, he thought to himself, what a shining example you are. Burying his face back in the magazine, he continued to read another article while something fluttered at the periphery of his senses.

The article, about the Chechen rebels in Russia, was fascinating, and he was too engrossed in the story to notice the orderly come out of the room and head down to the end of the corridor where room 310 was located. It was only when the powered door of 309 banged shut did he realize that the man had finished and gone. Riordan got up and looked down the corridor to see the orderly exchange a few words with the police officer, then push the cart into Allan Brown's room.

Setting down the magazine, he stood up and stretched and the thing fluttering outside his senses came into focus. The lady at the car rental had said that Mister Fleming had been dropped off at the office by an oriental gentleman with a pony-tail who was driving a black 4-wheel drive truck, similar to the one Riordan had seen in the hospital car-park. Fuck tolerance, that's too much of a fucking coincidence, thought Riordan, sprinting down the hall towards Brown's room like an Olympic athlete exploding from the blocks. At the sound, the police officer stood up and immediately went for his pistol on seeing Riordan bearing down on him like a Dallas Cowboy's linebacker.

"I'm Daniel Riordan," Riordan shouted, "and I think that orderly is trying to kill Allan." A look of disbelief crossed the man's face, hearing the name of the person he was supposed to give access to the room, but wary of Riordan's method of approach.

"I need some ID," he said, planting himself firmly in Riordan's way.

Riordan said, "Sorry mate, don't have time," and slapped the man in the throat with the back of his hand. The blow sent a miniature shock wave up the man's carotid artery and into his brain, inducing momentary paralysis. He pushed past the stunned man and kicked open the door of the room. The orderly, an Oriental man in his mid-thirties by Riordan's estimation, was standing beside Brown's bed, holding the port from Brown's intravenous drip in one hand and a large needle in the other. The man's head jerked up at the unexpected intrusion, he stopped what he was doing and immediately rushed across the room, holding the needle like a dagger.

Riordan feigned fear, creating an expression on his face, which was exactly what the Yakusa would have expected to see, and rocked back on his heels as if preparing to flee. The Yakusa snarled in anticipation of victory in midstride, but then Riordan sprang forward, exactly the opposite reaction to what his attacker obviously expected. The Yakusa, confused, hesitated for a second, which gave Riordan the opening he was looking for. He parried the arm holding the needle with his forearm, and in the same fluid motion rammed the heel of his hand upwards against the bottom of the man's nose, the punch driven by a hard twist of his hip. Riordan heard the satisfying crunch of bone as the man's nose shattered upwards in a splash of blood, driving needle-sharp shards of bone into his brain. The blow killed the Yakusa instantly, and the needle and the man's body dropped to the floor.

"Pretty impressive," said a voice behind him, and Riordan spun on his heel, a guttural snarl escaping his lips, fists up and ready for another confrontation. It was the police officer, who holstered his pistol and put up his hands in mock defense. "No, no, I'm one of the good guys," he protested. "I saw what he was trying to do."

"So why the fuck didn't you shoot him?" gasped Riordan, staring down at the spreading fingers of blood on the floor that were reaching out towards the syringe. He took a tissue from a box on the table, stepped over the lifeless body, picked the syringe up gingerly and handed it to the police officer.

"I couldn't get a clear shot at him," answered the officer, rubbing his neck. "Besides, you didn't exactly have a problem dealing with him. Is he dead?" Riordan glared at the man, several biting responses on the tip of his tongue but resisted the urge.

Riordan said, "What do you think? I'm going to sit with Allan until the homicide guys come. Go and put the syringe somewhere safe, and call it in." The officer left the room and Riordan went over to his friend's bed, staring down at the ashen pallor of Brown's face and the feeble, almost gasping pants of breath making his chest rise and fall. It seemed like every breath was about to be his last.

Multi-hued wires snaked out of round, plastic disks attached to various points on Brown's body and flowed across the bed and up to a shelf of equipment above. A set of monitors, duplicates of those at the nurse's station poured out their constant flow of information, none of which Riordan understood. He took his friend's hand in his own, frightened by the cold, clammy texture of Brown's skin and understanding only too well that Brown's heart was weakening, not having the strength any more to drive blood to his extremities.

"Don't go, Allan," he said quietly, tears filling his eyes and spilling on the pristine white sheets. He remembered another time while he was still at University, driving through the dark, rain-splattered streets of Belfast towards the Royal Victoria Hospital. Beside him on the floor of the car, his girlfriend, an art student named Annie and the reason for the trek through the rabbit warren, had been complaining about the need for the precautions. That was up until the first bullet twanged off the hood of the car and went zinging off into the night like an angry bee–then she was only too happy to be on the floor.

She had lived in the little village of Clones, on the other side of the border, and really had no great exposure to the 'troubles' until she had come to study in Belfast. Two brothers from the same village had gone to Belfast to work at the same time, and she had kept in touch with them as she had baby-sat several times for the older of the two.

That same morning, while Riordan had been preparing to go to lectures, a bomb exploded under the van that took the brothers to work, killing the driver and severely wounding all those in the back. Riordan had heard about the explosion around suppertime, accepting it like most people did with the same fatalistic shrug of the shoulders and a 'thank God it wasn't me.' Shortly after the announcement, a tearful Annie had shown up at his door, wanting to know how to get to the hospital, explaining how it was her friends who had been in the van.

Riordan, knowing what he was about to face, explained the rules to her and reluctantly set off into dangerous territory. When they reached the hospital, much to the chagrin of the policemen behind the barricades, a young, harried doctor told them that the older of the two brothers had died on the operating table and the younger one had a slim chance of recovery. Annie went to see him, and Riordan sat beside her, holding her hand as the enormity of the violence came home to her in a very frightening and personal way.

She cried then, shoulders trembling while Riordan lied to the young lad, telling him that his brother was in the recovery room downstairs and was going to be okay and he'd soon be out of here and they'd all have a pint together. And the lad clenched his hand tightly and whispered through lips puffed and cracked, "Thanks mate," and Riordan felt the chill in the lad's fingers and knew then the light would soon go out. A tragic waste, but one Riordan was to see repeated over and over again until he became numb to it all.

The vision faded and he hung his head for a moment, like a repentant receiving communion. Tucking Brown's cold hands inside the blankets to try to keep them warm, he sat down beside the bed and waited.

He did not leave Allan's side until one of the homicide detectives who had come to his house, the man named MacGregor, showed up and assured him that two officers would be posted at Allan Brown's bedside on a constant basis. Riordan gave a brief statement to the detective, then continued his vigil at Allan's bedside while the forensic people came and went, taking photographs and measurements.

A little while later the coroner showed up, checked the body with the detective, then took it away to the mortuary where he promised to perform a full autopsy as soon as possible. There was little doubt in his mind what had killed the man; all he needed was the medical corroboration. Finally an orderly came and mopped away the bloodstains. It was as if nothing had happened.

Eventually two officers showed up and posted themselves inside the room like sentries at each side of the door, armed with magazines and flasks of coffee. The aroma of the fresh coffee made Riordan's stomach twist like an eel, reminding him that he had not eaten. The plate of pasta was still in the microwave at home.

"Got a spare cup?" he asked, and one of the officers poured a mug for him. It was steaming hot but tasted wonderful. "You wouldn't by any chance have some Bushmills?" he quipped, and the two men grinned at him, sharing the joke.

"We're on duty," said the man, and Riordan gave him a "you must be joking" look. Sitting back beside Allan's bed, he sipped the coffee gratefully, his eyes getting heavier and heavier until he eventually drifted off into a light sleep. At three a.m. he was startled by the constant high-pitched whine emanating from one of the machines, followed by the ICU nurse crashing through the door followed by two others pushing a crash cart.

Blinking his eyes several times to get rid of the fug, he realized that the monitor for Allan's heartbeat had just flatlined.

Allan was dead.

The door crashed open. Two doctors sprinted into the room, ordered him brusquely to get out of the way and immediately went to work on Allan. Riordan had seen such things on television, but could not make out what they were doing. He heard the word 'Clear', followed by a muffled thunk, and Allan's body jerked spasmodically on the bed. A nurse prepared a huge syringe that she handed to one of the doctors who rammed it directly into Allan's heart.

Riordan watched the monitor in disbelief, his eyes watering from the burning sensation caused by the interruption of his slumber. Tears streamed down his cheeks as the monitor continued its monotonous whine. The doctor said 'Clear' again and once more the monitor spiked, Allan's body jerking like a dead frog connected to a battery. The whine turned into a slow beat. The regular sine wave returned to the heart monitor and the doctors slapped each other on the back and the nurses smiled with relief. Riordan sighed and stepped over to the bed.

"What are his chances?" he asked, and one of the doctors turned to face him. The man, barely into his thirties, with red-rimmed eyes and a day's growth of beard, smiled gently.

"He's a tough customer," the doctor said, making some quick notes on Allan's chart. "Anyone else in his condition wouldn't have survived what he just went through. Don't be alarmed but I'm going to put him on a ventilator, to give him a bit of an assist with his breathing."

"Thanks Doc," said Riordan. "I'll stay with him for a while, just to be sure. We Irish are a wee bit superstitious, don't you know. He was there for me when I went through a bad spell, so now's my time to return the favor."

The room returned to silence, following a brief interlude while the respirator was wheeled in and Allan was hooked up via a long pipe connected to the pump. To Riordan's untrained eye it appeared as if Allan's breathing was stronger, and that a little bit of color was returning to his cheeks. Wishful thinking, he thought to himself. Sliding his hand under the sheets, he felt Allan's fingers and to his great relief they were once again warm to the touch. A tiny smile crossed his lips. "Hard to kill a bad thing," Riordan said, and returned to his vigil.

Shortly after three o'clock in the morning Slade's phone rang, dragging him reluctantly from sleep. He rolled over, switched on the bedside lamp and examined the illuminated buttons on his phone console to see which light was blinking. The red light, which was reserved for clients, winked at him. Taking a quick sip from a bottle of mineral water on his night table, he swallowed hard, pressed a switch to activate the tape recorder built into the unit and picked up the phone.

"Slade here," he said.

"Your messenger didn't deliver the parcel," came a voice he recognized instantly. It belonged to the Chief of Police for the region, another of his clients, yet different from the others as the Chief's 'visits' were free, in return for information and protection. A scowl crossed Slade's face.

"For fuck's sake stop speaking in riddles," Slade growled. "This is a secure line. What happened?"

"Your man was killed before he could get to Brown," came the contrite reply.

"Killed?" Slade sat bolt upright in bed, his mind trying to comprehend how his bodyguard had been bested. Of the six Yakusa who acted as his elite guard, the man ranked about a three in terms of martial skills and all-around nastiness. "How?"

"I read the report that came in from the detectives and it says that Allan Brown's friend, a bloke by the name of Daniel Riordan, came across your fellow in Brown's room. According to the preliminary coroner's report, he was killed by a blow to the nose that drove splinters of bone up into his brain. Riordan says it was a fluke."

"Fluke, my ass," snorted Slade, scratching his scalp to remove an errant itch. "That is a killing blow applied by the heel of the hand. Used by Special Forces groups and those highly trained in martial arts. Have you checked out this Riordan in the VICAP system?"

"There's no info on him at all. A few parking tickets, but other than that he's a model citizen."

Slade scratched at his chin thoughtfully. There was far more to this than his caller realized. Slade had a sense for these things. He said, "Thanks," hung up the phone and called up his on-line directory. He had asked Oliver Wentworth to get him information on Riordan and Featherstone, but had not seen anything as yet. It was time to apply a little pressure.

CHAPTER 9

Kaleidoscope

By morning Allan Brown's vital signs were improving, albeit slightly, and the doctor was cautious, guarded in his appraisal, but Riordan was reassured. He knew his friend, knew his determination and spirit and intuitively understood that the worst was behind them. "It's all about corners turned," Riordan said to the sleeping figure, and at that moment Featherstone walked into the room, acknowledged both cops by name and made his way over to the bed.

Featherstone looked down at Allan Brown for a moment, then said, "Nancy told me you'd be here. Heard it was pretty much touch and go during the night. The doctors are encouraged by his vital signs though."

Riordan lowered his voice a notch. "How did things go at the lodge?"

Featherstone smiled. "Pretty much as I expected. The Provincial Police are a bunch of incompetent boobs when it comes to this sort of thing, so they pretty much deferred to me when it came to the process of investigation. They asked me to keep in touch but they agree it was a murder and that I was a somewhat innocent bystander, so now they're way in over their heads. I imagine they'll probably ask for help from the Homicide department here in the city, which wouldn't at all be a bad thing for us, given the circumstances."

Riordan noticed Featherstone unconsciously touch his side gently, and remembered the man taking the shots in his bulletproof vest. "How's the chest?" he asked.

"Two broken ribs, all trussed up like a Christmas turkey, and I feel like I've been kicked by Phar Lap. But other than that..." Featherstone turned his head and Riordan felt the intensity of the man's eyes boring directly into his own. "And how are you holding up Daniel?" Featherstone asked, "I hear you had a little bit of excitement during the night."

Riordan yawned. "One of Slade's goons tried to kill Allan by injecting something into his IV and I stopped him, permanently. Other than that I don't feel too badly," he replied, truthfully. "I've slept in fits and starts during the night and the officers eventually supplied me with some reinforced coffee. A bit of breakfast wouldn't do any harm though."

"Great," exclaimed Featherstone, rubbing his hands together. "I know a greasy spoon not too far from here where we can get a good fry-up. Plenty of greasy bacon and eggs, your basic Mick diet from what I remember.

Don't worry about Allan here. I'll give the nurse my cell-phone number and she'll contact me if there's any change."

Riordan patted Allan's leg, then for a joke, which only Allan would understand, tied a name tag around his big toe, the same as used to identify dead bodies in the morgue. "You're a sick bastard," exclaimed Featherstone, when he saw what Riordan was doing. "I like you even more."

Following a quick call to Nancy, Riordan tucked into his steak and eggs and home fries with the relish of a condemned man eating his last meal, as did Featherstone, after pouring a couple of mugs of steaming coffee into his system.

"Feel more human now," he said, chewing contentedly on a piece of steak that tasted like it must have come from the sole of an old army boot. He swallowed the piece, then took a long swig of coffee. Featherstone was right about the cafe. None too elegant, but clean and tidy inside, with a row of stools along the counter and booths along the wall. Tiny jukeboxes intruded into each booth. A tall waitress, with peroxide blonde hair and her roots showing, yet with a shapely figure had greeted Featherstone by name. The other booths were filled with patrons, mostly blue-collar workers either heading to work or coming off the night shift. The tantalizing aroma of frying bacon hung heavy in the air, commingled with a sizable cloud of cigarette smoke–no political correctness here.

Sitting at the counter, an older man with gray hair, a gray beard and sad watery eyes raised his coffee mug in a salute to Featherstone. "Who's that?" asked Riordan.

"He's a grumpy old bastard, but he does the occasional job for me. He runs his own computer firm and has a tremendous amount of internet experience which I draw on from time to time. I don't have my own expertise in that field as yet."

"So what do we do about Slade?" Riordan asked, anxious to be doing something. Sitting around waiting for another attack was not exactly tempting and, as he had been taught many times, it was always best to go on the offensive, no matter what the odds.

Featherstone thought for a moment, then set down his utensils and wiped his mouth with a napkin. A tiny piece wore off and stuck to the stubble on his upper lip. "I think we have two choices, neither of which has much appeal. First option; we contact the authorities and tell them what we know. If they buy it, and that's a big if, they will have to get a search warrant for Slade's house, which means involving more and more people. If his tentacles extend as far as I think they do, he'll be tipped off and anyone on that island who could incriminate him will be killed and dumped at sea. So that's not a good option." He extended two fingers and continued. "Option two, I assemble a team and we go in under cover of darkness and have a look for ourselves. A bit of a recce, you might say. If we find enough evidence then we shoot the fucker and call in the authorities after we get away."

"I like plan B," Riordan said. "After what he did to Allan, I'd like to shoot the fucker too."

"Thought you might," grinned Featherstone. "To that end I've called a meeting in my briefing room for three o'clock this afternoon. Some of the lads from the Counter Revolutionary Warfare wing who work for me now will be there and they've got a lot of experience at this sort of thing."

Riordan paused from sawing off another piece of steak. "I'm coming too," he said, his tone making it certain that this was not up for discussion. "I have a wee bit of experience in this sort of thing too!"

"Never doubted it for a moment," quipped Featherstone, and started once more into his food. "I've got one of the lads going up later this morning in a private plane to take some piccies of the island, and we'll get them developed in time for the briefing. I'm also trying to get my hands on the plans for Slade's house–that will give us some idea of what we will be facing. In the meantime you can go home and see your missus. There's not much else you can do for now."

"Do you have any background on this Slade character?" Riordan asked, more curious than anything. Slade had framed and tried to murder his friend Allan, killed Allan's girlfriend, and Riordan would no more hesitate from pulling the trigger than shying away from killing a rabid dog.

"All I know is based on whispers," replied Featherstone. "His official military record is sealed and his tracks lead all the way back to Saigon, to the underworld there. He is a very rich, very powerful, reclusive man, and takes advantage of all the secrecy his money can buy. I do not have an up-to-date photograph of him, only an old one from..." Featherstone paused. "...No matter," he continued. "Slade may even have changed his appearance. There are stories from long ago that a Vietcong whore sliced off most of his dick."

Riordan nodded. "That would make sense to me. From what I've read, serial killers are often sexually dysfunctional, so he may get his kicks from killing the girls or watching them being killed. No matter, he's as good as dead when I see him."

"Just like that," said Featherstone, staring across the table.

Riordan shrugged his shoulders.

"Just like that," he said.

Featherstone picked up the bill, leaving the waitress a generous tip, and headed off to the washrooms. Riordan, full of trepidation, drove to his house trying to think of a way to tell Nancy what he was about to do. A fire of indigestion burned in his chest. On the stereo, Jimmy Nail blasted out the haunting strains of 'Big River' and Riordan sang along, knowing the words by heart. It was one thing to help a private detective try to track down clues about who had framed Allan Brown, but a covert assault on an island which was probably well-protected was another matter entirely. Then there was Slade.

Nancy was in the garden watering her flowers, a huge denim maternity dress billowing in the wind like the sail on a cutter, when Riordan pulled into the driveway. He climbed out of the car, and the hose mysteriously twitched in his direction, making him yelp at the impromptu cold shower. Nancy grinned and he dashed over and grabbed the hose from her hand.

"Daniel, don't you dare," she spluttered as he slipped a hand behind her back and kissed her fiercely. She responded in kind, her mouth opening against his and her warm tongue slipping past his lips. It was several moments before they broke away, breathless, and he felt her hand brush against his groin, where his intentions were clear to see. "Come in the house you bad man," she ordered, "or that old biddy across the street will be calling the cops on us. You certainly seem to be in good form."

Inside the house she dragged him across to the couch and started opening the buttons on his shirt, kissing his chest as button after button popped. Dropping slowly to her knees, she undid his belt, opened his trousers and dragged them and his underwear to the floor. "Oh my," she grinned, "I must have been neglecting you."

"Nancy," he groaned, "we need to talk."

"Later Daniel," she said, "I want to fuck."

That was one of the things that Riordan loved about her. She was a bright, well-educated lady who could hold her own in any form of intellectual debate, but there was this raunchy, earthy side about her that would probably surprise most people with whom she was acquainted. And then her warm lips encircled him, tugging and teasing, her tongue tracing tiny circles and he involuntarily began to gyrate his hips in time to her ministrations. It had been a while, and he felt his orgasm build quickly, but he pulled away, wanting to prolong the pleasure.

Nancy turned around on to her hands and knees, the only position which she found comfortable at her advanced stage, and Riordan tossed the denim dress up over her back, revealing the fact that she was not wearing any panties. "My God," he exclaimed, "what a wanton woman."

"Well it was either you or the milkman," she shot back. "Good thing you got home first."

Riordan positioned himself behind her and entered gently, gasping at the velvety warmth, and the way her muscles clenched around him. A tiny grin played across his lips; she must have been practicing her Keigel exercises in preparation for the delivery. It was one of the things they had learned at the Lamaze class, about how a woman should practice clenching the muscles of her vagina.

The young instructor, much to Riordan's delight, had suggested that the husbands or significant others offer to be the Keigelometers. The conversation had then descended into a bawdy pantomime, much to the amusement of the others in the class. A lesbian couple in the class, who, much to Nancy's chagrin, Riordan kept referring to as 'Fuzzy bumpers', did not share in the merriment, which only served to encourage Riordan.

"You can go a wee bit harder Daniel," she ordered, her voice deep and husky. "I'm not going to break."

With her muscles clenching against him, it was not long before Riordan could sense the tiny tremors in his wife's legs and she moaned aloud. He had to fight to hold back his own, wanting her to share in the pleasure. The tremors built to a shattering crescendo, and Nancy screamed aloud, her nails digging into the carpet all the while thrusting back against him. "Now Daniel, now Daniel," she cried, and he erupted inside her, that ecstatic release which seemed to go on and on.

They stayed connected for some time, enjoying the feel of their bodies entwined, and Riordan gently massaged her back. "Time for the cream Daniel," she said, "and before you say anything, I know you've given me all the cream you've got at the moment!" He climbed out of his clothes, helped her to her feet and led the way to the bedroom.

When he came out of the washroom she was lying naked on the bed, her huge belly threatening to overturn her tiny body. He opened the jar of cream and began to massage her stomach, rubbing the cream into the stretched skin. Almost instantly a tiny foot slammed against his fingers and Nancy gasped at the blow that left her almost breathless. Riordan marveled at the sensation and continued to rub while the tiny digits made contact.

"What did you want to talk to me about, Daniel?" she asked. Riordan stopped his ministrations and looked into his wife's eyes. He could never lie to this woman, nor did he want to.

Without hesitation he replied, "We think this guy called Slade is behind Allan's frame-up, and the attempts to have him killed. There was another attempt during the night that I managed to foil, but it was a lucky break. A few more seconds and Allan would have been dead." Nancy reached out and touched his cheek gently.

"And how is Allan?" she asked, her voice hesitant, as if she really didn't want to know the answer.

"Actually he's doing just fine," Riordan said, brightening. "They've got him on a respirator, but the doctor thinks he's turned the corner. So do I."

"That's great sweetheart," she said, beaming, her smile like a cloud uncovering the sun. "Now, what about this Slade character?"

"He's the problem," Riordan said sternly, while continuing to rub in the cream. "We think he's connected up the ying yang, so any formal attempt to investigate him may bring disastrous consequences to anyone he's holding out on his island. Feather thinks it would be best if we took a sneaky look at what he's doing, and see if there's any evidence we can use to call the cops. That's what would be best for Allan."

"You're going with them, I presume," she said, her voice firm and strong.

"Moi," said Riordan, feigning innocence, and received a slap on the arm in return.

"Be serious," Nancy snorted.

Riordan nodded. "I think I can help. Besides, Allan is my friend and I want to do everything I can to prove he is innocent. I'm going to go back down to the hospital in a little while to spend some time with Allan, and then this afternoon I'm off to Featherstone's office for a meeting. We'll probably go after Slade about two or three a.m. tomorrow morning."

"Daniel," she started. "You know how much I abhor violence, but I am pragmatic enough to realize that in certain circumstances violence is warranted. Go and prove your friend is innocent. But be careful and come back to me in one piece, you hear me–one big piece. And don't injure any of the good parts." Her hand slid down his body and grasped him gently in her hand. It came as a surprise to both of them when he stiffened immediately.

"Ohhh," she smiled. "Seconds?"

"Fuck," groaned Nancy Riordan, as a tiny foot lashed into the side of her abdomen with all the power of a CFL kicker, draining the breath from her. "God, are you ever going to come out?" she said, rubbing her stomach in an attempt to calm the tiny footballer inside her. "You're just like your father, too much energy." Pouring herself a cup of herbal tea–caffeine was bad at this time though she craved a mug so badly–she sat down on the sofa and switched on the television to see who was on Oprah today. Daniel was gone off to the hospital when she eventually wakened.

They had had a second bout of playful lovemaking after he had massaged the cream into her skin, and afterwards she had drifted off into a deep peaceful sleep.

She fidgeted about on the couch and just about the same time as she managed to find a suitable, comfortable position, the doorbell rang. Sighing loudly, she set the tea down and eased herself up off the sofa, no easy feat considering her situation, and waddled over to the front door. A large shadow filled the frame, blocking out the light which normally filtered through the stained glass window, and she felt a momentary pang of fear, like a tiny pinprick in her psyche.

Opening the door, she was confronted with a tall, well-groomed Oriental with short dark hair and a serious expression on his face. "Are you Nancy Riordan?" he said, without any trace of an accent.

Nancy's stomach churned. This was not good news. She nodded, afraid to speak.

"Missus Riordan, I work for Mister Featherstone. There's been a bit of an accident during an impromptu training exercise and Daniel asked if I would bring you to him. It's not too serious, and a doctor checked him out, but he wanted you to come."

"Oh my God, what happened?" she exclaimed, and ran back into the house to get her handbag.

Riordan was at Featherstone's office promptly at five minutes to three, understanding now how anal Featherstone could be about time–once a soldier, always a soldier. The receptionist waved him on into the office and he was walking past the coffee station when the reflection of a woman's face appeared in the mirror above the door. It was Nancy. Startled, he spun on his heel and went into the kitchen where she was holding open the fridge door and peering inside.

"Nancy," he said, and the woman peered over the top of the door, a carton of cream in her hand.

"Excuse me?" she said, and he felt his face redden in embarrassment. He realized it was not Nancy, but the two women could have been sisters. There were the same high cheekbones and the short dark hair and that smile that could melt your heart.

"I'm sorry," he mumbled, the heat rising in his face. "You're the spitting image of my wife, so you can imagine my surprise."

"Are you making coffee?" he asked. "I'm here for the three o'clock meeting with Feather."

The woman held out her hand. "I'm Christine Doran," she said, her grip firm and strong. He could feel her sizing him up.

"I'm Daniel Riordan," he said and she grinned, her eyes twinkling mischievously.

"Ah yes," she replied, " Feather told me all about you at our weekly briefing. I may be along this evening to keep an eye on you lot, and to make sure the coffee is just right!"

"Okay, okay," he protested, "you don't have to rub it in!" Chastised, Riordan examined the woman closely now, admonishing himself for thinking she was one of the secretarial staff. She was in her early to mid-thirties, lines around her eyes giving her a world-weary look, and had that almost imperceptible aura of a soldier about her. He guessed that this was one of the ladies from the 14th Intelligence unit, and as such was as deadly as any of the men whom Featherstone employed.

"I'm just going into the briefing room," he said. "Are you coming?"

"Not to this one," came the reply. "I have another client meeting in a few minutes but I may see you later, if Feather decides he needs my help." She closed the fridge door and set a carton of fresh cream on the counter. "Anyway, it was nice to meet you." She turned and went out of the kitchen, leaving Riordan to admire the shapely figure that looked like it had been poured into a pair of faded denim jeans. He nodded approvingly to himself.

There were three men in the briefing room, all dressed casually, sipping on mugs of tea and munching away at digestive cookies when Featherstone led him through the door. Riordan instantly identified them as soldiers by their posture, the way they coolly appraised him, and the firm handshake of each.

The three men stood and Featherstone said, by way of introduction, "This is Tony Scapelli, aka Capo, Brian Henderson, aka Tosser, and Jean-Marc Raffine, aka the Frogman." Riordan smiled at each of the unflattering sobriquets, par for the course for the SAS, singling them out one at a time for attention. He gave each man a quick once-over, the policeman's special. Capo, dark-skinned, with a mop of black, shiny hair, a ragged scar beneath one eye, and a thin mustache above a pair of full lips. Tosser, over six feet, closely cropped blonde hair and a gold stud in one ear was the most well-built of the three, full of menace, and had several scars criss-crossing his lower-forearm. The Frogman had a smattering of brown hair on his head and a pair of the currently fashionable sideburns reaching to the bottom of his ear. There was an almost Gallic look about him, and Riordan's suspicions were soon confirmed,

"Tosser," Riordan asked, "you wouldn't have done time in Belfast by any chance." The man shook his head, no. "Good thing," Riordan replied. "Tossing in Belfast is playing with yourself. I wouldn't feel too comfortable working with a wanker!" The others burst out laughing, as did Tosser himself.

"Capo and Tosser are from the CRW, which I'm sure you are familiar with," said Featherstone. "God knows there's been enough books written about the regiment at the moment. I can't go in a bookstore anymore without seeing a photograph of my body with a little black rectangle over the eyes."

"But isn't that the way your girlfriend likes it," said the Frogman, in a heavy French accent, and they all laughed again.

Featherstone laughed loudest. "The Frogman here came from the GIGN, an elite French anti-terrorist unit, who bravely sunk Greenpeace's Rainbow warrior, a feat of tremendous daring."

"I did not do thees," came the indignant reply, and the Frogman realized he was being wound up yet again and quieted down.

"This is the team I have chosen for the surveillance," said Featherstone. "I'd trust any of them with my life." Riordan acknowledged the comment with a nod, knowing such statements were not made lightly. Sometime in the past Feather had probably done just that, put his life in their hands. Featherstone continued, "I've briefed them about Slade and his island–we have some ordnance survey charts here of the place–and now we'll plan what we are going to do this evening. The aerial surveillance photos will be here in a few minutes. Anything you want to say?"

Riordan said, "I met Christine in the kitchen and she said she might be joining us. I made a bit of a fool out of myself because she and my wife Nancy could be twins."

"That's Chris for you," smiled Featherstone "Can turn a man's head in a heartbeat. We've used that to our advantage once or twice, haven't we lads? But, no, she won't be coming tonight, we've got enough coverage now."

Riordan recognized the quality of these three men immediately, knew there was nothing more he could add. Featherstone unrolled one of the charts, placed a heavy ashtray at one end and held it down at the other. Riordan peered at the plans.

Featherstone said, "The house is situated in the center of the island, about half a mile from the jetty. It is completely open for several hundred yards around and then the place is trees all the way to the waterline. I sent a boat there this morning to test the perimeter and, surprise, surprise, they were quickly given their marching orders by a couple of heavily armed Orientals." His finger traced an arc around several of the bays. "I imagine they have some sort of radar or detection devices or even cameras mounted around the island to keep on the lookout for intruders. So getting on the island may be a bit of a problem. The next..."

The door opened and Featherstone's secretary came in carrying three computer disks and set them on the table. Four sets of eyes followed her to the door. No one spoke but each man knew what the other was thinking.

"Quelle domage," said Jean Marc, holding a hand over his heart. "It is a shame I am taken."

"Taken," mocked Capo. "I thought they changed the French wedding vows to allow the word mistress in there somewhere."

"Come on, lads," growled Featherstone. "Pay attention here. These are the most recent images from the island– they're only about an hour or two old. We'll take a look at these photos first and then see if we can figure out how to get on the island." He slipped the disk into a notebook computer sitting on the table, and then switched on the overhead projection unit. "Daniel, the lads have all seen this software before but for your benefit I can frame a portion of the picture and zoom in on it. We can actually focus on a golf ball lying on the road, the resolution is so good. So I'll give us a quick tour of the island."

For Riordan's benefit he added, "I got a bootleg version of this software from the green slime at Hereford... I've done them a good turn once or twice." Riordan knew Featherstone was referring to the intelligence officers at SAS headquarters, who had been given the unflattering sobriquet of 'green slime' by the regular soldiers.

The aerial photographs were easy to match to the survey charts lying on the table, so after a slow circuitous pass around the island, Featherstone focused on the house. Zooming in on the courtyard, they saw a four-car garage with three black Pathfinders sitting outside, and one of the guards with a bucket of soapy water in the process of cleaning the cars. He was looking upwards at the plane, so Featherstone zoomed in on the man's face until the harsh oriental features filled the screen, and then printed out the image. Another guard was standing on the steps of the house, also looking upwards, so Featherstone repeated the process and printed out another image.

"That's two more," Featherstone said, retrieving the images from the printer. From a manila envelope on the table he extracted two more photographs and laid them beside the others. "These are the two guards who shooed away the boat this morning. As you can see they are not the same. So we now have four guards." He took out the first disk and inserted the next. The picture showed one of the pathfinders parked at the front of the house and several people standing around. "Great!" exclaimed Featherstone,

"Let's see who's there now." Several more images rolled out of the printer, and Capo took them and laid them beside the others.

There were two more guards, different from the others, and two well-dressed individuals whom Riordan thought looked like businessmen. When he stated this fact, a frown crossed Featherstone's face and seconds later Riordan realized what the man was thinking. Given the business that Slade allegedly carried out, these probably were customers–which meant that there were potential victims on the island.

Riordan said, "Are you sure we just can't call the authorities and the press at the same time? They can't ignore an official complaint, especially if it has to do with the death of a police officer."

Featherstone shook his head. "The way this guy is connected, they'd be long gone before the PC Plod's got near the place. No, we've got to go in there ourselves. At the back side of the island is another jetty with a very large boathouse, in fact one which is big enough to house a float plane. There is a plane, a Cessna 152 registered to Slade's company, and it has been insured with floats. If he gets a whiff that we're after him, he'll be out of there in the blink of an eye. And if I was him, I'd have the place wired with explosives to cover my tracks long enough to get away."

Featherstone slipped in the final disk and pulled the first picture up on to the screen. He zoomed in on the back of the house where he noticed a large wired area, and the images of several large rotweilers swam into view. As a man the team groaned. Each of them was skilled at dealing with guard dogs, but it was an unpleasant task, unpredictable, and all of them had been bitten at some stage of their training.

Capo asked, "Do you think they run free?"

"The lads on the boat this morning said that the guards who shooed them away were accompanied by dogs, but they didn't hear any barking," said Featherstone, rubbing his chin thoughtfully. "I've come across these types before–they have had their vocal cords surgically severed for a completely silent approach. If you're not aware that these things are about, you can have a hundred pound guard dog attached to your throat before you know it. Or your groin, depending on how they have been trained. The South African police force were masters at training their dogs to do just that. You've heard the joke about what's long and black and hangs between a South African's legs–a South African police dog!"

The men winced, and hands moved towards groins, an involuntary defense motion followed by sheepish grins on their faces, Riordan's included. "So this is the dreaded SAS," he commented sarcastically, and received several withering looks in return.

Featherstone moved the mouse on the notebook and brought up the next photograph, which showed another group of people standing around a Pathfinder. The picture blurred as Featherstone framed the tiny group on the screen and allowed the system to refocus, a kaleidoscope of images was thrown on the screen and then it was clear.

Riordan gasped and a great pain sat in his chest like a leaden weight and another breath would not come. He put out a hand to the table to steady himself, cold fingers of fear trailing down his spine, and he shivered. He saw the puzzled look on Featherstone's face, and the man's hand reaching out to support him. Then he saw Featherstone's eyes travel back to the screen and the image displayed there. Bile rose in his throat. He knew what Slade was capable of doing, knew there was no fear there, and was at once terrified for the safety of his wife.

There was Nancy, in all her pregnant glory, standing between two of the oriental guards and a large, menacing figure directly in front of her.

Slade.

Dead man.

"Cunt," Riordan hissed, fingers clenching and unclenching around an imaginary neck. The others turned to look at him. "That's my wife Nancy," he explained. "She's due to give birth at any moment, and I can't imagine that bastard being too concerned if she goes into labor. I need a phone."

Featherstone pointed to a unit in the corner of the room. "Any of the three bottom lines."

Riordan, trembling, dialed the digits for their call answering service and waited until the system checked and responded with the fact that there was one new message. Pressing the digit one, he listened intently to the message, then saved it for playback. The muscles under his cheeks tensed and released like a live creature under his skin as he scanned the console unit for a hands-free button. "Listen to this," he said, and pressed the button. A deep voice boomed across the room.

"Mister Riordan, I have a piece of your property. I need two days to complete my business here and then I will be gone. If you attempt to interfere, or go to the authorities, I will rip your bastard child from your wife's belly and feed it to my dogs. I will return her unharmed in two days." Riordan took a deep breath, a cleansing breath learned at the Lamaze childbirth classes, and hung up the phone. His mouth was dry, his head spinning.

Featherstone and the others looked at him and Riordan could see the pain in their eyes. They were hardened warriors, of that he was certain, but they too had feelings and he knew they were putting themselves in his shoes, wondering what they would do if they were in a similar position. Featherstone said, "This is your call now, Daniel. What do you want to do?"

Riordan did not hesitate. The fury had abated to be replaced with cool, focused thoughts. There was to be no room for error, and to do that his mind had to be clear of thoughts of vengeance. To lash out in anger would be a futile act, and would probably result in Slade killing Nancy. It had to be meticulously planned, down to the very second, so that his wife could be rescued. Slade's big mistake was in thinking that Riordan would sit back and do nothing. Then again, Slade had no notion of the violent acts that to Riordan had been commonplace.

Riordan said, "We go in tonight as planned. Except we take the guards alive first to find out whereabouts in the place they are keeping Nancy. Our priority is to find her and get her out of harm's way. Then I'll deal with Slade." The men nodded.

"Now," Riordan continued, "I have a way of getting on to the island without being detected." He could see the interest in their eyes and he grinned. "My friend Allan and I are experts with paramotor equipment–powered parachutes, if you like. If you've ever jumped they are easy to use."

A match flared and the Frenchman lit up another cigarette. The heavy scent of the Gauloise filled the room. "I've jumped once or twice," he said off-handedly. "This will be a treat." The others laughed, knowing that he in fact he was an expert in HALO (High Altitude Low Opening) jumps, and had used the technique many times in hostage situations.

"Right," said Featherstone. "You guys get your kit ready and checked–you know what we'll need. Capo, you take care of the logistics for exfiltration, there will be six of us, plus any strays we find on the island. I'll take Daniel here over to the warehouse and get him kitted out, we'll have a de-brief about eleven and then we'll be off."

The men nodded and left the room. Featherstone turned to Riordan. "How long has it been since you've fired a pistol?"

"A few years," replied Riordan truthfully. "But it's like riding a bicycle." Featherstone touched him gently on the shoulder.

"Don't you know about the 7 P's Daniel–prior perfect planning prevents piss poor performance? Shooting is not like riding a bike," said Featherstone, his tone friendly, "it's my life out there and those of my men. And if we need to depend on your shooting abilities you need to practice a bit. You'll be popping off a few hundred rounds at the warehouse until I'm satisfied that I'm not going to get hit."

Riordan said, "You're pretty safe on that score. The only one who needs to be concerned is Slade."

Slade leaned back in his chair, put his feet up on the desk and took a long sip of his drink. He'd just finished making all the arrangements to get his other house on the Central coast area of California opened up and ready for him. It, too, was located in a remote area, far away from prying eyes, and as such was an ideal location to continue operating his 'business'.

He had spent most of the afternoon on the phone, and the sun was starting to slink behind the Rocky Mountains, casting a surrealistic reddish glow over the city of Vancouver in the distance. It was a shame to have to move, but things had run their course here, which he knew would happen one day, and he was well-prepared to deal with that circumstance. Besides, he was getting fed up with all the fucking rain. All it ever seemed to do in Vancouver was rain, and it also was the main topic of conversation with the locals.

Riordan, however, was the wild card in the deck, but Slade felt that having kidnapped Riordan's wife would keep him at bay for the two days he needed to have his clients do their business and leave.

Still, there was no point in taking any chances. Leaning forward he pressed a button on the phone console. "Slade here," he said. "Increase the patrols tonight and let the dogs have free rein." He was rewarded with a guttural grunt and the speaker went dead. Looking at his watch he saw it was almost seven o'clock, the time he had arranged to have dinner with his guests.

No expense was spared in the preparation of dinner, with the finest wines, brandies, whiskies and cigars available to complement the meal. After all, the men were each paying one million dollars for the pleasure of having a human life in their grasp for two days, to do with what they wished. And all on CD for them to replay their fantasies time and time again when they returned to their homes.

He was about to rise when a knock came to the door. His brow furrowed–he was not expecting anyone. "Come," he shouted and the door opened and an oriental entered, dressed in his ceremonial Samurai robes. The man shuffled across the room. Toshi was one of Slade's regular customers, coming to the island once a year for his few days of pleasure. He was the only one to take any "souvenirs" home with him, tokens from his victims; Toshi had a large collection of ears.

"Mister Toshi," Slade said, and stood and bowed in greeting. Waiting until the man returned the bow, Slade sat down and motioned for Toshi to do the same. "What can I do for you?" Slade asked.

"Slade san," came the reply. "I was having a swim this afternoon and I saw a new lady come into the guest wing of the house. She is very much pregnant, no."

Slade nodded, wondering where this was all going. "She's due at any moment."

"Is she for one of the other guests?"

Slade exhaled slowly. Now he knew. "Yes," he lied. "It was a difficult request to satisfy but the fee of two million was enough to ensure delivery."

"I would like to have her instead of the girl I asked for," replied the man. "I will pay you two times what the other guest paid."

"It will not be easy," said Slade, his mind racing with moves like a chess master. A few loose ends would have to be tied up quickly over the next two days, especially Daniel Riordan, and that bastard Featherstone, but the profit margin was enormous. "She is yours," said Slade. "Do you want her at the usual time?"

"Yes. At exactly four a.m. I will bathe her before the ceremony begins. And this time I will have four souvenirs to carry home."

CHAPTER 10

Assault

Riordan inhaled deeply, then stilled his breathing. He assumed the modified Weaver stance and squeezed the trigger gently, feeling the recoil in his arms and the familiar scent of gunpowder in his nostrils coaxing the feral animal that was the Raven back to life. The targets at the far end of the range danced as bullet after bullet plowed through the eyes and heart of each of the black silhouettes, brass casings dancing on the concrete, the reports reverberating around the large room. Featherstone looked on in astonishment while Riordan ejected a magazine, slammed home a new one and continued firing all in one fluid motion.

"I take it back," Featherstone said, when Riordan had fired his last round. "You can watch my back." Pulling off the ear protectors, he grinned at Riordan. "That was unbelievable. And you say you haven't fired in years."

Riordan ejected the empty magazine, set the pistol on the table and began refilling it from a box of shiny brass cartridges. Shrugging his shoulders he said, "Well, maybe the occasional round or two up north. I take the pistol with me when I go fishing, for protection from bears, and the odd time I might set up a few beer cans. Other than that the pistol stays in its case."

Featherstone said, "The lads will be here soon. We might as well load the gear into the van and be ready to go."

The others arrived shortly afterwards, checked their weapons and climbed into the van. Featherstone drove, heading out of the city and driving north to a secluded beach where they could launch in relative secrecy. Using a pair of night-vision binoculars, Riordan could make out the faint outline of the island, about three miles away. Nancy was there, probably frightened out of her wits, and she was to be rescued no matter what the cost. And Slade, as for him...

Filled with silent fury, Riordan stowed the binos, donned a pair of night vision goggles and, filling the chute with air, started the engine and guided the parasail up into the cold night air.

The plan was to use the parasail engines to give them some altitude and then glide directly on to the island, landing in a clear area at the back of the house. The darkened chutes would provide camouflage and their dark clothes ensured they would blend into the trees. Each man was armed with a 9-millimeter Browning Hi-Power in a cross-draw holster, a silenced Heckler and Koch MP5S with a laser aiming device, and a large commando knife strapped upside down on the strap of their Kevlar combat vest.

In heavy black cloth satchels they carried small packs of plastique explosive with radio-controlled detonators. Riordan declined the offer, not being familiar with the equipment. The explosives were to be used to destroy the electricity generator at the back of the house, and the backup unit as well.

There were other personal weapons which Riordan had seen in the warehouse; the Capo had a wire garrote, the Frog carried a menacing looking switchblade, and Tosser wore a cartridge bandolier across his back with a cut-down Remington 870 pump-action shotgun held inside by bands of velcro. Strapped to the inside of his wrist Riordan himself carried several well-balanced throwing knives. Dispatching Slade was going to be up close and personal with a blade–Riordan wanted to see the lights go out in the bastard's eyes.

Like geese flying in formation, the men approached the island, and Featherstone ordered the engines to be shut off. They were all in direct contact with one another through a set of combined transmitter/receiver earpieces, each of which had been checked thoroughly at the warehouse. Riordan watched the ground appear through the night-vision goggles, the entire area cast with a greenish tint. Suddenly the trees were rushing by in a blur and he hit the ground hard, stumbled a little and broke into a light run when he regained his balance. The others landed close behind, unhooked their gear and set it back in the trees to retrieve later.

Breathless, he shrugged out of the harness, gathered up the parachute like a fisherman hauling in his nets, and stowed it away with the others. Riordan felt the rush of excitement, the tingling sensation in every fibre of his being, co-mingled with fear for Nancy's safety. His pulse raced. Tonight there could be no mistakes. Unhooking the MP5S, he touched the trigger gently and watched the red beam from the laser sight stab out into the darkness. He switched the fire selector switch to three round bursts and moved over to join the others. All ready.

Featherstone gave the men the order to split up into their pre-assigned approach areas and then set off, Riordan following closely behind. Featherstone had taken him as a partner, but Riordan easily deferred to the big man's experience. The scent of pines hung heavily in the air, and a soft cushion of needles lay on the ground, quieting their approach. They moved quickly but carefully, as a twisted ankle at this point could jeopardize everything. An occasional firefly danced in the trees ahead of them, like someone tossing a lighted cigarette into the air.

As they neared the house, they were forced to remove the night-vision goggles due to the excessive amount of light flooding the back area. The house was much, much larger than Riordan had imagined from the surveillance photographs, with two large wings running off a central area. The back of the house was almost covered by a large swimming pool, surrounded by brightly colored patio furniture. Putting a pair of tiny binoculars to his eyes, Featherstone scanned the buildings for any forms of surveillance equipment. Riordan did the same.

Waiting at the tree line while scanning the area, Featherstone was looking off to one side when Riordan saw one of the guard dogs appear at the side of the house, raise its nose to the air and then bound across the lawn directly at them. Its mouth was opened wide, and there should have been a loud snarling sound, but the animal made no sound save for a light pounding on the grass.

He gasped, attracting Featherstone's attention, and was amazed when the big man stepped out to meet the huge animal. It launched itself directly into the air at Featherstone's throat, but he calmly stepped to one side, grasped its two front legs and yanked them apart. There was a ripping sound, like tearing open a large sheet of velcro, and the huge animal fell to the ground, twitched for a few moments and then was still.

"Fundamental flaw in the bone structure," offered Featherstone, his teeth gleaming whitely through the black and green striped camouflage paint.

"You're a braver man than me, Feather," commented Riordan. "I'd just have shot the fucker."

"The bullets might have gone through and hit the house," said Featherstone, "and we don't want to alarm them just yet. Besides, I needed the practice. My neighbors complain when I kill their dogs. Let's go, we need to grab one of the security guards."

Riordan covered the big man's back as he sprinted across the grass to the house. Given the hour, it was not likely that anyone would be up, except for the guards, so they were going to wait by the back door until one of the guards showed. Featherstone pressed himself flat against the house and beckoned for Riordan to follow.

Slipping out from behind his cover, Riordan had taken one step when he heard a crunching sound behind him and turned to see another of the huge dogs rushing directly at him. There was something totally incongruous about the jagged rows of teeth and the slavering mouth and not a sound coming from its muzzle. He did not hesitate. The silenced MP5S coughed three times and the beast dropped in its tracks as though felled by a poleaxe.

"Come on Daniel," came the urgent command in his earpiece.

"Just doing some doggie training," quipped Riordan, and ran across the grass to where Featherstone waited.

"What now?" whispered Riordan, pressing himself against the wall beside Featherstone. At that moment their earpieces whispered and the Frenchman's voice said, "Got one, mon capitane, but he didn't want to talk. Said he'd rather die so I obliged. I'm moving in towards the house."

"Feather," came another voice over the earpieces. Riordan couldn't tell if it was the Capo or Tosser speaking, but they certainly seemed to be out of breath. "I've taken out two guards. One is still alive and says the woman is being held in the basement area along with the other girls. The client suites are on the second floor and the video room is in the far east wing of the building. The guards hang out in the kitchen, which is the door off the back where you are heading. There are eight guards who patrol every thirty minutes in teams of two, and Slade has two personal bodyguards."

Featherstone's hand went instinctively to his earpiece. "Frogman, Frogman. Be careful, they're patrolling in twos." Riordan listened intently but there was no reply. Featherstone continued, "Capo, Tosser, get over to the house. And watch out for those fucking dogs."

"No problem Boss," came the reply, "We got a couple of the woof woofs already. Tosser got bit in the arm but it's not too bad–he's just happy it's not his wanking arm!"

Featherstone shook his head and Riordan grinned. "Always taking the piss," Riordan said.

"You have no idea," replied Featherstone, and the door opened and two men, dressed in black fatigues, walked out, weapons cradled under their arms while they lit up cigarettes. They were totally oblivious to the two men hiding behind the door. It slammed shut behind the guards and Featherstone raised his machine pistol and loosed off several three-round bursts into the men, their bodies jerking and twitching like demonic marionettes by the force of the heavy rounds slamming into them. There was no noise save for the quiet rattle of the HK's bolt and the tinkle of brass casings on the patio tiles. When the guards had collapsed to the ground, blood pouring from shattered bodies, Riordan dashed over and removed the magazines from their weapons and tossed them away into the garden.

"Good," said Featherstone, replacing the magazine in his pistol. Smoke curled lazily from the barrel. "That means there's just two more inside. If we can get them quietly we'll be able to go on into the house without raising the alarm."

Capo and Tosser were at the back door quickly, weapons up and ready following a quick look at the two bodies. "Any sign of Frogman?" Featherstone asked. The question was followed by a shake of the head from Capo. "Did you place the explosives?"

Capo nodded and extracted a tiny transmitter from his trousers. He flipped a switch and the green button on the front of the unit lit up. "All ready," he said.

Featherstone said, "Anyone in the house who is not female is to be considered a target. Questions?"

Silence.

"Let's go then."

Riordan stilled his breathing, ensured the earpiece was in place, closed his eyes and slipped the night vision goggles over his head. In his head he heard Featherstone's voice say, "Three, two, one," and there was a distant muffled crump and Riordan opened his eyes and followed the others into the now-darkened house. The men were well versed in the black art of house clearing, so Riordan held back and watched them dispatch the two guards efficiently and then take off into the other areas of the house. Heart pounding, Riordan headed into the main part of the house and found a set of stairs leading to the basement. He ran down the stairs, the red beam from his gun's aiming device settling on the first door.

He kicked it opened and ran inside, prepared to kill anyone he found there, but it was empty. Panic rising, he moved to the next and kicked it down also. Inside he found a young girl, dressed in a bra and panties and crouched in the corner of the room, whimpering in fright. "Stay there," he ordered, "we'll be back for you."

Outside in the corridor, Featherstone was repeating the process on the other side. Voices echoed in his head as Capo and Tosser efficiently eliminated anything with whom they came in contact. They were running out of rooms and still no sign of Nancy. Riordan felt his soul fill with despair. Where was Nancy? Had they killed her already? Featherstone kicked down the door of the last room and ran inside. When he came out he said, "Someone's been in there recently–the bed's still warm." Riordan ran inside, sniffed the air and recognized Nancy's perfume immediately… Jean Paul Gautier, her favourite.

"Christ, where the fuck is she?"

"They took her a few minutes ago," came a voice from behind. Riordan turned to see one of the young girls standing in the doorway. She said, "I couldn't sleep and I heard them take her. She's probably in the video room over on the other side of the house."

"Shit," spat Riordan, feeling on the verge of panic. He knew what went on in those rooms. "How do we get there?"

The girl said, "This corridor runs across the house. Go all the way to the end and up the stairs. The video rooms are there. There's two, one on each side of the corridor. I've been in both."

Riordan touched the girl gently on the arm. "Get back into your room and stay there. We'll be back in a few minutes." He ran off down the corridor.

Nancy Riordan was terrified. She had been dragged from sleep and brought to this room by two of the oriental guards. Mounted high on the wall near the top of each corner was a large video camera with a blinking red light, showing it was recording. Lack of sleep and a wave of nausea washed over her in the large room when an oriental man appeared, dressed in a traditional warrior's costume. His hair was slicked back and tied up in a bun, and he wore a long, neatly trimmed mustache. A long bladed sword and a smaller dagger, katanas, were wedged in his belt–she recognized them from part of Daniel's collection. A large bowl in one corner of the room was filled with steaming, scented water. Puzzled, she stood up from the large bed and faced the man.

"Who are you?" she asked, her voice quavering.

"I am Toshi," replied the man. "Please remove your clothes and lie down on the bed so that I may bathe you."

Nancy could barely believe what she was hearing. "Go fuck yourself," she snapped and was rewarded with a brutal, stinging slap across the face which sent her reeling backwards on to the bed.

The man stepped forward and drew the katana from its scabbard. The gleaming steel moved slowly towards her face. "Please do as I say or the punishment will be worse."

Reluctantly, she sat up and removed her nightgown, then lay back on the bed, her face burning with shame and anger as the man stared at her nakedness. The man replaced his sword in its scabbard, then carried the bowl of water and a cloth across to the bed and set it beside her. Rinsing the cloth, he muttered some words to himself and then began to wash her skin with the scented water. She saw he had small, pudgy fingers, but there was a ridge of hardened skin along the side of his hands. It looked like the side of Allan Brown's hand.

Nancy closed her eyes, her mind racing with what possibilities were to come. The man called Slade said she was a hostage to keep Daniel from going to the police for a couple of days, but this was something different. She felt threatened by this man. Opening her eyes, she saw the man reach across her body to wash her other arm, and in front of her face was the pommel of the sword and the tiny dagger.

She shivered.

Then the lights went out, throwing the room into complete darkness.

At the sound of the first explosion Slade slid his hand under his pillow, grasped the butt of the automatic he kept there and rolled out of bed. Someone was carrying out an assault on his house. It wasn't the police either, because they would have announced their presence first. Crawling across the floor to the window, he peered outside in time to see the backup generator explode in a ball of orange flames.

"Riordan," he spat, and quickly pulled on a pair of track pants and a fleece top. Sliding his feet into a pair of running shoes, he pressed the intercom for the kitchen but the power was completely cut. He grabbed the walkie-talkie atop his nightstand and pressed the transmit button. "Come back, come back," he yelled. "Identify yourselves." There was a hiss of static and one of the guards acknowledged his call and informed him the others were dead. He ordered the man to get back to the house as quickly as he could.

As he stood up, a knock came to his door and he heard the guttural voice of his bodyguards. "Come," he said, and the two men, both armed to the teeth, ran into the room and waited for his orders. "It's time to leave," he said, and went over to the wall-safe in his bedroom. Using a small flashlight, he spun the dial and extracted a set of documents, several passports and large packets of high-denomination US currency. "Did you take the woman to Toshi?" he asked over his shoulder and a wide grin split his face when he heard the acknowledgment. Riordan would get his wife back in pieces.

At the back of the safe he pressed a red button and a digital timer began a countdown from 30 minutes. The entire house had been wired with explosives, a deadly combination of Semtex and Thermite, sufficient to completely demolish the place and then incinerate the remains, so it would be several days before the police could piece anything together, if there were any pieces left.

By then he and his guards would be long gone. Slade was a planner by nature, so every detail, down to a secret escape route had been set up long before he started his 'business'.

"Let's go," he said, pulling back a bookcase to reveal a set of stairs.

Riordan charged along the corridor and raced up the stairs, taking them two at a time. At the top there were two doors. Riordan did not hesitate, crashing into the first with his pistol up and ready. A large bed sat in the middle of the room. Nancy lay there, sprawled across the bed, but even in the greenish glow from the glasses he could see the dark blood across the sheets and her stomach. Riordan froze, and in the corner of his eye he saw a man dressed in long flowing robes heading for the corner of the room.

In the same instant Featherstone shouldered him to one side and opened fire. Riordan saw the robes pop back as if the material had snagged on a nail, then dark patches like ink blots appeared. He turned his head back to the bed, afraid to take a step. Featherstone grabbed him by the arm, his fingers digging painfully in Riordan's bicep and startling him out of the trance. "Go check on her," Featherstone said, and ran over to ensure her assailant was dead.

Riordan ran over and looked at the mess of blood on his wife, searching for the wound. At first he thought that she had been stabbed in the stomach but there was no sign of a wound. Turning her gently on her side he examined her back but there was no wound there either. "What the fuck?" he said aloud, and at that point Nancy groaned and put a hand to her head. Riordan followed the fingers and felt a huge bump growing at her temple. A wave of relief washed over him and he grabbed her tightly, feeling her body tense like a cat about to spring.

"Nancy, it's me," he said, and instantly her arms wrapped around him.

"Oh Daniel," she sobbed, "I thought you might not come. I was so afraid and that man..."

Riordan said, "You're safe now. We'll get you out of here. Put on the nightgown and come with me. There are some young girls downstairs who need help."

Featherstone came over to the bed. "Thanks Feather," said Riordan, and Featherstone laughed aloud.

"You needn't thank me. Our friend here was well on his way to the hereafter before I helped him along. There's a ten inch knife buried in his guts." Riordan turned to look at his wife.

"You did that," he said.

Nancy slipped on the nightdress and stood up. "He was bending over me when the lights went out. I was terrified, so I grabbed it and shoved it as hard as I could into him. He hit me with something and I passed out, and the next thing I know my white knight is here."

Featherstone stepped out into the passageway, checked both ways and motioned for Riordan to follow. They ran as quickly down the stairs as they could, Nancy waddling along assisted by Riordan, picked up the remaining girls and headed back up to the kitchen.

"Capo, Tosser, come in. We're heading for the kitchen," Featherstone said.

"Boss, Capo. There's no sign of anyone about here. The beds up here have been slept in recently but we can't see anyone. There's a safe open on the wall here so it looks like they left in a hurry. The safe is cleared out but there's a display... oh fuck. It's a timer."

Riordan turned to look at Featherstone. "What sort of timer?" asked Featherstone.

"Don't know boss," came the reply, "but it's set for twenty-three minutes and counting. Looks like the bastard has got the place wired."

"Get down here," ordered Featherstone. "Tosser, where are you?"

"Boss, I'm in some sort of computer room. There was some little bastard in here who tried to jump me but he's out cold. Someone's took his hand off recent like. There's several large computer servers and equipment for making CD's and all sorts of video equipment."

"Are there any cabinets with tapes and the like?" asked Featherstone. Riordan knew that the man was looking for evidence to tie Slade to the killings and the murder of Susan Delgado.

"Oh fuck," exclaimed Tosser, and Riordan heard the panic in the man's voice. "Boss, all these cabinets are wired with thermite charges, and it looks like they have been activated."

"Relax Tosser," Featherstone said. "We've got about twenty minutes. Grab as many of the CD's and tapes as you can and meet us in the kitchen."

"I'll help him," said Riordan, making a quick decision. "I know about computers, and I know what to look for. Keep your eye on Nancy. I'll be back in a moment."

He sprinted down the hallway listening to directions from Tosser in his earpiece. The computer room was on the second floor near the room where Nancy had been held, and Tosser was standing in the doorway when Riordan, breathless, arrived on the second floor.

"Winded a wee bit," came the sarcastic comment, and Tosser stood back to let Riordan into the room. "I'm going to have a poke about the rest of the place," Tosser said. "I haven't seen hide nor hair of Slade or his bodyguards." There was a low level of light in the room, and all the equipment purred gently fueled by a large un-interruptible power supply (UPS) that took up one corner of the room. A quick glance showed Riordan the walls were covered with pornographic images held in place with tape or large, multi-colored pins.

"Forget him," Riordan spat. "He's probably long gone by now. Help me inside–we may have to take one of those servers you were talking about. Where's the geek?" Tosser pointed over at a desk in the middle of the room.

Riordan peered over the desk at the prone figure lying on the floor, taking in the growth of acne on the young man's cheeks and the fresh, bloody bandage on the stump of his arm. A purplish lump was growing on the man's forehead, testament to the self-defense skills of Tosser. "Can you bring him around quickly?" Riordan asked.

A vial of pungent smelling salts appeared from a first aid package in one of Tosser's voluminous pockets, and the man was soon shaking his head groggily, his one good hand massaging the bruise on his forehead. Riordan poked him on the cheek with his pistol, leaving an angry red ring below his eye.

"You don't have a lot of time," Riordan spat, his voice harsh. "Do you hear me?" He poked viciously again.

"Please," came the pathetic moan. "Slade took my hand off with a sword for contacting the police. It really hurts. Don't hurt me."

"Police, what police?" Riordan asked.

"Susan Delgado. I sent her some images and asked to make a deal but Slade found out about it and cut my fucking hand off and fed it to the dogs."

At last, Riordan thought, hard evidence to exonerate
Allan Brown. He shoved the pistol against the man's face.
"Where are the backups?" Riordan asked. "And then your
personal backups. A weasel like you will have made copies
of all the important stuff." A trembling finger pointed to a
line of CD's on the bottom shelf of the cabinet, all tagged
with a red sticker, then another row tagged with blue
stickers.

Riordan grabbed all the red-marked CD's and tossed
them into a sack, then loaded another bag with all the
others in the cabinet. "Make yourself useful," he shouted,
handing the bag to the youth. "Get on down to the kitchen.
Put one foot wrong and you'll get capped." The youth got
to his feet, grabbed the bag and ran out of the room, the
injuries all but forgotten.

"Feather," Riordan said quietly, and heard the words,
"What's up?" in his earpiece. Riordan said, "I've sent
someone down to you with a bag of evidence. Tosser
scared the shit out of him so please try not to kill him when
he runs into the kitchen. Over."

"Euch," Tosser spat, having taken a closer look at the
pictures on the wall. Riordan looked at the expression on
Tosser's face and stepped beside him. Immediately a knot
turned in his stomach at the sight of the pictures that
appeared to have been downloaded from the internet. There
were several internet mail addresses and user ids written on
post-it notes and attached to each of the images. The
pictures were of pre-pubescent girls and boys having
intercourse with adult men and women–there were even

some bestiality pictures, which forced a column of bile to rise in his throat.

"Little fuckin' pervert," hissed Tosser, "no wonder Slade took his hand off. I'd like to top the little bastard!"

Riordan nodded, his teeth grinding together in revulsion of the display before him, images of the children, especially some of those whom he estimated to be only six or seven, indelibly burned in his mind. Their expressions were... his mind searched; Auswitz–like the haunted faces of the prisoners in the camps before being liberated–little lost souls. "I know, Tosser," Riordan said quietly, fingers tightening around the butt of his pistol. "I'd finish him myself, but unfortunately he's the only link to Slade and the only witness we have to prove that Allan Brown was framed. I have to keep him alive. Now, bring that computer along." Ripping away all the connections at the back of the unit, Tosser hefted the machine on to his shoulder and set off down the corridor.

When they reached the kitchen, Featherstone, who was waiting with the others, raised his arm and looked at his watch. Riordan, instinctively, walked over to comfort Nancy but Featherstone intercepted him and took him off to one side, out of earshot of the others he said, "Daniel, there's not too long left now on the timers. And don't be draping yourself over Nancy in front of the others–that will just raise complicated questions later. We'll take the jeeps outside, drive down to the jetty and nick the cruiser. Then we'll drop this lot off at the docks and go on up the coast to where we started out."

"But what about Nancy?" Riordan asked. "I'm not leaving her with this lot." Riordan felt Featherstone's fingers dig painfully into the fleshy part of his arm as if to emphasize his words.

"Listen Daniel," came the low voice. "We have taken tremendous risks here tonight and I don't want this coming back to me or my men. These are fucking street children who've been beaten and abused and Nancy is the only one who can explain what happened. When the police let them go I'll see that they are cared for properly–I've already spoken to them about that. You've got to go back to your house and wait until the police call to inform you that she is safe, then you can play that little tape recording of Slade's threat to them. They will understand why he was trying to keep you quiet. You should know the drill by now–always tell a story which contains a grain of truth and stick to it."

"Makes sense to me," Riordan reluctantly replied. He knew Featherstone was right.

Featherstone turned to the others. "Time to go," he said, and opened the back door. Instantly a burst of fire raked the bricks beside his head and he leapt back into the room, slamming the door shut. The other dropped to the floor. "Fuck," he exclaimed, touching his cheek gingerly with his gloved fingers. A piece of shrapnel had gouged a furrow about an inch long under one eye. "There was one guard we missed."

Riordan, peering out the window through his night vision goggles, saw movement beside the pool cabana. The remaining guard, following orders to the bitter end, was concealing himself behind the back wall of the tiny wooden structure. Riordan thought for a moment, set his pistol on full auto, then opened the back door. A burst of fire answered his movement, but the door remained open.

As soon as the firing stopped Riordan was on his feet, racing through the open door straight for the cabana. God help me, I hope I'm right about this, he said to himself. The guard, hearing footsteps, immediately moved out of concealment and Riordan squeezed the trigger, the 9-millimeter rounds passing through the thin structure like paper and tearing the guard to shreds. Riordan continued running and firing until he stood directly over the guard's body. He kicked away the man's gun as a precaution, a movement borne out of habit. It was not necessary.

"All clear," he said aloud, and turned to see Featherstone rush the others out of the house and around to the front where the three vehicles were parked. The engines purred to life and they were soon racing towards the jetty. Featherstone and Riordan took the first 4 by 4 and sped down the dirt trail, lights ablaze and yelling like banshees with relief. The vehicle slid to a halt at the top of the jetty, and Riordan and Featherstone were out and sprinting towards the boat, guns raised in case there were any more surprises. A thin plume of smoke reached to the night skies from the engines at the back and Riordan leapt over the side, his gun up and ready while Featherstone provided cover. Riordan took in the scene immediately and called "Clear!"

The Frenchman was lying beside the controls, his gun falling to the ground when Riordan approached. "I hoped you'd get here," the man said weakly, blood trickling from the corners of his mouth. "The other guard got me, and then one of the fucking dogs wanted a bite as well."

Featherstone had a penlight out and quickly examined the wounds while the others got into the boat and went into the forward cabin. "Not too bad. Missed the lung," Featherstone commented, taking out a syrette of morphine and slamming it into the Frenchman's leg. "As for the doggie bite, we better get you a tetanus shot, just to be on the safe side. Tosser," Featherstone said, his voice crisp, a voice used to giving orders. "Get us under way quickly. We've got a few minutes before the place blows. I want out of the way before the cops get here."

"Okay boss," came the reply, "Capo's just arrived. I've put the girls in the forward cabin. There's some blankets and stuff there to keep them warm."

Riordan helped Featherstone move the Frenchman away from the console and onto one of the seats. Featherstone carefully cut away the black sweater to reveal a puckered wound high up on the Frenchman's chest. A first aid packet materialized and the man's wounds were bandaged quickly to staunch the bleeding. The boat rocked gently and the throaty hum of powerful engines filled the night air as Tosser examined the controls.

"Shit," Riordan exclaimed, and Featherstone turned, startled.

"What's up?" Featherstone asked, concern in his voice.

"What about the paramotor equipment? That stuff can be tracked back to us."

"What the fuck do you think Capo was doing? I'm not just a pretty face you know, Betty. Betty?" Riordan marveled at the man doing Michael Crawford impressions from a program Riordan had long since forgotten, his hands covered in blood, on board a stolen boat with one of his men seriously injured. These men were surely the stuff of legend, men whose tales would never be told except within the closed ranks of their warrior society. Once sworn enemies, Riordan had come to respect these fierce men, and he owed his life to one of them, a man called John Waters.

There came several loud clunks at the stern of the boat, Capo loading the equipment on to the deck none too gently, then casting off the lines. The boat moved away into the night, cresting against the light swell until Tosser had a feel for it, then he gunned the engines and sent the craft hurtling towards the coastline.

They were just approaching the tiny dock when, in the distance, a huge fireball lit up the night sky, and a miniature atomic cloud rose into the heavens. The booming reverberation carried across the water, buffeting their ears.

"That was a fuck of a lot of explosives," commented Riordan. "There won't be anything left of that place but a huge fucking hole in the ground."

"I think that was the intent," replied Featherstone. "The chances of getting any physical evidence out of the that place now is zero. It's a good thing you brought those CD's." Tosser guided the boat gently to the dock and Featherstone led the others out of the cabin and helped them onto dry land. One girl threw up. The scrawny young man was none too happy being manhandled by Capo, but quieted down when Featherstone handed Nancy a gun and said, "If he moves, shoot him in the legs. And make sure the police get that bag of CD's! I called them a few minutes ago and they will be arriving shortly with an ambulance."

One by one the girls stepped over and kissed Featherstone on the cheek. "Thanks for saving us mister." Nancy, who did the same, winked at Riordan on the way past. "I'll thank you later," she whispered, her lips trailing across his cheek.

"Let's go," Featherstone ordered, and leapt down into the boat. Riordan did the same and Tosser guided the boat away from the dock and back into the dark waters.

CHAPTER 11

Encryption

Just over two months later, Riordan stood at his kitchen sink, smiling as he watched the crowd on the outdoor patio sipping champagne, munching hors d'ouvres and mingling on a beautiful summer's day. There could not have been a more perfect day for the christening, and the two boys, David and Allan, lay sleeping peacefully in the nursery upstairs, a fact attested to by the gentle breathing emanating from the intercom on the counter. Nancy, resplendent in a white cotton dress, moved from group to group receiving hugs and kisses from the gathering of friends and acquaintances. Allan Brown, just a little bit the worse for wear, sat in a deck chair, a hand-carved, Irish blackthorn walking stick resting across his knees. And as usual a pretty young thing sat beside him, entranced by one of his many yarns.

Featherstone and the three stooges, as Nancy had nicknamed, Capo, Tosser and the Frenchman, were all deep in conversation with respective 'targets', some of the single nurses from Nancy's work. Talk about a fox in the henhouse, thought Riordan, twisting the wire on yet another bottle of Veuve Cliquot. Totally focused on opening the bottle, his conscious mind registered the patio door sliding open and soon a warm pair of hands encircled his waist.

"Oh, don't do that," he moaned, "Nancy will see us," and the fingers pinched the skin at his waist. The fingers grabbed a roll a little too big for his liking and he resolved to get back to the gym as soon as possible, although the children had thrown a wrench into any sort of normal routine. It was a difficult adjustment to make. The cork popped and he turned into the smiling face of his wife, glowing as only a new mother can. Her face was tilted up for a kiss and he obliged, feeling her full lips part and her tongue slide provocatively into his mouth. He responded in kind, holding her as tightly as he could with one arm. "I think maybe we could try it tonight," she said. "The stitches have healed and the pain is gone so maybe, y'know... If you're still interested, that is!" A hand slid down his chest and trailed slowly across his groin, fingers tugging against the raging erection in his trousers. "I have my answer," she grinned, and held up her glass for more champagne.

Riordan filled the glass, and looked around for a fresh strawberry. "Want one?" he asked, knowing only too well the answer. "Only if you do it," came the reply.

Holding the strawberry in the palm of his hand, he squeezed gently, allowing the juice to trickle through his fingers like red raindrops and drip into Nancy's glass. When he was finished he dropped the pulp into the glass as well, and then held out his hand. Nancy lifted his hand to her mouth and slowly, ever so slowly, sucked the remaining juice off his fingers one at a time, producing a series of strangled moans from Riordan's lips. "If you don't behave yourself you're going to get jumped here and now," he groaned, his voice thick with lust.

The patio door slid open again and Featherstone appeared in the doorway, followed by the head nurse on Nancy's ward, a stunning redhead wearing denim cutoffs and a halter-top that left little to the imagination. "Ah, Daniel, my good man," said Featherstone, in a very posh British accent. "We've come for replenishment. The champers is running out so we absolutely must have some more, and some more of those super little munchie things." The nurse went into fits of giggles and wrapped her arm around Featherstone. "Don't look at me like that," he continued. "This darling lady is hungry as well. If you don't feed her she might eat me!"

Riordan lifted one eyebrow. "I thought that was the plan," he said, and Nancy punched him in the ribs.

"You weren't complaining a minute ago," Nancy said, lifting her glass and breezing out the door to join the others. Riordan filled Featherstone's two glasses, and was filling his own when Featherstone said, "Darlin', why don't you go on outside and I'll join you in a moment. I want a quick word with Daniel here." Riordan watched the cutoffs disappear out through the door, the nurse's hips moving tantalizingly under the material.

"Thank you Lord," commented Featherstone, raising his glass in a mock toast. "I'm there."

"So Feather," Riordan said. "This must be important as I'm obviously eating into your skirt-chasing time. What's up?"

"Nothing with me lad," Featherstone replied. "I was just wondering if you were getting anywhere with those CD's. I haven't heard a whisper about the ones we sent to the police along with that little pervert, and given the fact that it's been almost eight weeks, I was expecting some huge hoopla or other in the press—you know what they're like when it comes to kiddy-porn, let alone snuff movies. Other than the fact that they've issued a country-wide warrant for Slade to assist in their inquiries, I haven't heard a peep, which intrigues me."

Riordan shook his head sadly and took a sip of champagne. He too was perplexed by the lack of activity. "The little bastard has used some sort of encryption on the CD's and I haven't been able to break it as yet. Until I do, I won't be able to view them. But it's just a matter of time. I've been working on it when I get the opportunity, but between my regular work and helping Nancy with the kids I haven't had as much time as I would have liked."

Featherstone rolled the chilled rim of the glass against his brow. "There are still a few questions which are puzzling me, and I think the answers may lie in the images on those CD's. Like how the guy got popped at the lodge, and how the killer knew we were there."

Riordan nodded. "I agree. It's been troubling me too. There's something floating about in the ether but it hasn't crystallized into anything tangible as yet. I'm going to ask Allan to take a look for me cos' he's a bit of a techno-weenie and loves this technology stuff. He might be able to come up with some ideas I haven't thought of. By the way, what happened to the girls we brought off the island?"

A frown crossed Featherstone's face like a cloud blocking the sun and Riordan could tell the news was not good. "We did what we could. The police took their statements and gave them some money for shelter. One girl decided that after her ordeal, life with her parents wasn't too bad after all so she went back to them. The others are just faces on the streets, lost souls in the big city."

"Too bad," commented Riordan, "but at least they are still alive." Featherstone drained his glass and held it out for a fill-up. "What did your last slave die of?" Riordan muttered, slowly filling the glass with the golden liquid.

Outside, Allan Brown was chatting up another nurse, offering to show her his scars when Riordan interrupted. "Allan, I have a problem with my computer and I was wondering if you could take a look at it for me," Riordan said, looking down with concern at his friend's emaciated appearance. The stabbing and the brush with death had taken a tremendous toll on Allan, but there was still the mischievous twinkle in his eye. The fake toe-tag was now in a tiny boxed frame above Brown's desk, a grim reminder of how close he had come to death. Patting the nurse on the bottom, he said, "Ah love, duty calls, but I'll be back in a few minutes and then we can resume our conversation." The nurse smiled disarmingly, and Riordan helped Allan to his feet and handed him his cane.

When they were out of earshot Riordan said, "What the hell are you up to? You know a good shag would probably kill you at the moment."

Brown shot back, "Look mommy, given the choice between a shag and a knife, trust me, I'll have a shag any day. Now tell me, what's your problem?"

Riordan opened the patio doors and led the way to his study. "I've got a problem with some encryption on a CD and I'm trying to break it. The last person to own this machine was a computer nerd, much like yourself, so I thought that since warped minds generally think alike, you might be able to help me."

Brown muttered something un-intelligible and eased himself with all the speed and grace of a senior citizen into Riordan's chair. The computer sitting on the desk whirred quietly and Brown began to stroke the keyboard, his dexterous fingering like that of a classical pianist. "I need to break out to DOS," he said, and Riordan grunted in assent. It was something he had tried several times in his search for a clue. Brown continued, "These guys usually put their entire LOGIN procedure in a script form, and, given their general approach to matters of security, they often hard-code their password right into the script. If you have the right password then you can easily break the encryption. And sometimes the password itself actually unlocks the encryption."

Brown did a file search for anything that ended in .BAT, then checked the dates on the files as well to see when they were created. His finger trailed down the screen leaving a greasy smear. "This looks like a possibility," he said, and went to the DOS editor and keyed in the name of the file. He browsed through the file, looking in detail at the instructions, nodding to himself knowingly at some of the commands embedded there. "These look like responses to password prompts to me," he said, pointing to words like 'clitoris' and 'vulva' followed by the symbol <CR> for carriage return, a simulation of someone pressing the 'ENTER' key on a keyboard. "Whoever set this up is certainly into female anatomy in a big way!"

Closing down the editor, he keyed the file name at the C:/ prompt and almost instantly the script unfolded, password windows appeared and shortly afterwards the password appeared as if written by an invisible hand. A few seconds later a menu appeared on the screen with various icons for manipulating and replaying CD's. "Bingo," smiled Brown, displaying the menu with a flourish that would have put Pavarotti to shame. "I'm going back to the party, and if you have any sense you'll do the same."

Riordan patted his friend on the shoulder and shook his head in astonishment. "I should have come to you sooner," he said, "I never thought to look for the obvious, but at least now I can take a look at what's on the CD's."

"Should I ask?" said Brown, "or is this another 'need to know' situation?"

Riordan handed his friend the cane and smiled. "Baldrick, you didn't see this computer and you definitely didn't see that pile of CD's on the desk," Riordan said.

Brown nodded. "What CD's?" and limped off down the corridor.

Riordan stood for a moment, looking at the screen and the pile of CD's he was going to have to wade through, steeling himself for the images he knew he would have to face. Not tonight, he said to himself. Not tonight.

After powering off the monitor–he didn't want anyone stumbling into the system by accident–he was replenishing his glass in the kitchen when the doorbell rang. He went down the hallway, expecting to see some other well wishers come to join the celebration. On opening the door, he was surprised to see Brian Dymond, Susan Delgado's partner, standing on the steps holding a gift-wrapped package in his hand.

The detective fumbled for words and Riordan guessed that he was awkward about the situation. Riordan felt sorry for the man and empathized with him as the evidence, coupled with Allan's original confession, had convinced Dymond that Allan Brown killed Susan. If he had been in

Dymond's shoes he would probably have felt the same way.

"Daniel," Dymond said, holding out the gift. "I found this in Susan's desk when I was cleaning out her things. She had mentioned several times about your wife's imminent delivery, and had picked these up one day when we were out on a call. They caught her eye in a tiny antique store, and there was no holding her back. I wanted to bring them over."

Riordan saw the pain in the man's eyes when he spoke about his ex-partner, and smiled and took the package. "That was very kind of you," Riordan said. "Would you like to come inside and have a drink? There's quite a party going on in the back."

Dymond shook his head. "Thanks, but I have to get down to the office. Perhaps later. There are still some leads we're following up."

Riordan asked, trying to be as nonchalant as possible, "How is the investigation going? I mean I haven't heard anything in the news at all, and I know Allan is curious."

Dymond chewed his lip, as if pondering whether to disclose any information. "There's not much I can tell you. Slade has vanished off the face of the earth, and that computer specialist managed to get out on bail and he too has vanished, even though we put him under twenty-four hour surveillance. We had hoped he would help us with the CD's that your wife brought in, but the encryption has our guys stumped. They've been sifting through the ruins of the house, hoping to find some documentation or even some

pieces of the computer the prick used to create the CD's."
Riordan swallowed hard. It's sitting not 15 feet from where
we are, he thought to himself, feeling the slightest twinge
of guilt.

Dymond continued, "So at the moment we have
precious little to go on. At least he corroborated Allan's
story, and showed that Slade was behind Susan's death.
But I have thirty-seven CD's sitting on my desk, all waiting
to tell their story, and I'm frustrated as hell. I'm sure there
will be many clues on those."

Thirty-seven, thought Riordan, trying to keep the
shock from his face. There were forty in the bag that I gave
to Nancy. Somewhere along the line the chain of evidence
had broken down. But interfering with evidence was not an
easy task, and only personnel within the station would have
had access to the evidence locker. Which meant... He
frowned, the thought process leading him to the possibility
of a corrupt individual within the police department who
would have known what was on the CD's and had removed
them.

Biting back the obvious question, which would
incriminate him as being part of the team who rescued
Nancy, Riordan said, "Thanks for coming by, Brian. And
please keep us informed about the investigation. I'd like to
see Slade get what he deserves." He shook hands with
Dymond and went back inside the house, his senses reeling
with the fact that three of the CD's had gone missing.
There were many questions he would have liked to ask

like, "Where the fuck are those three CD's, and just who
was in the images on those CD's?"

Carrying the package, he went out the back and
handed it to Nancy, leaning over to whisper in her ear.
"Brian Dymond just dropped this off," he said. "Susan
apparently had this in her desk drawer for us. Don't
mention it to Allan for now. I'll tell him later." Nancy
nodded, her bright eyes misting a little, and went inside the
house to open the gift.

Taking a long sip of his champagne, Riordan sat down
beside Featherstone and quietly recounted the story.
Featherstone listened intently; his piercing eyes focused on
Riordan's, a frown appearing when Riordan had finished.
"Something is rotten in the state of Denmark,"
Featherstone said, in his best Lawrence Olivier accent, but
there was no humor in the words.

"I know, Feather, I know," said Riordan, "but finding
out what it is will not be easy."

The party carried on for several hours until a chill
crept like a thief across the garden. In the distance, the sun,
a majestic reddish orb, sank slowly under the horizon and
the festivities, much to Featherstone's dismay had just
moved inside the house, where he had commandeered
Riordan's leather recliner.

"Daniel," he said, holding out his glass with a
sorrowful look on his face. "It's a shame we couldn't stay

out a while longer. What a wonderful array of nipples there were. That lady from the obstetrics department, you could hang your coat on those puppies!"

Riordan scowled at him, good-naturedly. Featherstone, a mellow drunk, got up, demanded directions to the location of the spare bedroom and wandered off to find the ward sister who had been so entranced with him earlier. Riordan poured himself another glass of champagne, emptying the bottle, and went into the kitchen to get a replacement. He smiled on hearing Nancy's voice emanating from the speaker on the counter. She was upstairs breast-feeding the babies, and, given the amount of champagne she had consumed, Riordan was hoping they would sleep all the way through the night.

The strains of an old Scottish lullaby drifted through the kitchen and Riordan hummed along, knowing the tune by heart. He had commented once on Nancy's singing to Featherstone who simply grinned and said, in a thick Scottish accent, "Not that old famous lullaby, the one that goes 'Fuck up, ye wee bastard, and get to sleep!' sung while intoxicated."

The doorbell rang, interrupting Riordan's reverie, and he set down his glass and went to answer the door. He was puzzled–most of the people they had been expecting had shown up already–perhaps Bryan Dymond had decided to return for a drink after all. A deliveryman stood on the doorstep, resplendent in a brand new, well-creased UPS outfit, and handed Riordan a large cardboard box, which was fairly heavy. Riordan signed the form and looked closely at the label–the delivery had come from the United States and appeared to be a hardware component for his computer. He was always getting stuff in the mail for evaluation purposes, so some new board or disk-drive manufacturer had sent him something to review.

He had been making a fairly respectable name for himself as a freelance reviewer, in addition to his day job, and his well-thought out, in-depth reviews and analyses of software and hardware products were attracting the attention of those who were interested in having his 'Okay'. The volume of work was such that he was contemplating giving up the day job to concentrate on the review work on a full-time basis, but that was a long discussion yet to happen with Nancy.

Taking the package to his office, he tossed the box onto his desk and was surprised by the dull thud it made upon contact, like the sound the sand-filled promotional balloon he used as a paperweight made when it landed. He was about to leave when some inner sense made him stop and pick up his letter-opener, a pearl-handled switchblade with six inches of well-honed steel he had bought while in vacation in Marseilles. Slipping the knife under the corners of the box, he quickly cut away the tape, eased the blade back into the handle of the knife and with some amount of trepidation opened the top.

A faint, yet unpleasant odor caressed his nostrils as he eased both hands into the tiny pieces of styrofoam, a sense of alarm rising slowly within his being. Both hands had almost disappeared when his fingers touched a stiff, plastic bag commonly used by computer component manufacturers to vacuum seal their products. It had the same feel as the myriad zip-lock freezer bags Nancy kept in the fridge.

Crumpling the edge a little, he drew the bag up through the styrofoam and his eyes focused on the clear bag and its contents. The odor increased and he turned away and retched violently, still holding the bag in his fingers. His eyes widened in horror at what he now had recognized–the misshapen head and the tiny fingers and toes of a premature baby, suspended in clear fluid. Setting the bag delicately on his desk, he went outside into the hallway, wiping long strings of saliva from his mouth.

"Feather," he called, and the large ex-soldier appeared quickly, recognizing a voice full of tension.

"What's up, Daniel?" Featherstone asked, his voice and facial expressions full of concern. Any sign of the alcohol-imbued haze had disappeared.

"Have a look in my office," Riordan said, resting his head back against the wall. "And try not to stand in that puddle of puke on the floor."

"What?" Featherstone grunted, and brushed past Riordan. A few moments later he returned, his face ashen. "I've seen some pretty fuckin' awful sights in my time but that takes the biscuit. Strange that the ears are missing. Any idea..." A glare from Riordan silenced him.

"It's hardly a coincidence," spat Riordan. "This thing shows up on the day I'm having the boys baptized. It's that bastard Slade, playing fucking mind games. The oriental guy who was going to cut the baby out of Nancy probably has some sick friend who likes to do the same thing. Slade is back in business somewhere and he's laughing at me. That box could just as easily have been a bomb, and Christ alone knows what would have happened if Nancy had opened the damned thing."

Riordan took a long, deep, breath and slammed his head back against the wall. A heavy weight constricted his chest, the frustration building like steam in a pressure cooker. He wanted to lash out in retaliation, but there was no target, no focus for the anger. He clenched his knuckles until they hurt, his forearms shuddering with the effort. "Jesus, Feather, what am I supposed to do now? He's not going to frighten me out of my home, but I'm concerned for Nancy's well-being, and the children as well."

Featherstone rubbed his chin thoughtfully. "Is there any family she can stay with, or can she even take a mini vacation?" Riordan thought for a moment. There were not too many options.

"She could go and stay with her sister for a while, but I don't know how long that would work. You know how sisters are! They don't get on all that well at the best of times. But I'll think of something."

"She's got a sister," Featherstone repeated, one eyebrow rising. "You never mentioned this before!"

"Dear God Feather," exclaimed Riordan, the black funk dissipating, "don't you ever give up?"

The rest of the evening passed quietly and Nancy, true to form, when everyone had left, had dragged Riordan up to bed and had made love to him as if he was a soldier going away to war. Nancy loved sex, which delighted Riordan immensely, as there was nothing he liked more than heading off to bed for an afternoon with a bottle of chilled champagne and a bowl of strawberries to make love for hours.

Their relationship was almost spiritual in that sense, and they would explore each other's bodies like lovers finding each other for the first time. And after two or three hours of foreplay they would indulge themselves in a frenzied coupling, two people arriving at the same place while focusing on the journey, not the destination.

Nancy had few inhibitions, and Riordan's cock ached from all the attention it had received. Afterwards, she drifted off into a peaceful slumber, while Riordan's mind raced from one scenario to another barring him from the luxury of sleep. He tossed and turned for a little while, then resigned himself to the fact that he was not going to sleep and got up, slipped on his dressing gown and went downstairs into his study.

The computer he had stolen from Slade's house winked at him in the darkness, a palpable entity waiting like a mugger in the dark. He exhaled slowly, then sat down and switched on the monitor. The software screen for manipulating images bounced into view, and he took the first CD from the pile and slipped it into the player.

Pressing the 'PLAY' icon, the screen filled with the image of an oriental man, dressed in white robes, and carrying two swords that were held in a red sash around his waist. In front of him, a naked young girl cowered in fright on a bed, her hands bound and a black blindfold over her eyes. She was trembling, and her head darted birdlike from side to side listening for signs of the man approaching.

Riordan watched in horror as the man drew the katana in a blur of movement, and the girl's head went spinning off into one corner of the room while her torso pumped a red spray into the air like a open fire hydrant. The man whirled around in the spray, arms outstretched like a child playing in the rain. His face, hair and robes were soon sopping from the flow and the camera zoomed in on his face to show a close-up of an expression of pure bliss. Eyes clenched tightly, his tongue lapped up the droplets of blood from his face and his teeth were stained red. The spiral ceased, and the man lifted the girl's head and held it up for the camera to see, blood dripping from the severed stump. Then, again to Riordan's horror, the man drew the short knife and sliced off the girl's ears.

Blood pounded through his head and he trembled in fury at the sight. He paused the CD and with shaking fingers printed off the man's image and a close-up of the girl's face. The printer whirred and the pages slid out. Riordan removed the CD, stuck a label on the case and a similar label on the two prints for cross-referencing purposes, marked them with a pen, and inserted the next CD, which this time he played at high speed.

It showed a tall man of middle-eastern origin, who violently whipped, raped and sodomised another young girl into unconsciousness. This time however, the man did not kill the girl. Riordan printed out the images, but this time made a second copy of the girl's face that he left lying on his desk in a pile on the left side. He wanted to know how many girls had been murdered immediately, and how many appeared with other clients before meeting an untimely death.

By morning the pile had grown and Riordan was profoundly shaken to the core of his being at the extent of the brutality. A half-consumed bottle of Bushmills whisky sat on the desk, an anesthetic for the brain. It was like watching a scene from one of the 'slasher movies' that were all the rage with teenagers today, but this was not acting. These scenes were real and there were no special effects or make-up to create these bruises and scars.

Growing up in Belfast, he had grown accustomed to what he termed 'casual violence', grown men fighting and brawling in the streets for some perceived slight, or the brutality inflicted in so-called 'punishment' beatings. He thought he had become inured to the violence, but in truth he had not. He felt numbed by it all. The pile of pictures of dead girls now numbered 27, and many of these had been used and abused by numerous clients before joining the pile on the right.

Light filtered through his window, heralding the arrival of a new day, the first rays of sunshine stealing across the garden to kiss the flowers. A huge bumblebee spat in the eye of the laws of gravity as it bounced from flower to flower and a gentle tapping emanated from the bird feeders Nancy had hung outside his window. Rubbing the sleep from red-rimmed eyes, he put the CD's in the back of his desk drawer, inserted the piles of images into large envelopes and locked them away in his cabinet. There were 5 CD's left to go, but he was determined to watch them later. His ability to cope with more of the violent images had vanished.

Hearing a wail from the nursery, he looked at the clock on his table and saw that it was almost 6:00 a.m. Soon he heard Nancy's footsteps on the floor upstairs. A smile creased his face for the first time in hours–the children had slept through the night–and he went upstairs to join his wife and hold his precious sons, to love them and protect them from the evil in the world.

Willie, 'The Razor' Lewis sat in his brand new black and gold Lexus GS400, the engine quietly purring and a soft cool breeze from the air-conditioning unit protecting him from the searing midday heat of downtown Los Angeles. In his pocket lay the original whalebone mounted straight-edge razor from whence his nick-name had been derived. He had posted himself on the curb across from the bus station, where long dusty aluminum tubes disgorged their cargoes from the hinterlands of America, bringing those in search of fame and fortune to the movie capitol of

the world. Those people he ignored. What he sought were
the young strays, boys and girls barely entering their
teenage years, who had run away from their homes for
reasons real or imagined, hoping to find... something in the
big city.

These were Willie's treasures and his appearance, that
of a friendly grandfather, belied the evil below the surface,
and easily lured the innocents into his clutches. They were
so careful about the black pimps that prowled the area like
scavengers. They had heard stories about such men and
avoided them like opposing poles on magnets, but were
easily conned by the man with the white hair and the well-
trimmed beard who ran a pimping operation that filled his
coffers to overflowing.

Willie earned enough money in a day to put most
CEO's to shame, but even he was amazed by the offer
made to him less than a month ago. An oriental gentleman,
well-groomed and with amazingly good English, had
approached him with a suitcase full of cash and a request to
procure five, 12 to 14 year old girls, who were clean–no
diseases, no drugs–and a promise of further transactions if
he complied. Willie, careful as ever, checked out the man
as best he could using his wide and varied network of
contacts, in case it was a 'sting' operation, but all searches
came up clean. It was impossible for the police or feds to
mount such an operation without Willie hearing a whisper,
so he agreed and met the man who requested the
transaction. Or rather, met the man's shadow.

The meeting had taken place in a darkened hotel room, the man sitting behind a lamp that was tilted in Willie's general direction. All Willie could see was a powerful outline, and a voice that could have belonged to the devil. On a projection screen set up against the wall, the man showed Willie frame after frame of surveillance photos of his life, from the office where he worked to the Brownstone in Newport beach where he lived most of the time to the condo in Rancho Del Mar, where Willie entertained the rich and famous.

At the end of the show, the man simply said, "I have chosen you to be my supplier. You have no scruples that I can see–these are all pieces of meat to you–and if you abide by my rules I will make you incredibly wealthy. If you cross me, or attempt to find out who I am, this will happen to you." On the screen flashed an image of a Oriental man holding a girl's freshly-severed head. Willie, although not a stranger to violence, almost swallowed his tongue, and that image had been indelibly printed on his mind for a long time.

The first four girls had been easy; a simple number to contact and the oriental came and took them away from his condo, drugged and unconscious from the tranquilizer he had put in their glass of coke. Where they went and what happened to them did not matter, their plight was of no concern to him. His only concern was the next suitcase of cash, almost two hundred grand for each girl.

The doors of the greyhound swung open in a puff of dust and the weary cargo disembarked, Willie eye's scrutinizing each and every face like the SS in front of the concentration camps. Too young, too old, too weak, wrong sex... and there she was, a beautiful young thing with a mane of red curly hair, dressed in a pair of cutoff jeans and a white T-shirt and carrying a bag almost as big as she. He watched her scan the area, eyeing the black dogs warily, looking away from the policemen who patrolled the station, and generally looking like a lost soul. Like a hyena moving in on a wounded animal, Willie opened the door, picked up the bunch of flowers he was 'taking home to his wife,' and set off.

Slade   was   about   to   be   back   in   business.

CHAPTER 12

Barracuda

The following afternoon, when Nancy and the boys were lying down having their naps, Riordan returned to his office, having spent part of the morning mulling over the series of events that had brought him to this place in time. Odd thoughts niggled at him, like minnows chasing a worm, but he was frustrated when he tried to fixate on them and they moved out of reach of his consciousness. He was also still puzzled by the fact that the computer specialist, a known pedophile whom Slade had hired to make the CD-ROMs and who was a material witness in a murder case, had managed to find bail money and then had vanished.

Maybe he's gone to ground with Slade, Riordan thought to himself. And then came a flood of thoughts, one building on the next with a fury that sent him scrabbling for his pen. One of the curses of getting older was that his desk was littered with yellow post-it notes of things to do, random musings, and the odd 'do this tomorrow' instruction. Pedophiles, he wrote, photographs, binaries, newsgroups, where to get videos, check userid on server, check service provider, AOL?

Eventually, the brain dump finished and he sat back, drained, yet satisfied that at least there was something useful he could do. Having read several articles about pedophiles, given their profile in the press of late and the security agencies' concern that these monsters were using the internet to freely distribute their material, he remembered that there was little or no hope of reforming their behavior. Using that as a basis, he hypothesized that Slade's technician would be up to his old tricks soon. Given the fact that Slade had expected all the equipment to be destroyed in the explosion on the island, there was a good chance that the geek would resume his activities using his old identification. While on the island, Riordan had torn some of the kiddie porn pictures off the wall of the computer room and tossed them in the bag with the CD-ROMs, each having a name and a contact typed across the bottom.

Powering up the computer, he had re-programmed the auto-exec batch file to run the canned program the man had created, and it took only a few seconds for the system to boot up. Riordan explored some of the other applications hidden behind windows on the screen, and quickly found the icon that provided access to the internet. Excited by the prospect, fingers trembling in anticipation, he took the phone connection from his own PC and connected it to the communications jack at the back of the machine before him, fumbling several times before hearing the reassuring 'click' as the plug slid into place.

The two modems were soon executing their handshake process, hissing and spitting at each other like tomcats in an alley, and an internet screen popped up in front of him–the geek had programmed his password into the internet access system as well. Thank you Lord, he whispered, and started to examine the screen in detail.

A quick scan showed that cookie protection was in place–a security program to check that no foreign matter was surreptitiously being sent down the line when the user was downloading files. Cookies were the name for miniature 'spy' programs, a trick that internet vendors routinely used to get information about people browsing their web-pages, and nowadays police forces were using such devices to track people issuing porn on the net. The only problem was that as quickly as people could come up with methods of tracking individuals, the denizens of the net who did not take kindly to such intrusions responded with a safeguard. Riordan had long known of such things.

Loading the program called FORTIFIE, which showed the active news groups on the net, Riordan scanned them for subscribed groups and sure enough, the geek was tied into a group called

ALT.BINARIES.EROTICA.LITTLE.ONES,

and several others dealing with bestiality, teenage erotica, tasteless binaries and a variety of deviant fetish groups. This program allowed people to download binary images with the file extension of .JPG, and then there was usually a complementary program to view the images. Riordan minimized the icon and went searching again using the file manager for anything with that extension. He was not expecting such an overwhelming response and the screen filled up and then refreshed time and time again with binary images. Feeling like he was going to be waiting forever, he pressed the 'BREAK' key and the search stopped.

Another fact he had read about pedophiles was that they treasured their collections of pictures and went to great lengths to keep the images safe and protected, often compromising their own security and anonymity. Known pedophiles were often targeted by police surveillance teams and from time to time were involved in minor traffic 'accidents' because of a suspicion that the offender was moving his 'stash'. Possession of child pornography was usually sufficient to have the offender incarcerated for a long time. Riordan assumed the geek would be missing his pictures, and would want to build his collection up again. Which meant that he would be scanning the newsgroups for the pictures he liked and downloading them for his own deviant purposes.

Riordan grinned, anticipation building.

Time to set a trap.

Heat from the midday sun caused the parched earth in front of Slade's sprawling Hacienda-style home to shimmer like liquid in a glass. Putting the cold beer to his lips he drained almost half of the bottle, then set it on the table beside him. Tiny rivulets of condensation ran down the sides of the bottle and pooled on the glass top. Slade did not mind the heat. From the stinking jungles of Vietnam to the searingly hot, humid streets of Saigon, he had grown acclimatized to extremes of heat. Here, over the mountain from Santa Barbara and a few miles from the strange Norwegian village of Solvang where he had made his new base, the midday sun was torturous, hitting the high nineties routinely.

Slade liked the place. Located on some 10,000 acres, the house was many miles from his nearest neighbor and out of the line of sight from the nearest road, a dirt track running off a feeder road leading to the main highway 101. The earth had little to offer in terms of nourishment for plants, and the main income for the locals was either from growing grapes, which required a complex watering system, or breeding ostriches for meat. Slade was interested in neither; his business was far too lucrative for him to be a gentleman farmer, but he kept horses in a specially air-conditioned stable, and rode them around his land like a rancher of old.

A trail of dust appeared in the distance and a tiny black dot appeared, the Pathfinder carrying his final requirement to get his business under way again. The first 'client' was to arrive in 3 days time, flying from Norita Airport to Los Angeles International, a few hours drive to the south of where Slade now lived.

Brushing aside a sheen of sweat from his brow, he took another long sip of beer and picked up the series of black and white photographs from the table. The photos showed Riordan signing for the parcel, some of the guests arriving and leaving from the christening party, and some photographs of the back garden taken from the air. A cruel smile split Slade's face as he imagined how Riordan must have felt on opening the box. He would have given anything for a picture of that expression.

Getting the fetus was not a problem. Slade had driven to San Francisco and visited several office towers until he found what he was after, a place with a separate parking garage elevator. At closing time he sat inside, waiting until he spotted a pregnant woman getting into the elevator carrying a huge briefcase. He followed her, and when she got out to go to her car, Slade, ever the gentleman, held the door for her. He asked questions about the baby and how far along she was and what was she going to name the child, and could he help her with that enormous bag. The woman, charmed by him, dropped her guard and handed over the briefcase.

When they reached her car he looked around, saw no one in sight and knocked her senseless, then dragged her into the back seat. He climbed into the passenger seat in the front and, kneeling down, leaned over and pulled up her dress. An ugly purplish bruise was beginning to form on her chin. All it took was several deft strokes of his hunting knife and he got what he wanted of her, dropping his struggling, wailing prize into a large plastic bag. The cries stopped soon. He cleaned the thing up when he got back to the ranch, removed the ears, and then vacuum-sealed the rest. One of his bodyguards packaged it up and went to a UPS center, where he mailed it to Riordan. The overnight special would be sufficient.

"Ah Riordan," Slade said aloud, staring hard at the photograph. "What shall we do to you next? Perhaps I'll mail one of your own brats to you in a bag." The patio doors slid open bringing a waft of cool air like a lover's touch from inside the house. Slade tilted his head to one side to see who had come out. It was the computer geek, dressed in a pair of outrageously colored shorts and a T-shirt with a logo that said 'Butthole Surfers'. A Walkman CD player was clipped to his waist and the ever-present pair of headphones hung around his neck. The faint odor of an unwashed body reached Slade's nostrils.

"Dickson," Slade growled, "would you like a beer?" He handed the young man a cold bottle from a cooler by his side. The bottle was not a twist top so Dickson stood there, looking thirsty with the bottle in his one remaining limb. "Oh, I'm sorry," said Slade in an exaggerated voice, knowing only too well the man could not remove the top. It was a subtle reminder of the punishment Slade had meted out for Dickson's act of betrayal, and Slade knew that the man was totally subjugated to his wishes. Besides, the little prick was good at what he did, and it would have been difficult to replace that specific set of skills.

"That's alright," replied Dickson in a thin reedy voice. "I forget all the time as well."

Slade popped off the top, handed the bottle to Dickson who guzzled it greedily, and said, "Is all the equipment set up and working?"

Drawing the back of his hand across his lips Dickson replied, "Everything is ready and waiting. I have tested each item of equipment several times."

For Riordan the workday passed slowly, with some of the users his team supported complaining about late delivery of reports and a thousand and one other petty gripes that made up the usual business day. The clock hands moved with the inexorable slowness of a clock watched. He hated the politics of it all; the corporate backstabbing, the wearing of a shirt and tie–the corporate uniform, and the endless games that needed to be played to progress up the 'ladder'. His patience for such crap was waning and the words 'fuck you' were more and more on the tip of his tongue these days.

At times his mind hearkened back to the days in Belfast when he, as the Raven, meted out punishments to all and sundry for the greater good of the movement. From a 'Black and Decker job'–a drill bit through the knee-caps, to a 'hood job'–a more permanent sentence, whatever the old man had ordered he had done without question. If any of the morons he had to deal with on a daily basis knew the truth about the man they regularly belittled, they would tread a lot more lightly. The fact that he could snap a neck with as little effort as snapping a twig gave him a sense of inner calm, and he often fantasized about telling some of the more unpleasant customers just exactly what he could do to them. But that was all it was–a fantasy.

That was the main reason for the desire to go totally freelance and become his own master. Having to answer to no one but himself and being paid well for his efforts held much more appeal than working like a slave for a raise of maybe 2 or 3 percent a year, a pat on the back and the promise of more misery in the coming year.

Unconsciously, his hand wandered to scratch an imaginary itch on his chest, his fingers tracing their way over the brace of scars running down his chest, a souvenir from an evil man called Elder who had thought to feed him to a school of barracuda. That was another time when his past as the Raven had caught up with him, tearing him from what he considered a normal life, ripping away the facade of normalcy and exposing the violent creature that lived in a dark corner of his being.

The Raven was always there, sitting quietly until summoned. Suddenly, an image of Featherstone drifted into his consciousness and at once Riordan envied the man, envied the freedom and the exciting life he had, master of his own domain.

Perhaps it was time for a change.

CHAPTER 13

Fury

Riordan took a long sip of his glass of Bushmills, savoring the golden liquid before swallowing. From the CD player came the sweet strains of Van the Man singing 'Brown-Eyed Girl', and Riordan sang along, losing himself in the music.

The aftertaste and the aroma from the whisky invoked memories of days by the coast of Ireland, the scent of seaweed heavy in the air and the spray from the tide splashing his face as he sat with his fishing rod on a outcropping of rock, a favorite spot near the town of Cushendall. He sighed, his Celtic heart warm with the all-too-brief reverie, then leaned forward and clicked on the 'PLAY' icon on the computer screen.

Coming home after a long day at the office, he had had a quick bite to eat with Nancy, played with the boys for a few minutes and then started to watch the last three CD's. He was expecting more blood and gore but this time the girls were merely violently abused with whips and canes before being sexually assaulted. Riordan froze specific frames as before, taking those with a good, well-defined image of the protagonist, and a shot of the girl as well. One man's face, in the second-to-last CD seemed familiar to Riordan, a profile that he had seen in the newspaper or television or somewhere recently. He would show that one to Featherstone–the man had an excellent memory for faces.

Merely assaulted, thought Riordan. Jesus, I am getting inured to this stuff. The final CD started playing while he was making notes on the back of the other photographs, and it had been playing for a few seconds before he looked up and saw the figure, dressed in a black leather mask, black leather shorts and carrying a whip. The man's penis protruded at full-mast from a hole in the front of the shorts and Riordan shivered on hearing the first lash from the whip rip into the girl's flesh. A prolonged wail of agony followed and the girl fell forward on to the floor, writhing like an eel. Her hands and feet had been chained together to restrict her movements, and the two sets of shackles had been joined together. The stainless steel manacles gleamed like new.

The camera zoomed in on a long red slash becoming visible across her back and the tiny red tears spilling from the cut. Riordan ground his teeth together at the girl pleading for mercy, and reached forward and turned off the sound before the second lash fell. Closing his eyes to shut away the images, like a child wanting something bad to go away, he waited for few moments before opening them again. This time the girl was draped face-down across the bed, and the man was shoving his penis into–Riordan couldn't see where, but the man obviously succeeded in penetrating the girl because he started a rhythmic humping motion which lasted for only a couple of minutes. The man withdrew, ejaculated over the quivering body, and then followed up with several lashes across the girl's buttocks.

Riordan clicked on the 'FAST' button, annoyed at not being able to get an image of the man. The CD ROM sped forward and the man paced around the room and Riordan squinted at the motion–there was something about the man's gait, and the long flailing limbs–like a preying mantis. Suddenly the pieces floating around in the ether started to fall into place. "Bastard," Riordan hissed, and pressed the 'PLAY' button to slow the motion down, waiting until the man abused the girl one more time before urinating on her. The man's last action was to tear off the mask and leer into the camera, knowing that this was his special moment.

Freezing the close-up, he printed the image, and then shaped his fingers into the shape of a pistol. The barrel he put against Oliver Wentworth's forehead and said, "Bang, Bang, you're dead." Putting the images into the file he had already created, he pulled open the drawer of his desk until it was all the way out. At the back, a light pressure from his fingers and the spring loaded compartment popped open. His fingers touched the keys, hanging on tiny golden cup-hooks, and he mentally counted down until he found the one for the locker in Vancouver airport. It was time to perhaps remove some of the fake identities and documents and a substantial amount of money.

These had been put in place many years ago when he, as the Raven, had set up escape routes and safe houses for Protestant paramilitary members who were on the run from the police. Canada, with its lax security, was a safe haven for them. It might now become necessary to flee with Nancy and the boys, although that was a step he would loathe to take. Still, it never hurt to be prepared.

This time there was no hesitation. Taking the key from the hook, he slid the drawer back into place and shut down the system. In the back garden he could hear Nancy singing to the children. Running upstairs, he changed clothes quickly, strapped a throwing knife to his inner forearm, and went out to join her for a little while. The sun was beginning its downward journey towards the horizon as he sat down on the bench beside her. She leaned over and kissed him full on the lips, then smacked her own.

"Having a wee one, were we?" she smiled. "So where's mine?"

"You just had it," Riordan replied, and she punched him playfully in the ribs. Looking down at the two tiny faces, barely visible in the bundles of clothes, Riordan felt a lump in his throat, and the key in his hand seemed to increase in temperature as if threatening to burn him. He knew it was only his imagination, but it seemed as if his conscience was trying to tell him something. Maybe it would be better to pass the information on to Featherstone, or even anonymously to the police, but he knew that was a cop-out. This was his problem.

Nancy saw the pain on his face and slid her arm gently through his own, pulling him tightly against her. "What's up Daniel?" she asked. "You've got the weight of the world on your shoulders." And at once she knew, without him even saying a word. "No, don't tell me," she said, sitting up and looking him directly in the face. "You've got some things to deal with at the moment, something relating to this mess with Allan. How long will you be gone?"

Riordan heard the emotion in her voice, heard her trying so hard to be brave, and loved her for it. She understood him better than any other human being, and knew more of his secrets than he, in any other times, would have been comfortable with her knowing. She knew of his past, of many of his exploits when he was the Raven, but there were those he did not share. That vault of demons was locked tightly shut and would be forever.

"I'm not going away anywhere at the moment," he said quietly, taking her hand in his own, fiddling with her wedding ring. "But I may have to at some point." He patted her arm reassuringly. "No matter what happens, I will be back. I have too much to live for now." Their fingers entwined tightly and she kissed him deeply, passionately. They sat that way, two souls touched by one another, until the glowing orb disappeared below the horizon and tugged a blanket of chill air across the city. "I'll help you put the boys to bed," he offered, and pushed the tiny carriage into the house, thankful for the momentary respite from the task that lay ahead.

Riordan stood quietly back in the shadows, waiting for Wentworth to appear. Dressed all in black, he was totally invisible in the corner of the room, a dark wraith armed with a .22-millimeter automatic fitted with a Carswell silencer. Breaking into Wentworth's house, an old brownstone in the ritzy area of the city, had been a breeze, and he had even left some fresh scratches on the brass lock to show how the 'robber' had entered the house. In the library where Wentworth had his office, several briefs lay open on the desk. It appeared Wentworth was preparing to do some evening work.

A quick search had revealed a safe behind a set of fake books, and a wry smile broke Riordan's stony countenance. A robbery gone awry was always a good reason to find a dead body in a room. The safe, a common or garden variety, was no match for Riordan even though his skills were somewhat rusty. Inside lay several bundles of large-denomination bank-notes and at the back, much to Riordan's surprise, concealed under a bunch of documents lay a snub-nose, .38 caliber, hammerless revolver.

Riordan went back and partially unscrewed the main light bulb in the room, so that the only muted light came from a banker's lamp on the desk. From a tiny tin he removed some strands of blonde hair and a cigarette butt he had picked up in a local bar, and placed them near the desk. It was always good to send the cops on a wild goose chase. The light spilled around the desk but did not reach the back corners of the room where he pressed himself against the wall and waited. He did not have long to wait.

A car pulled into the driveway, its headlights briefly illuminating the room, and Riordan closed his eyes quickly to preserve his night vision. A door slammed shut, then there were keys in the front door and he heard footsteps in the hallway. The library door opened, and in the silence Riordan heard Wentworth fumbling with the light switch. There was a muffled curse and Wentworth was in the room, striding over to his desk.

Expensive cologne wafted over and touched his nostrils. Riordan stilled his breathing, even though his heart was hammering so hard he felt there was no way Wentworth could help from hearing it. He waited until Wentworth had taken off his jacket and sat down, then stepped forward out of the shadows.

He was almost at the edge of the desk before Wentworth realized there was someone else in the room. There was a momentary flash of panic; Riordan saw the eyes widen and the change in body posture, but then Wentworth was back in control. Riordan was impressed. Not many people could regain their composure so quickly after being confronted with an armed, masked man. But then again, Wentworth probably thought he was dealing with a common housebreaker, and that his years at the bar defending such criminals would stand him in good stead.

"What do you want from me?" asked Wentworth calmly, the arrogant aristocratic voice producing the same reaction in Riordan as nails drawn down a chalkboard. Riordan pointed the barrel of the pistol at the fake set of books and Wentworth grinned. "So you found my safe, did you?" Raising his hands, Wentworth stood up from his desk and eased back the fake front. His fingers flew across the dial and the safe was soon open.

Riordan smiled a knowing smile inside the mask. Wentworth was using his own body to effectively shield the inside of the safe. He tossed bundle after bundle of bank notes on to the desk and then, as soon as Riordan moved forward to pick them up, the revolver appeared in a blur of motion. "Don't move or I'll kill you, you bastard," hissed Wentworth. Then, in a more relaxed voice, said, "Or maybe I'll kill you anyway. Take off your mask."

Riordan allowed the pistol to hang loosely by his side and used the other hand to draw the black ski mask from his head, tossing it on to the desk. Wentworth was speechless. "You, you," he spluttered. "What the fuck are you doing here? You're not a thief!" Riordan slipped his free hand into his pocket, extracted a CD ROM and tossed it on the desk. Wentworth's eyes followed the disk, recognition dawning, and a wolfish grin split his lips, the same as Riordan had seen on the video. "Ah," Wentworth said, "you've seen my little performance."

"You set up my friend Allan," Riordan said, his voice calm and even. "And then you put my wife and children in danger." Wentworth shrugged his spindly shoulders and the motion, the casual dismissal of what he had done set the hairs on the back of Riordan's neck on end. A cold fury coursed through his veins at the lack of respect for human life.

"I fell into bad company," laughed Wentworth, by way of explanation.

"So what now?" asked Riordan. "Do we call the police?"

"Not on your life," Wentworth said. "At least not yet. I've never killed any of the little bitches yet, but that was my next treat. So I'm curious to see what it feels like to kill someone." Raising the revolver, he aimed directly at Riordan's chest and pulled the trigger.

Once - click.

Twice - click.

Click, click, click.

"So much for the hard-on. Now, where's Slade?" Riordan asked, looking directly into Wentworth's eyes.

"Fuck you, who do think you are anyway?" Wentworth spat, flecks of spittle at the side of his mouth. The facade had cracked. Riordan could smell the fear, and to him it was fitting that Wentworth should sample some of what his victims must have felt.

"I am the Raven," Riordan said, and shot him in both eyes, the muffled shots blurring over one another. Wentworth's body slammed back against the bookcase, long strings of blood from his shattered head splashing across the many legal tomes on the wall. Riordan shot him two more times. Clawed fingers tore at the books for support and they slipped out and Wentworth crumpled to the ground. The old familiar odor of gunpowder filled Riordan's nostrils, bringing back memories of other times. For a brief moment he hesitated, then instinct took over and he started the cover-up.

Taking the set of shells from his pocket, he replaced them in Wentworth's revolver, and then placed the weapon in the dead man's hand. It was good thing Wentworth wasn't a pro or he'd have known by the weight of the gun that the shells had been removed. The CD went into the safe and the money went into a black pouch. The casings from his pistol he left behind–only a professional hit man would pick up the shells. A panicked robber would never think to search for the shells, especially if he had not been expecting to face the owner of the house. Using a piece of cloth, he screwed the main bulb back tightly in place, then left by the rear door.

On the way home he drove down by the docks and tossed the pistol, the balaclava, and the gloves into the ocean. There was one more quick stop by the airport to replace the satchel, the money bundle now significantly larger than before, then he was on his way.

CHAPTER 14

Torment

"So anyway," said Featherstone, leaning back in his chair and resting his feet on his desk. The rest of the team who had stormed Slade's house sat in a semi-circle around his desk, an unofficial morning break; the adult version of show and tell. Jean-Marc, the 'Frogman' had had his bandages removed and this was cause for a minor celebration, so there were several gifts all pertaining to the injuries he had sustained; dog-leads, doggie-biscuits, poop & scoop bags, and a dog-whistle. All of which he took in his usual good-natured manner, by offering to buy the first round in the pub later.

Featherstone continued, "These guys from the tactical team get a tip about a huge shipment of coke and so they storm the drug-dealer's house, knowing that the guy's been seen carrying weapons. Unfortunately he's scarpered and this guy on the team, a fuckin' madman by all accounts, goes into the dealer's bedroom and sees a pair of Lederhosen and a French horn mounted on the wall. By this time they've all been told to 'stand down' and, thinking that a bit of fun was necessary to relieve the tension, he takes his clothes off and comes down the stairs, wearing only the Lederhosen and blowing the horn. All the tac team fall about the floor laughing their bollocks off and he gets pissed off at them. He's doubly pissed when they show him the photographs of the dealer, who turns out to be a homosexual, wearing the Lederhosen and shoving the French horn up his partner's ass. It took him a long time to get over that one."

The others laughed until tears ran down their faces, and were still laughing when his secretary brought in the morning pot of tea and croissants and the daily newspaper. When she left the room there were several suggestive comments about the length of her black leather mini-skirt and the rapid-pulse rate she had caused among them. Featherstone played mother, all the while scanning the headlines. His eyes alit on the section which said that a prominent lawyer named Oliver Wentworth had been found dead in his home, and was presumed to be the victim of a hold-up gone awry. Featherstone did not notice that the cup was overflowing, so engrossed was he in the article.

"Boss, boss," came the excited yell from Capo, "you're pouring the stuff all over the table." Featherstone looked up and eased back the pot, realizing his error.

"What's the matter?" asked Jean-Marc, holding up a soggy croissant with a look of utter despair.

"The lawyer for Allan Brown was found dead in his house last night, suspected to be the victim of a bungled robbery. Chance would be a fine thing," said Featherstone thoughtfully, scratching his day-old growth of beard and absent-mindedly stirring his tea. "I think I'll have a quick word with my friend in the station–he'll know what is going on."

Picking up the phone, he punched in a few digits and waited. When he heard a voice on the other end he simply said, "Hi there, this is Feather. I'd like to get some details about Wentworth's death, especially about how he died. And yes, there will be a bonus in this for you." He hung up the phone, sat pensively for another few minutes before picking up the phone, a decision made.

It was some two hours later that Riordan walked down the corridor towards Featherstone's office, nodding to those people he recognized in their offices on the way. He made a point of stopping in to say 'hello' to Christine, for no other reason than she was a pretty lady and some old habits were all to hard to kick. She seemed genuinely pleased to see him and they exchanged a few pleasantries before he moved on. When he finally arrived at Featherstone's door, the 'three stooges', Capo, Tosser, and the Frogman had filed out of their offices and were all behind him, trailing like goslings following their mother. They too were interested in what was going on with Wentworth since the mission had involved them all, and they had been briefed on the details.

Featherstone opened the door of his office, nodded hello to Riordan and looked past him to the others. "Oh all right," he said, resignation in his voice. "You can come too. We'll go over into the boardroom. Tosser, get Susan to make us a brew, will you, and some digestives as well!"

Riordan felt a smile creep across his face–brits and their tea. Even in the middle of a war there was always time for a quick 'brew'. Featherstone led the way to the boardroom and Riordan took a few minutes to scan the photographs and mementos on the wall. Of particular note was a silk map of Iraq, neatly framed and signed by 'Stormin' Norman Swartskopf, head of the allied forces during the Gulf War.

Beside it was a copy of the document in which the Chief Constable of Scotland Yard had passed responsibility for control of the Iranian Embassy siege to the SAS. Photographs of the subsequent assault, where the publicity-shy regiment was thrust in the public eye, were mounted in splendid gilt frames. At the subsequent inquest, each of the members of the 'Pagoda' team had been given a letter of the alphabet to identify themselves when giving evidence. Impressed, Riordan wondered which letter had been given to Featherstone. He wandered around the room scanning each of the photographs, noting several were of areas in Belfast that he recognized immediately.

His tour complete, he sat down, as did the others. When they were all seated Featherstone said, "There have been some developments in the case which may or may not affect us. As you know, Allan Brown's lawyer, Oliver

Wentworth was killed last night in a robbery attempt. Seems like he tried to pull a gun on the robber and got wasted. At least that's the official police story at the moment. When the police checked his safe, which the robber had left open, they found some obscene material, namely Wentworth abusing some young girls, one of whom has subsequently turned up dead. The cat is now among the proverbial pigeons as this information has been leaked to the press and rumors of a high-level pedophile ring are beginning to circulate." Featherstone gave them all a moment to absorb that information before continuing.

"There is going to be a lot of attention focused on this case, especially if it has links to what went on at the island, so be careful if any of the cops come snooping around. They have no idea it was us, and the story about a team of mercenaries rescuing the girl seemed to placate them at the time. So just be on your guard. Slade is still..." A knock came to the door and Featherstone's secretary entered, the mini-skirt again having Jean-Marc gasping for breath. He made the sign of the cross when she bent over the table to set the tray down, turning his eyes heavenward in a mock plea for guidance. Riordan enjoyed the view of the well-tanned expanse of thigh as well.

"Who's being mother?" she asked, and took a heavy cardboard envelope from under her arm. "This just came in the mail from UPS, Feather, addressed to you," she said, "so I thought I'd bring it in. I'll open it for you." Capo picked up the teapot and started pouring.

The secretary held the heavy envelope against her stomach and pulled at the tab across the top to open the container. The movement served only to accentuate her ample bosom, a fact that did not go unnoticed by the assembly. "There's something heavy in it," she said, struggling with the tab. Featherstone grinned at her struggles. "Maybe it needs a man to open it," he offered and was rewarded with a "fuck off" expression.

Tosser, rising from his seat said, "Here, let me help you." He received the same glare and sat back down, somewhat contritely.

There was a ripping sound and the tab moved a little and she smiled, "Thanks, Tosser, but I've got it now."

Riordan felt something prick at his senses, and the concern must have been plainly evident on his face because Featherstone yelled, "Don't open it, don't..." Time slowed down like in the movies and Riordan felt like he was moving through molasses. Intuitively he knew the girl was a goner, that her card had been marked; and unless he moved quickly he too was marked. He burst forward out of his seat like a steeplechaser out of the starting gate, and, a fraction of a second after his hand hit Featherstone on the chest, he heard the click of the detonator's contacts hammering together.

The package exploded in a burst of yellow and red flame. The force of the explosion, focused because it was contained in a small piece of copper piping–a shaped charge–cut the secretary neatly in half. Riordan hit the floor at the same time as both halves of her torso, blood gushing from the shattered body in a red tide across the wooden floor. Steaming, ropy coils of intestines snaked across the varnished hardwood planks towards his face and the two fingers remaining on her right hand trembled for several seconds before abruptly stopping.

The nauseating stench of scorched flesh touched his nostrils and he retched, then a hand grabbed him and pulled him up and away. His ears rang from the percussion. A quick look showed him that the secretary was the only victim and the others were climbing to their feet, doing a quick self-examination looking for shrapnel. Riordan knew there would be none–the package had been precisely created to do what it had done, except it had found the wrong target.

Riordan looked up into Featherstone's flinty eyes and the expression on his face was one of pure unadulterated, fury. "That was meant for me," Featherstone said, but the words came only as a whisper to Riordan's ears. People crowded around the boardroom to see what had happened, to ensure that everyone was all right. They knew only too well the sound of a detonation, and the faces of the former warriors first paled at the sight of the young girl's body, then, to a man they hardened, their protective masks sliding into place.

They had witnessed first-hand the casualties of war, the victims of bullets and bombs, but this was a friend, someone they knew and cared about. For them the vault had been opened once more and tonight the demons from their own private hell would come and torment them.

Others, simple civilian office staff took one look and immediately ran away clasping hands over mouths in a futile effort to staunch the bile surging in their throats. For them, it was their first exposure to violence of any kind and their senses simply could not cope. Riordan had seen it many times before.

"The police will be here soon," Featherstone offered, brushing dust and debris off his clothes. Looking directly at Riordan, he said, "If you don't want to be interviewed about this I would make myself scarce. Besides, I don't think you want to talk to them at the moment. You can explain it to me later when we get together to decide how we get at this Slade character."

Riordan felt Featherstone's eyes boring into his own, met the man's stare and in that instant, not even the space of a heartbeat, realized that Featherstone knew he had killed Wentworth.

It took several hours for the ringing in his ears to subside. Riordan had just settled into a booth in a corner of Clancy's pub with a pint of Guinness in front of him when the gloomy interior was invaded by a blast of street noise and a spear of sunlight from the doors opening as Featherstone stepped inside. Featherstone looked around, saw him, waved and went to the bar.

Clancy's pub was a bit off the beaten track, frequented by locals and British and Irish ex-pats who had come to

know of its existence. The scent of stale beer and stale
smoke hung in the air and the decor had not changed in
years. In one corner a dartboard hung, its once-black
surface virtually erased by constant use. Two men played
pool quietly in the corner, the click of the balls an old
familiar tune to Riordan, who had spent many hours at
University playing the game.

Dressed in a white silk shirt and a pair of faded
denims, there was something almost feral about the way
Featherstone moved, the paucity of movement and the fluid
motion of a man who seemed always prepared to spring.
Heads turned as he walked past, especially those of the
female patrons. The barman took his order and moments
later Featherstone sat down with a pint of lager, pointed at
Riordan's Guinness and said, "Never could get used to the
taste of the stuff so I just stuck to Harp, and the occasional
shot of Bushmills."

Riordan looked at the worn face, the tension and
world-weariness written there for all to see as Featherstone
raised the glass to his lips and took a long draught. A foam
mustache disappeared with a flick of his tongue. "What a
horrible fucking day it's been," Featherstone said wryly.
"Homicide, forensics, fighting with assholes who want to
look into our cases to seek a motive. I told them who I
thought was behind this but they seem to be a bit skeptical
about Slade. Then I had to face Susan's parents–they're a
retired couple. I've met them several times and she was
their only daughter. They were devastated by the news, so I
offered to make the funeral arrangements for her."

Featherstone's knuckles whitened around the glass and Riordan half expected it to shatter from the pressure. Shaking his head slowly, in the dim filtered light Featherstone looked to Riordan like a beaten man. Featherstone said, "This has brought back a lot of horrible memories about Belfast for me. Especially about the time when all those tit-for-tat killings were going on - you remember, a Protestant gets killed so the Protestant paramilitaries have to kill a Catholic and so on and so on. I remember the fear in peoples' faces because there was neither rhyme nor reason to it all. All innocent victims, in the wrong place at the wrong time. And now, it happens again."

Riordan nodded. The last few hours had not been easy for him either. Featherstone put the glass to his lips and drained it, then waved at the barmaid to bring another. He sat staring at the concentric rings and cigarette burn-marks on the table's surface, like a fortune teller staring into a ball looking for answers, quiet, unmoving for a few moments, then tilted his head to one side. The flinty eyes again focused on Riordan.

"Why did you kill Wentworth?" he asked.

Riordan saw no point in lying. "He was the one who set us up at the lodge, and he also was responsible for helping Slade abduct Nancy. Wentworth was one of Slade's clients, but I didn't discover this until I got to the end of the CD's–his was the very last one I looked at in the pile. I figure that Slade has killed about 25 girls, given what I saw on the CD's, and I have them cross-referenced with an image of the person who killed them. Many of the girls were abused by several of the 'clients' before being killed."

Featherstone took a deep breath and said, "I would've topped the bastard as well!"

Riordan was glad that the barmaid came up at that particular moment with another pint, breaking the tension. She had shoulder-length blonde hair and wore a green lycra body-suit under a pair of skin-hugging jeans. The accent was English, and she had an extremely engaging smile, something which Riordan had noticed when he first came in the bar. It was the first time he had seen her, so he guessed she must have been a recent hire. Riordan estimated she was in her mid to late twenties and was unashamedly interested in Featherstone, chatting him up without the slightest hint of embarrassment. The two exchanged some small talk, the usual minutiae between ex-pats, and she finally wandered off after giving Featherstone a matchbook with her phone number and address.

Riordan grinned, and Featherstone looked a bit sheepish. "Seems almost sacrilegious," Featherstone said, "to be chatting up a barmaid after all that's gone on today."

Riordan shook his head and sampled some more Guinness. "It's a celebration of life, Feather," he said. "You and I have seen so much bloodshed that it wears you down, especially when someone so young gets killed, but we must go on because that is all we can do. Either that or eat a bullet. The innocent victims are the toughest of all, but people like Wentworth I won't lose a minute of sleep over."

"I knew it was you the minute I heard the results of the autopsy–one bullet in each eye–trademark of the Raven. The Major provided me with that little tidbit of information," said Featherstone, playing with the matchbook.

Riordan laughed aloud. "Surprise, surprise, good old Major Skinner. How is the old bastard these days?"

"Oh, he'll never change," grinned Featherstone. "He truly is one Machiavellian bastard, and was asking after you. He faxed me a bunch of information about you from his private scrapbook. I was extremely curious about the episode involving the Prime Minister, not to mention your little visit to Cuba–you certainly get around, don't you. For someone who's supposedly retired, that is!"

Riordan snorted. "It seems my past is always determined to catch up with me, but this time, since I met Nancy, things have been really good and then it all went to hell when Allan was framed. I feel like I will always have that albatross to carry. But you asked about the Prime Minister..."

Featherstone frowned, trying to recall some piece of information. "That was a few years ago, wasn't it? This wouldn't be about the Prime Minister admitting to having that jet shot down, and the subsequent cover-up."

Riordan nodded. "Yep, that was me. My wife and daughter were on that plane and when it was hijacked, the Prime Minister ordered it to be shot down. The terrorists were threatening to crash it into downtown Toronto if their demands were not met. Three hundred and twenty people lost their lives in that disaster and then the Prime Minister and the head of security, an animal called David Elder, tried to cover it all up to protect their own skins. I didn't like the answers I was given, so I uncovered a trail all the way back to the PM's office. They tried to kill me to protect the cover-up, and when that didn't work then somehow the IRA found out about me and they tried to off me as well. That's when an SAS SABRE team inadvertently saved my life, although I think the Major would have been delighted if I'd taken a round or two in the head. All this only made me more determined to get to the bottom of it, so I was the one who kidnapped the PM's wife and children to force him to confess."

Featherstone nodded, now having recalled the entire story. "Yes, I remember it well. The CRW (Counter Revolutionary Warfare) team reviewed the tapes of the incident courtesy of the RCMP's special emergency response team. It was not well handled, but I thought they did get the kidnapper and the case was closed, if memory serves me right. Seems he was the head of one of the Proddy paramilitary outfits."

A lump rose in Riordan's throat, and he could feel the warm flush of a tear in his eyes. "The RCMP killed my father, the old man–everyone in Belfast knew him as the 'old man'–thinking he was the kidnapper. He trained me after my parents were killed, and made me into the Raven all the while insisting that I get a proper education. I think he knew that one day I would leave it all behind, and he wanted to prepare me for something other than violence."

He paused for a moment, and took a long sip of beer as the memories came flooding back. Setting the glass back on the table, he continued, "I contacted him to get some information, and next thing I know he shows up on my doorstep and insists on helping me. He sacrificed himself to give me a chance to get away, so the authorities still believe there was only one person involved. After all that I came to Vancouver to settle down. Things were fine for a few years and then a dear friend of mine and his family were murdered. The police put it down to accidental death because of the circumstances, but I knew differently. I poked around a bit and turns out the people responsible were working for the Prime Minister's former head of security, David Elder."

"I remember him," said Featherstone, putting the glass to his lips. "He was found dead in a hotel in Toronto. Some big scandal about young male prostitutes."

Riordan's mouth crinkled up at the corners.

"No," said Featherstone in disbelief. "That wasn't you as well, was it?"

Riordan nodded. "The man was an animal, on a par with this character Slade. I didn't give it a second thought."

"You're in the wrong line of business, mate," offered Featherstone. "When all this is over you should come and work for me. The hours are good and the work is... challenging." Riordan laughed aloud and finished his pint. He waved at the barmaid who was only too eager to come over to their table for another chat with Featherstone. He ordered another round, and when the waitress had gone, turned to Featherstone.

"Feather, I have an idea about how to get to Slade," Riordan said.

"Tell me," said Featherstone, his face brightening, "especially about the bit where I get to off the fucker!"

"This is not going to be easy, and I need some 'stuff' that you might be able to procure for me. I imagine you have contacts in low places, very low places, and this might be a bit risky."

"Doodness," said Featherstone in a mocking tone. "Dangerwus. But I'm fwum the dweaded SAS."

"Fuck off," Riordan snorted, then lowered his voice. "I need you to get me some kiddie porn videos."

Featherstone choked on his beer, sending a spray of foam all over the front of his shirt, and then went into a jag of coughing. "Explain," he ordered, dabbing at his shirt with a napkin.

So Riordan did.

CHAPTER 15

Surveillance

"I think the guy is on the internet again, pulling off images of young girls and wanking himself to death," Riordan said. "I have re-posted the images we took from Slade's house, and advertised the fact that I have more images and also tapes for sale. If the bastard is true to form he'll take the bait, but he'll be careful about how he does it. These guys can track down the Feds with uncanny accuracy, so if there's any hint of a sting I'll never get to him. I had thought of slipping a cookie in the files but he would catch that too easily."

"Cookie?" asked Featherstone, a puzzled look on his face.

Riordan smiled. The internet was totally foreign to many people, and Featherstone was no exception. He said, "It's a little present you can send down the line to anyone who signs on to your web page. I have one set up with a fake id, just in case the authorities try to trace me, and I bring it up at specific hours during the week. Renegade web masters usually do such things."

Featherstone shook his head and took another swig of his beer. "Daniel, my respect for you just grows and grows. You're just as bad as I am!"

Riordan lifted his glass in a toast to the compliment, and then drained it in one go. At the same moment, Featherstone lifted his head and scanned the room, his eyes roving back and forth like the beam from a lighthouse, a motion he had repeated many times since entering the bar. Riordan grinned–it was a behavior hard learned in the streets and bars and hedgerows of the North of Ireland–one of self-preservation. "Checking your six, Feather?" Riordan asked, and was rewarded with a sheepish wince. Six was an old patrol protocol where you checked your position by the hands of a clock, and six was checking your back.

A wave of Riordan's arm attracted the barmaid, and two more pints were soon on their way. When she was out of earshot, Riordan said, "I haven't been contacted directly yet, but I'm hopeful. I've put out the bait so now I need to be able to deliver on the promises if someone asks. Hence the need for the tapes. I admit it's a long shot but it's one avenue I'm following."

"You've got more up your sleeve?" asked Featherstone incredulously.

"But of course," laughed Riordan. "I'm the notorious Raven, aren't I? I told you before that Allan Brown works for a consulting firm who specialize in writing software." Featherstone nodded. "Allan wrote some of the billing programs for BC Tel, and as he supports the system, he has access to their production system and hence all the billing records for everyone in British Columbia. He's helped me out once before, so I thought I'd have him retrieve all of Oliver Wentworth's calls for the last few months and match the numbers he called with the billing system. That way I can see who and where he's called. If he called Slade after the escape, then I might get lucky and find an address for the bastard, and then we can pay him a visit."

Featherstone rubbed his chin thoughtfully, as if delaying the raising of a touchy subject. "Daniel," he said eventually, a serious look on his face. "I meant what I said about coming to work for me, even on a freelance basis. Your skills would be a tremendous asset to my company, not to mention your devious mind. So please give it serious consideration. On another subject, when do you get the stuff from Allan?"

Riordan was genuinely flattered by the offer, as it sort of fit in the direction he had hoped to take. Still, it required a fair amount of thought and discussion as it now involved more than one person. He said, "Probably tomorrow evening. He's coming over for dinner again."

"What about the discussion we had about Nancy moving for a little while, given that Slade's attacks seem to be escalating? And the tapes, I take it you need them as soon as possible."

Riordan nodded. "As for Nancy moving, we talked about it and decided that we can't be driven from our home by the asshole. We'll have to be a bit more vigilant but she's holding her ground."

Featherstone continued, "No problem–that sounds like Nancy. If you see a strange car in your area from time to time that'll be one of my guys keeping an eye on your place as well. I took the liberty of helping out a bit since the explosion today here at the office. I'll make a few phone calls and pick up the tapes this evening if I can. I know people who know people who deal in this stuff."

Riordan said, "That's very good of you Feather. Eases my mind, it does, and I'm sure Nancy will appreciate it as well. I better be off now. I promised Nancy I'd pick up some fresh meat and stuff from the market for dinner."

There seemed to be an almost wistful look on Featherstone's face as Riordan downed the last dregs of his pint. It seemed to him that Featherstone was envious of the fact that he had some semblance of a family life. He stood up, patted Featherstone on the shoulder and said, "Don't worry pal, I don't think you'll be alone for dinner this evening either." The barmaid winked at him on the way out and Riordan smiled at her and said, "I've got to run, so he's all yours."

After a hurried supper and tucking the children into bed and promising Nancy that he'd nudge her awake when he got home, Riordan climbed into his car and set off for the warehouse district of the city. It was here that he had rented an office under an assumed name and had created his web server for testing purposes. The district was the only part of Vancouver not yet developed by real-estate speculators, and had a reputation as a no-go area, especially at night. The disused warehouses and broken-down offices were home to the dregs of humanity, and any self-respecting citizen would not be caught dead in the area. For Riordan, these people did not bother him in the slightest. They kept their distance from him like weaker animals avoiding a jungle predator, as if they recognized that he was someone who should be shunned at all costs.

His rented space was in one of the more secure areas, and even still was well protected with deadbolts and alarm systems. It was always useful to have a place where he could hack away to his heart's content and not have it traced back to him. Ever a cautious person, he did a quick tour around the immediate vicinity to ensure that there were no 'strange' cars about, then pulled up at a warehouse some two hundred yards away from his own and walked back. If there was surveillance about he could easily elude them, but car number plates—that was another matter entirely.

Letting himself into the office, he quickly disarmed a little 'surprise' he had wired up under his desk. The C4 charge was not sufficient to destroy the warehouse, but enough to blow the computer and the boxes of files to shreds–and of course anyone who sat at the desk for more than 2 minutes. He tapped the space bar on the keyboard and the dark screen saver disappeared and the main icon page appeared. Clicking on the Fortify reader icon, which loaded all his active newsgroups, he went down the list until he found the pedophile group. He pressed the button to tell the system to retrieve all articles, and waited, seeing a message, "retrieving 131 headers" appear on the bottom of his screen.

He watched the percentage grow by 10's, then the screen was filled with all the articles and images posted to the pedophile newsgroup. There were the usual SPAM messages about 'you sick perverts', 'Jesus can save you all', 'Canadians suck', and a few other choice missives. Amongst these were some stories and several binary images, some of which he had posted. Scrolling down the items, he saw several messages for his on-line handle 'Dirty Danny', requesting him to post some more of his collection of images. These were from the usual freaks who communicated on a daily basis within the pedophile newsgroup, people he had recognized from his observing the daily interaction of the netizens, and he continued to scroll down, feeling that today, like the others was going to be another waste of time.

As each message appeared, and he reviewed the sender, dismissed it, and went on to the next. The system was excruciatingly slow, and he loaded the next message, which was another SPAM piece of hate mail, and went on to the next. The scroll bar reached the end, and the final message made him sit bolt upright. It was from the computer nerd, code name 'tricky.dicky@fucksalot.com' requesting more images from the set he had posted previously. Checking the time and date he saw that the message had been sent less than ten minutes ago.

He almost bit through his lip. The guy was active and on-line again. Stay calm, he admonished himself, time to play with the catch. Taking another image from his hard drive, he created a header that said, "Here's one for you Dicky," and enclosed another of the images he had stolen from the island. He sat in silence, waiting to see what would happen, having set the Fortify software to refresh the screen every five minutes. There was no way of knowing how often the guy would check the newsgroup so Riordan, born with an immense amount of patience sat unmoving, staring into the screen, waiting for something to happen.

There were the usual postings on a regular basis from nutters who wanted to kill anyone who signed on to this particular newsgroup, and Riordan sympathized with their tendencies. Grown men wanting to have sex with underage children and those barely into puberty, turned his stomach. A swift 9-millimeter in the back of the head was too good for them, he mused to himself.

He continued his vigil and was scanning down the list when his portable phone rang, startling him. Taking it out of his inner pocket he said, "Hello," and waited for the response. The line crackled for a few moments and then he heard Nancy's voice. "Daniel, It's me. Feather was just here looking for you. I told him you were working and he went off in a huff, saying he couldn't find you anywhere. Perhaps you could give him a call. It sounded pretty urgent."

"Okay love, I'll give him a ring," Riordan said, his voice gentle. "How long ago did he call by?"

"It was about twenty minutes ago. And Daniel...."

"Yes, love?"

"Hurry back. I'm so wet I'm starting to slide about in the sheets."

Riordan's mouth went dry. Ever since they had been able to resume their sex life, Nancy had been absolutely insatiable, waking him up at all hours for a quick 'shag'. He laughed aloud as one of her comments the other day popped into his head. She had been watching a Britcom on PBS about two girlfriends who were trying to find dates without a great deal of success, and their summing up of men was; 'A quick shag and a ride to the airport'. Nancy had adopted this as her own and used it frequently, especially when Feather was around. A surge of heat filled his nether regions and he squirmed on his seat.

Folding up his phone, he turned back to the computer screen. It had just reached the five minute limit and was starting to re-load the newsgroup. Riordan went straight to the end and there, much to his surprise was a request from the computer nerd. It simply read, "Loved the Binaries, Dirty Dicky."

Riordan clicked on the message and the system retrieved it from the internet. Using a newsgroup reader, he called up the item and saw that the nerd was wanting to buy some tapes, as long as Riordan could prove he wasn't a cop or FBI agent.

Riordan thought for a moment, then typed a quick message for the nerd. "I've been posting kiddy porn on the net, mate. Fed or no Fed, that is an indictable offense, and federal agents are forbidden to do anything that would bring the agency into disrepute, especially committing a felony offense. That's why it's so difficult for the Feds to infiltrate biker gangs. Each of those gangs require you to commit a felony offense: rape, armed-holdup, car-theft, as a way to get in the gang. The feds can't do that. So I'm clean. What other proof do you need? If you want to buy some tapes, set yourself up with a drop-box in some postal outlet, then have some punk kid go in pick them up. That way you have a couple of cut outs–other people I deal with on a regular basis do this, and I have a long list of customers."

Riordan posted the message, then signed off the internet, allowing the nerd to stew for night or so. He had an ulterior motive as well–Nancy's words were echoing in his mind, and his body was reacting like that of a 16-year old teenage virgin. He had one more stop to make at Feather's office to pick up the tapes, and he'd give him a quick call from the car to arrange to meet.

Feather was in the office and buzzed Riordan in by the rear entrance. They went into a back room where Featherstone had set up a video recorder and TV monitor, and the three tapes sat on the table beside the remote control. A pot of tea, some cubes of sugar, a jar of honey, a small carton of milk, a plate of digestives and two mugs sat on a tray beside the tapes. "Thought you might like a brew," offered Featherstone. Dressed in a white sand-washed silk shirt and faded blue denims, he had that glow of someone about to head out on a date.

"Fall into the aftershave, did you?" asked Riordan, his voice dripping with sarcasm.

"I called the barmaid and she gets off at nine o'clock."

"And you'll be getting off shortly after that, I presume," laughed Riordan. He received a dirty look in response.

"Have you looked at them yet?" asked Riordan, pointing to the tapes.

A disgusted look crossed Featherstone's face. "No I haven't. Couldn't bring myself to do it on my own. It was bad enough having to touch the fuckin' things! Do you think it's necessary to look at them?"

Riordan nodded. "The guy contacted me tonight and is looking for tapes, wants to buy them from me. I've got to produce the real McCoy or that avenue will dry up, so the first tape has to be good enough to inspire him to buy another. He'll probably have a mailing address but that won't be sufficiently good enough for us to trail him. Some of these people open boxes in different towns or cities in order to protect themselves. We know he'll be close to Slade, but we need to know exactly where they are based. The first tape has to be clean, but in the second we should be able to insert a tiny tacking device–you know the kind.

Same as the ones you used when you were 'Narking' the IRA's weapons."

He was referring to a procedure whereby the SAS, on discovering a weapons cache, would insert a tiny transmitter into a rifle stock so they could track the weapons when they were moved. More often than not however, the SAS simply booby-trapped the entire cache and waited for the next terrorist to stop by. Boom and bye-bye Provo. Featherstone's eyes opened wide in amazement.

"Jesus, Daniel, is there anything you don't know?" Featherstone poured two mugs of tea, added a splash of milk to both and handed one to Riordan. Riordan sipped the strong brew, savoring the flavor, and munched on a digestive.

Riordan said, "I had a good teacher who helped develop the techniques you lot used in Ireland, so it wasn't difficult to find you when I wanted. And no, I didn't shoot any SAS guys!" Featherstone went to protest but Riordan waved it aside. "It's okay Feather, I could see the question on your face. I came across one of your guys one night when I offed 'Big Arthur Murray', a noted provo bomber. I just tied him up until I did the job and then we both scarpered."

"I heard that story," replied Featherstone, "but I thought it was just another of those 'folklore' stories about you that was circulating."

"No. It's entirely true."

Riordan loaded one of the tapes into the VCR and pressed the 'PLAY' button. The quality of the tapes was extremely high, the images crystal clear, and Riordan tensed when the young girl, who appeared to be no more than 10 years old came into view, walking towards a huge four-poster bed. A naked man lay on the bed, stroking a huge erection, but the camera studiously avoided the man's face. The girl slipped off the dress she was wearing, climbed on the bed and knelt down over the man's groin. The camera zoomed in on every possible orifice of the young girl's body, and then moved slowly around to where she was struggling to fellate the huge penis. Riordan looked away. "That's enough for me," he said, and stopped the film. He extracted the tape, slid in the next and played a small piece of it on fast forward until he was satisfied, then repeated the process on the next.

"That should keep the bastard happy," he said. "I'll take one of these with me and mail it to the nerd. Can you get one of your guys to put a wire into the cover of the next tape? When we find the address, we can find out exactly where it is and then go and stake it out. We can use the tracking device to monitor the tape's movement and if I'm right, this guy will lead us directly to Slade. This time we'll do the job right."

Across the city, the commando named Tosser stretched himself and moved position in the front seat of the Range Rover to prevent his butt from going numb. Surveillance was surveillance the world over, but at least this was better than lying under a hedgerow in the rain in South Armagh, smelling like a rancid goat while waiting for a bunch of IRA terrorists to visit an arms cache. Here he had two large thermos flasks of tea, a little plastic bucket to piss in and a good supply of digestive cookies for the evening. He could even listen to the radio. Luxury. If only all jobs could be like this. Across the road, he had watched the lights go out in Riordan's house, and had put on a pair of night-vision goggles from time to time to monitor the area around the building.

It was a quiet area, that was for sure, so any cars appearing were immediately scrutinized by Tosser as potential attackers. The model, color and license plate numbers were noted and filed away for reference. A repeat visit by any of the cars would immediately trigger an alarm and he would call for reinforcements. This would be a bad time for a burglar to make a move on Riordan's house, thought Tosser. He would likely find himself with a very large bullet wound.

Inside his jacket he carried a Browning 9-millimeter with a silencer, a totally illegal weapon, but he didn't want to be making too much fuss in terms of noise should anything happen at Riordan's place. That way the evidence could be disposed of without attracting the attention of the neighbors. In one trouser pocket he carried a switchblade and a set of plasticuffs, and in the other a stainless steel garrote. Tosser followed the boy scout motto of always being prepared.

His side hurt a little where a large, jagged splinter of copper pipe had embedded itself following the explosion, but the wound had been cleaned and the offending piece removed. The painkillers were starting to wear off, and he opened the packet, shook two pills into his hand and washed them down with a swig of tea. Pain was a good thing–it showed that you were still alive, but there was no point in suffering needlessly.

Two headlights appeared. A large black jeep turned into the street and drove slowly along as if the driver were lost or looking for a specific house. Tosser ducked down in the seat to give the impression that the Range Rover was empty and when the jeep drove past, put the night-vision goggles to his eyes and looked inside the car. There were two men, both Orientals, and the one in the passenger side was pointing towards Riordan's house. Tosser touched his earpiece to ensure it was in place, and spoke quietly. "Capo, can you hear me? Over."

Capo's voice came back quickly. "Tosser, what's up? It's getting pretty cold in these fuckin' bushes. I was hoping you might want to trade places."

"Not on your fuckin' life," snorted Tosser. "I've lain in enough wet damp places to last me a lifetime. Anyway, be alert. We got two Tango's in a black van just cruise past and they seemed to be very interested in Riordan's place. I'm waiting to see if they make a second turn. Oh, Oh." He watched the headlights turn on to the street again, and the black jeep came cruising past again. This time it stopped about a hundred yards down the road and the two men got out. They both wore long, Drover-style coats, with easily enough space to conceal a weapon.

"Stand to, Capo, our boys just got out and are walking back towards the house. My guess is since they don't have a wheelman they're expecting to go in quietly and shoot whoever's in the house. That means they'll go around the back. Try and take at least one of them alive, and wait until you actually see a gun before blasting at them."

Tosser heard an indignant grunt and the harsh metallic sound of the slide being pulled back on Capo's gun. "Trying to teach your grandmother how to suck eggs, are you?" said Capo.

"Sorry mate. Watch yourself, and be careful. I'll be right in behind them–friendly fire and all that nonsense. They're walking up the driveway now, and heading around the side of the house. I'm on my way."

"Got them," came the quiet whisper, and Tosser slid out of the Range Rover and into the street. He had already removed the bulb from the interior light so that there would not be a flash of white light when he opened the door. The pistol was out of its holster and held now in the folds of his jacket. He leapt over Riordan's low fence and into the garden, then ran quietly down the side of the house.

"They're at the back door," came the voice in his earpiece. "One of them has got a jemmy and is trying to force the lock. Time to take them down."

"I'm right with you," said Tosser, his heart racing, and stepped around the corner of the house. His pistol came up to focus on the two figures who were intent on forcing the back door. Tosser heard a loud splintering sound, then a low whistle from the bushes where Capo was concealed. Both heads turned at once, and weapons appeared. The man with the jemmy slammed back into the wall as if punched with a giant fist–once, twice.

The other man looked frantically into the darkness, searching for a target, and Tosser aimed at the man's legs and fired. The bullets found their mark with no more than a quiet cough, and the man smashed into the ground with a dull thud, his pistol flying across the patio. There came a rustling sound and a dark shape erupted from the bushes and sprinted across the yard to where the man lay. Capo fired another quick round into the first man's head for insurance. Tosser approached and saw that the second man was unconscious, bleeding from several wounds to his right leg and the upper arm. Capo had obviously been trying to take him alive.

"Good shooting," said Tosser, and took a emergency first-aid kit out of his coat. While he bandaged the man's wounds quickly to prevent any further bleeding, Capo ran across the street and reversed the Range Rover into Riordan's driveway so that the tailgate was facing the side of the house. The inside of the trunk had been lined with black garbage bags, just in case, and Capo took the dead man and threw him into the back. By the time he returned, the white bandages on the other attacker were stained through with red blotches. Capo picked the man up and tossed him like a sack of potatoes into the back of the Range Rover with his dead comrade.

"I'll take their jeep," Capo said, jangling a set of keys he had taken from one of the men. "Meet you at the dump." The dump was a swampy area outside the city where 'refuse' had been taken on more than one occasion.

"Okay," replied Tosser, looking around for a garden hose to wash away the bloodstains on the patio. "I'll give Feather a call and get him to meet us there. He'll want a quick word with yer man."

Featherstone had just poured another cup of tea for them both when his cell-phone chirped. Riordan watched Featherstone's face as he answered the caller with terse "yes's" and "no's" and then he hung up. He had studiously avoided any eye contact during the conversation, so Riordan felt sure the call had something to do with him. "Drink up your tea," Featherstone ordered. "I posted Capo and Tosser at your house tonight. You've just had a couple of oriental visitors who were trying to gain access to your house via the back door."

Alarm surged through Riordan's body, that sudden adrenaline rush with which he was only too familiar. His entire body tensed, ready for action. His voice shook, "You said, tried to gain access."

Featherstone smiled and replied, "One of the men is dead and the other was wounded as per my instructions. I want to talk to him to see if we can get any useful information."

"That's my territory," Riordan said, his teeth bared, and Featherstone moved back a little, as if frightened by the expression. "Where are they?"

"It's a swamp area way north of the city. Nothing but bears and mosquitoes."

"Wonderful," replied Riordan. "Just fucking wonderful."

A puzzled look crossed Featherstone's face. "Got something against swamps, have you?"

"I've been in one or two," Riordan replied, "but that's another long story."

Riordan drove out of the city, barely able to keep his speed at the limit. Now would not be a good time to get a ticket, or to have to explain where they were going. Featherstone patiently gave him instructions and they were soon in the thick of a heavily forested area to the north of Vancouver, driving down an unmarked road which took all of Riordan's driving ability to keep the vehicle from sliding off into the black abyss on both sides. The pungent scent of pines filled the car and the odd, straggly branch brushed across the front window like the fronds of a car wash.

"Are you sure they're down here?" he asked. "This track doesn't look like it been used in a while."

"That's the good thing about it," Featherstone said. "The ground is porous and it's hard to leave tracks. Trust me, the guys will be waiting for us about half a mile from here."

Riordan avoided the obvious question–You seem to have been here before–and focused on his driving, his speed now down to 15 kilometers an hour. After what seemed a very long time, he drove into a bit of a clearing, on the other side of which stood two other vehicles and beyond them a dark pool of water. Tosser stood by the Range Rover, smoking a cigarette, and Capo sat inside, sipping a mug of tea.

Riordan climbed out and made his way over. The volume of the crickets was almost overwhelming. A mosquito landed on his cheek and he slapped it dead before it had time to bite.

"Did these guys wake Nancy up?" Riordan asked, his breath misting on the night air. A shake of the head. "Okay, let's have a look."

Tosser opened the truck and Riordan peered down at the oriental features. "Feather said there were two," Riordan said, and Tosser nodded towards the water.

"One of them's taking a dip," quipped Tosser.

Taking the man's hand, Riordan slid the sleeve up to reveal the ornate 'Irizumi', tattoos along the man's forearm. "Yakusa," he commented. Letting the hand drop, Riordan slapped the man hard across the face, his fingers leaving imprints on the man's cheek. There was no response. Tosser stepped forward and held a bottle of smelling salts under the man's nose until he spluttered and came around. The man's eyes spun in his head, and his features immediately scrunched up with pain. "Got a syrette?" asked Riordan. Tosser produced one from his first-aid pack and Riordan jammed it into the man's leg.

"Morphine," Riordan said, and the man nodded in understanding. They waited for a few moments until the man's features softened, the morphine working its magic, and then Riordan tilted the man's face up to meet his own.

"I need some answers," Riordan said, not holding out a lot of hope for cooperation, and true to form the Yakusa stared defiantly back. "My name's Riordan. That was my house you were trying to break into." Riordan thought he saw the mask drop for a second, a moment of panic in the man's eyes, but then the defiance was back. "We can make this very easy or very difficult," Riordan said, repeating the words like a mantra from another life. "You are going to die tonight, that you cannot change. All you can alter is the method. I need some information, and then you get a bullet–quick and painless. Otherwise, it's going to be a long, painful death. My friends here tell me this place is infested with mosquitoes and bears, especially black bears which are quite nasty when they get annoyed."

Riordan pulled the small jar he had taken from Featherstone's office from his pocket and held it up so the man could see the label. The man's eyes widened when he saw the word 'Honey' and suddenly realized what Riordan was proposing. A look into Riordan's eyes told him that the man was serious.

"What do you want to know?" said the man, moistening his lips, his voice no more than a whisper.

Riordan questioned him for a few minutes but the answers were no more helpful than Riordan had expected; the man was just a foot soldier who had been following orders from his boss. When the man calmly said that they had been ordered to kill the woman and the two children and bring the ears of the infants back to their boss, Riordan saw spots dance before his eyes, and a long tremor shook his spine. He felt Featherstone's fingers dig painfully into his arm keeping him upright, and the pain drove away the horrible image of the fetus that had been delivered to his house.

"Out," Riordan ordered, and the man swung his feet shakily to the ground, testing the strength of the leg with the bullet. "I don't have time or I'd make you dig your own grave," Riordan said harshly, pointing towards the swamp with the pistol Featherstone had given him on the way out of the city.

The man limped slowly towards the fetid water and Riordan followed, angrily brushing away the mosquitoes dancing around his head. A tiny firefly arced off into the night like a shooting star from the heavens, and strange noises emanated from the deep woods. There was a splash and the man was in the water, limping straight ahead with his shoulders slumped in defeat, waiting for the bullet.

"Turn around," said Riordan, and the man obeyed. The pistol coughed twice in rapid succession producing one short blurred report and the man's head slammed back, his arms flung wide by the momentum. The water rippled for a few seconds, then was still, and after a moment the crickets resumed their nightly chorus. Riordan tossed the pistol after the man, and then turned and walked away.

CHAPTER 16

Maelstrom

After Featherstone had dropped him off, Riordan sat in his empty house, his pistol cradled in his lap and the eerie, haunting notes of a piper's lament echoing through the rooms. Old ghosts glided through his psyche, the faces of some blurred from lack of memory, others fresh and sharp although many years had passed. The music lifted his soul, took him to another place of green fields and rivers, the places of his youth, and for an all too fleeting moment he found the grail of peace.

In that moment, the eye of the storm, there were the voices of innocent children laughing, playing soccer with a pop can, skipping with ropes and singing songs before the violence came and robbed them of their youth. Now they threw stones and bottles and their faces were hard and they spouted vitriol like venom from a snake. Closing his eyes, he summoned pictures of better times, the faces of his newborn children and his wife. It was a difficult legacy he had brought them and now, once more, he was drawn back into the maelstrom of violence that had settled like a storm cloud around his shoulders.

Nancy and the children were gone, hastily dispatched under Featherstone's eagle eye to a hotel north of the city. In the morning, they would be moved to yet another secret location, a place that Featherstone's company used as a safe house. Riordan's stomach roiled like a bad day on the Irish Sea, nausea rising from the after-effects of the evening's activity. Another body, and no matter how legitimate or self-righteous he felt about topping the Yakusa, there were now several more people dead by his hand, the hand of the Raven.

Taking a long sip of his Black Bush, he leaned back amongst the shadows and old ghosts and savored the fiery liquid burning down his throat, a pleasant comforting warmth. The scent triggered another long lost memory, of another time waiting in the darkness, waiting for an informer to return home from a meeting with his British Intelligence controller. The man had been marked following a raid intercepted by the authorities, a piece of false information sent and passed on, the resulting ambush observed and foiled by the paramilitaries.

His adopted father, the old man, had had the look of the devil on his face when it had been reported back, and he dispatched the Raven to deal with the problem. Riordan knew the target, a lad no more than twenty years old, but also recognized that he was out of control and could have easily been turned by the brits. The target had been picked up and questioned by the security forces several times already, and that was sufficient to mark him. The brits exploited every possible weakness in anyone they felt was even remotely connected to the violence, often going so far as to set people up in a 'frame' so tight that they had no option but to assist the authorities.

Getting into the lad's flat was not a problem—a key under a plant pot in the back garden—and Riordan methodically tossed the place looking for information. Under a loose floorboard—there was always a loose floorboard—Riordan found a huge wad of cash in new bills. He also found a Canadian passport with a new identity, and a return ticket to Toronto dated for one week ahead, showing the informer was about to run with his eleven pieces of silver. Both money and passport disappeared into an inside pocket

There was an ample supply of Bushmills in the flat, and Riordan helped himself while he waited. He had removed the bulb from the solitary light in the center of the room, and a faint glow from the ruined streetlamps cast an eerie pall about the place. He sat in the dark corner, black on black, on a sofa that had seen better days, his nostrils twitching at the unpleasant odor emanating from the foil packets of stale curry from the carryout next door. Even the flat itself smelled of mildew, that peculiar scent of a home unkempt and uncared for, the dwelling place of a transient.

Shortly after closing time came a scraping of a key against the lock and the door opened, followed by the sound of a light switch flipping up and down. A muffled curse and a waft of cool air blew into the house like a wraith and the door slammed shut. A shadow crossed the room, none too steadily, feeling his towards the hearth and a table lamp like a blind man. The scent of alcohol on the man's breath reached Riordan's nostrils. Riordan closed his eyes as the lamp filled the room with yellowish light, then opened them quickly to see the lad's back turned towards him, only a couple of feet away. Riordan lashed out with his foot and sent the lad sprawling into the chair at the other side of the hearth.

The lad uttered, "What the fuck?" slurring the words, got to his feet and turned to face the intruder with the stance of a belligerent drunk. Bleary eyes blinking furiously, the lad stared at Riordan, trying hard to put a name to the face. "I've seen you in the pub," he said. "What the fuck are you..." and then he noticed the pistol lying in Riordan's lap, saw the silencer attached and in his alcohol-befuddled brain knew he had been rumbled.

"The old man sent me," Riordan said, tossing the money and the passport onto the floor.

The lad looked down at it, his body swaying from side to side like a stalk of corn in the wind, and then raised his eyes slowly to meet Riordan's. He swallowed hard.

"We lost some good lads because of you, you cunt," Riordan said quietly, the words all the more effective for not being screamed. "I want you to tell me a wee story. I know a lot of stuff already and if I catch you lying you will be a sorry wee man. Understand?"

"I'm done for," said the lad, his eyes filling with tears. "I didn't want to do it, it was the fuckin' brits, the bastards.

The police caught me with a couple of bags of pills and were going to put me away, but then I got an offer from a couple of guys from the army who were after the old man. They were going to top me if I didn't work for them. Please mate, you've got to believe me."

The pistol coughed twice, snapping the lad's head back and tossing him over the chair like a Raggedy Anne doll, legs and arms akimbo. Riordan got up, lifted the money and passport, then took off the lad's shoes and socks and left.

Touts were always marked as a warning to others.

Another sip of whisky as he strained to remember how many had gone before that lad, and how many after. Always bodies, so many bodies. And now there were more. Slade had threatened his family, and Riordan knew of men like him, men who killed for the sadistic pleasure of seeing the lights go out in another person's eyes. Slade would not let up until Riordan was dead. There had to be another added to Riordan's list, and added quickly, and then perhaps there could be some semblance of peace. It was not the first time Riordan had wished for that elusive dream, and given his track record it would probably not be the last. But he would try.

Setting the pistol and the whisky glass on the coffee table, he screwed the cap back on the bottle and went into his office to check his e-mail. Life had to go on, and there were several jobs outstanding that he was waiting to complete with special test results. He would do as much as he could get away with, then head off to the warehouse to see if Slade's little pervert had taken the bait.

Two hours later, following a frenetic test of a new piece of software, he was sitting in front of the computer in the warehouse, listening as the modems squawked and hissed at each other like a couple of Sicilian fishwives. The screen unfolded according to the script he had created, and the e-mail reader was logging into the pop server to check his messages.

There were 27 new messages, each of them from some idiot with a name like Mike.Hunt or Fuck.me and other sundry netizens all looking to purchase some of his kiddy-porn tapes. Knowing the authorities were constantly policing the net looking for pedophiles sharing videos and images, he absent-mindedly wondered which of the messages was the invitation from a fed. His scrolled down the list, message by message until he saw the name he wanted.

There was a message from;

"tricky.dicky@fucksalot.com," the one he was waiting to see. He pressed the 'enter' key and the message unfolded, his heart racing in anticipation of seeing a request for one of the tapes.

There it was.

His fingers jabbed the screen and slid down over the P.O. Box address, leaving a greasy smear like a snail trail on the glass. The address said Santa Barbara, California.

Picking up the padded envelope containing the tape, he wrote out the address using a black marker and tossed it into a plastic bag. In the morning he would drive across the border to Seattle, rent a mailbox to receive the payment, and ship the parcel by Federal express. The first step in the plan had been successful. All he had to do was hope the bastard liked the tape enough to ask to buy another, and that one would be bugged with one of Featherstone's tracking devices. Then they could hopefully trace him and the parcel back to Slade.

At the same time Riordan was climbing back into his car to go home, Slade was slamming his phone down on the cradle again and again until it shattered. He had just received word from the underworld boss in Vancouver that two men, who had been dispatched to get rid of Riordan's wife and bring him the ears of his children, had vanished without a trace. And that Riordan had been seen going into his house that very evening. The wife and kids apparently were no-where to be seen, the man implying that they had been moved. Which meant that Riordan was on his guard and the two thugs were most probably dead and disposed of by now.

"Fuck," yelled Slade, and threw the shattered remains off into the distance, silencing the cicadas momentarily. "Who is this guy?" He thought for a moment, the dark rage evaporating as his cunning brain explored the possibilities, and he wondered if Featherstone, the former SAS hard-man and his crew were protecting Riordan. He was fairly certain that it was Featherstone and his men who had stormed his house on the island–only professional soldiers could have gotten by his defenses. But why? What was the connection? It was time to go back to the first step, the key to the puzzle.

Allan Brown.

Brown was the person who had set the whirlwind in motion, and people and events around his incarceration were at the root of this problem. If anyone could know of the connection, it would be Brown. Picking up the intercom, Slade called one of his bodyguards. "Call the airport and have them get the plane ready for first thing in the morning. I need to pay a quick visit to Vancouver tomorrow."

Rubbing the last vestiges of sleep from his eyes, Allan Brown shuffled across the kitchen floor, naked save for a pair of black bicycle shorts, feeling a little light-headed as he put the kettle on to boil. He had been sleeping a lot, 10 to 12 hours each night, his body's natural reaction to the distress of the last few weeks. The bandage had been removed from his abdomen, and the tiny line of black stitches looked back at him like the threading on the side of a football. He could feel his strength coming back in waves, each day bringing little victories that added to his general feeling of well-being. The cane was now gone, had been for a couple of days, and each day the walk to the corner store for the newspaper was less and less daunting.

Opening a large can of protein powder, he started spooning the stuff into the blender, concocting his own form of shake to help him regain his strength. He cracked a few eggs into the blender on top of the powder, then added some vitamins, skim milk and a couple of bananas for good measure. In a few seconds the blender's contents had turned a strange shade of gray, and Brown smiled to himself. He could always see the expression on Riordan's face when he made the drink. Dispensing with any niceties, he put the blender to his lips and drained half the contents, smacking them noisily when he had finished.

Opening the fridge door, he took out a large packet of Starbuck's Arabica coffee beans and proceeded to grind up enough to fill the bodum. Riordan scorned the milkshake but never refused a good mug of coffee. Brown shook his head slowly. Since he had been released from the hospital, good old Daniel had shown up every morning for a 'quick coffee' and a visit under some pretext or other, never really being able to say that he wanted to keep an eye on his friend.

But that was how guys were, thought Brown. The tantalizing aroma of freshly ground coffee filled the kitchen, and right on cue the kettle started to boil. The clock on the stove said 9:30 a.m., which was usually around the time Daniel made his appearance, carrying a brown bag with fresh croissants or freshly baked scones from a tiny bakery on the mainland.

The doorbell rang and Brown pulled the plug of the kettle out of the wall, filled the bodum and went to open the door. The door swung open and Brown, turning back towards the kitchen, was surprised to see three men on the step; two Orientals and a large well-tanned individual with a closely cropped haircut. The fuzz was dark, highlighting a widow's peak, and the face was taut and angular like that of a body-builder. It would have been a handsome face, a pretty-boy, had it not been for the soul-less, dark eyes that seemed to suck the life out of their surroundings.

The two Orientals appeared to have been struck from the same mold; dark shiny hair pulled back in a pony-tail, greasy skin, and a few straggly black hairs on their upper lips like a pre-pubescent boy's mustache. Nicotine-stained teeth completed the tasteless ensemble. Their eyes, hooded like those of a snake showed feral intensity, anticipation of what was to come. A worm of fear crawled through Brown's guts.

Dressed in long, black leather coats, the three pushed their way into the house. Brown was too feeble to resist and the man grasped his arm painfully and guided him into the living room. A shove sent him sprawling onto the couch like a child tossing aside an unwanted doll. Brown groaned and put a hand to his side to see if the stitches had ripped open. There was blood on the tips of his fingers. The man stood on the other side of the coffee table and looked Brown up and down like some sort of lab experiment, the eyes focusing on the wound momentarily, before looking away. The other men flanked their boss, hands crossed in front of their coats. Brown could see the bulges under the armpits of the men.

Righting himself on the couch, Brown said, "You must be Slade." The calmness of his words belied the palpitations of his heart. This was not going to turn out well. The man smiled and nodded.

"Right in one," Slade said. "I have some questions about your friend Daniel Riordan. There is more to that man than meets the eye, and now we have a score to settle. So I thought I would come to the one person who seems to know most about him. Mister Wentworth, God rest his soul, told me that Riordan and you were best buddies. Tell me about him." Slade sat down on the armchair, crossed his legs with the air of a television interviewer, folded his hands about one knee and stared at Brown.

Brown could see that this was someone who was used to giving orders and having them obeyed. There was also no point in lying, but he didn't have to volunteer everything he knew. He had many suspicions about his friend Daniel, about what he had been, but he had never pried, allowing things to take their course. A little snippet from time to time and the jigsaw that was Daniel Riordan edged towards completion. But for now there were many, many empty pieces.

"There's not much to tell," Brown lied. "I met him about four years ago here in Vancouver and we became friends. He's into martial arts and fishing, and loves Irish whisky. And more than anything he loves his family, so you can imagine he was somewhat miffed when you kidnapped his wife."

Slade shrugged his shoulders. "An unfortunate circumstance, but I needed to buy a little time and I thought that would do it for me. I was wrong about that too. So who raided my house in the island? Was Riordan there?"

Brown shook his head and tried to be convincing. "No, that was Featherstone and his crew. When the police didn't believe my story, Featherstone started investigating and managed to track the killings back to you. He was taking some surveillance photos of your house and caught you holding Daniel's wife. When Daniel saw them he went absolutely wild and got Featherstone and his men to get her back. Seems he trusted the ex-SAS men more than he did the police."

"Hmm," Slade muttered, rubbing his chin thoughtfully. "Where's Riordan from?"

"I have no idea," replied Brown. "He has a soft Irish accent which sounds a bit Scottish at times, but he doesn't talk much about his past life. From the things he's said I have the feeling that his father was killed in the 'troubles' but I'm not sure. Other than that..."

"Where are his wife and children?"

Brown swallowed hard. "I honestly have no idea. Featherstone has taken them to some safe-house but that's all I know."

"You're not a great deal of help," said Slade, rising to his feet. "Still, you can be a useful message for me."

Brushing aside the flap of his coat, Slade slid his hand into the grip of an Uzi machine pistol. Brown saw the muzzle begin to rise, slowly, inexorably towards him, the end of the barrel like a tiny black 'O'. The Orientals leered, their mouths gaping open like spectators at a cockfight waiting for the kill. In his mind Brown thought of the unfairness of it all, how he'd been so close to death over the past while and survived. He closed his eyes and waited.

Riordan drove across the island, windows of the Range Rover down, tasting the salt air and feeling good about life. The black mood was gone, burned away like the early morning mist on a river. He had had a long chat earlier with Nancy at the safe house and listened to the boys gurgling to him over the phone. She was made of hardy stock and understood what needed to be done, wishing him luck in tracking down Slade. She too knew, from her long talks with Riordan, what type of a man Slade was, and how he needed to be stopped using unconventional means.

She was also in good hands. Jean-Marc had taken a shine to her, and Featherstone detailed Jean-Marc as her bodyguard to give him some time to recuperate from the wounds sustained on the island. It seemed as if he would never get over the stigma of being bitten by the guard dog.

On the passenger seat was nestled a brown bag, now faintly stained from the warm croissants inside. Riordan's mouth watered, and he hoped there was some jam left in

Brown's fridge. He had bought a huge jar of Walsh's strawberry preserve, specially imported from Ireland, to keep in Allan's fridge. However, Brown had a habit of putting the jam into his infernal protein shakes to give them flavor, which to Riordan's mind was absolutely impossible, not to mention a waste of good jam. Turning the corner into Brown's street, a row of townhouses which backed on to the bay, he saw a red Toyota Land cruiser parked outside Brown's house, and the back end of a long leather coat disappearing around the corner of the garage.

A flush of alarm spread through him, that old sixth sense pinging like the sonar on a submarine. He shivered and immediately pulled over to the side of the road, cursing aloud for having left the pistol in his house. All he had were the ceramic throwing knives strapped to his arm, but they weren't much use against guns. He leapt out of the car and ran around the back of the houses. Allan had two sets of French doors at the back, one set leading off the dining room, another off the kitchen, so he should be able to see what was going on inside.

Making his way slowly along to Brown's house, he lay down on the patio stones and snaked his way forward to the French doors off the living room. Moving a fraction of an inch at a time, he moved until he could peer in the bottom corner of the door. There were curtains on the windows filtering the images, but he could see three men in a semi-circle with Allan Brown sitting on the couch in front of them. One man sat down and started talking but Riordan could not make out what they were saying.

Saying a tiny prayer to himself, Riordan slipped back to the French doors off the kitchen and gently pressed down the handles. Usually, if the weather was good, Allan and himself would have their coffee on the deck, so he hoped the doors were open. Behind him, seagulls whirled and cackled in the thermals. The door cracked open a fraction and he heard voices. The man was asking Allan what he knew about Riordan and in a heartbeat Riordan knew it was Slade.

Slade the bastard, right here in the house.

Jesus, the man had balls. And the only person that Riordan and Featherstone had not thought of protecting was Allan. Easing the door open slowly, Riordan slipped off his shoes and stepped through into the kitchen; Brown was justifiably proud of his Mexican quarry-tile floor, but it was noisy. Riordan pulled the sleeve of his shirt up over the sheath holding the blades and moved forward. Through a tiny crack he could see the three men. Looking around the kitchen quickly, his eyes came to rest on Brown's collection of Henkel knives. Brown, a perfectionist in most things, always kept the knives as sharp as scalpels.

Bonus, thought Riordan and hefted the two largest, tested their balance and then judged the distance between himself and the three men. Throwing knives was an imprecise art, not at all like it was depicted in the movies, but Riordan practiced a lot. The two men on flank were always the most dangerous because they always carried the guns. The hard case was usually unarmed, but then again Slade was unpredictable.

Moving forward slowly, he heard the remains of the conversation and smiled to himself as he heard Allan Brown, once again, defend him. When he heard Slade say, "You can be a useful message for me," Riordan cocked his arm and stepped forward into their field of vision.

"Why don't you tell me yourself," Riordan said, and four heads immediately snapped around in his direction. The first knife had already left his hand, flashing past Slade's head by a fraction of an inch and imbedding itself in the Oriental's chest with a thunk. The man gasped, sank to his knees and pitched forward, both hands grasping the handle of the knife in a futile attempt to remove it. Riordan's eyes widened at the sight of the Uzi in Slade's hand, but then the other Oriental moved into Slade's line of fire. Slade, in an act of self-preservation, propelled him forward with his boot. It was a bad move because the motion forced the man's hand to slip off the butt of his pistol.

Riordan saw Slade turn and run but could do nothing as the other Oriental was bearing down on him. There was no time to raise the other knife so he did what he had been practicing for several months. He hurled the knife underhand, the blade leaving his hand horizontally like a projectile. The Oriental's sneer turned to a grimace as the heavy blade slammed into his stomach, penetrating all the way to the pommel. He gurgled a bit, took one faltering step and collapsed. Riordan did not hesitate. He dragged the man's gun out of its holster but it snagged, and he lost vital seconds trying to pry it free. It came away and he sprinted for the door just in time to see the Toyota disappear around the end of the street, tires squealing as it threatened to topple.

Bastard, he hissed, and went back inside.

Allan Brown was throwing up on the coffee table. "Told you those fuckin' protein shakes would be the death of you," said Riordan, and sat down beside his friend and held him until the spasms ended. Brown's skin was cold and clammy, and Riordan could feel his friend's bones pressing again his skin. Brown had that emaciated look of a long-term patient existing only on fluids.

"It's okay mate," said Riordan, stepping over the Oriental who was clinging to life by a slender thread, and went into the kitchen and brought back a glass of water and a roll of paper towels. Brown wiped a long string of vomit from his face with the paper towel and drank the water greedily. The man on the floor gave a long shudder, his heels beating a macabre staccato rhythm for a moment and then lay still.

"Jesus, Daniel," Brown managed to mutter. "What are we going to do with these two? The police will never believe that I killed them single-handedly."

Riordan grinned. "I think Featherstone will be able to help us there, and I'll get him to post a couple of his men outside, unless you'd rather go to the safe house with Nancy."

"I'd rather get away from here for a while, if it's all the same to you, and maybe go down south or something," replied Brown. "I can't take any more of this cloak and dagger shit, and I don't want to be cooped up in a safe house somewhere like a tethered goat. Just leave a message on my phone when you've gotten rid of Slade and I'll come back–that is what you are planning, isn't it? Putting him in jail wouldn't accomplish anything because he was able to reach inside and get me. Besides, this Slade is one evil bastard. The world will be a better place and all that."

"It will take just a little while longer to work this all out," said Riordan gently, his face serious, and Brown nodded. "Why don't you go and make the coffee?" Riordan said, "and I'll call Feather. He'll help us."

Brown stood shakily to his feet and looked at the two men lying dead on the floor. "My good knives," he said and shook his head, stepped over the spreading pool of blood and went into the kitchen. Riordan picked up the phone, called Featherstone's office, gave his name and the secretary put him right through. When he heard Featherstone's voice he explained what had happened, listened to the man's instructions and replaced the receiver.

"Good man Feather," he said, "you're a good man."

Featherstone arrived about two hours later with Capo and Tosser in tow, all three dressed in pristine white coveralls and caps and driving a panel truck with 'Joe Davey and Sons, Painters and Decorators' painted in green on the side. Riordan opened the door and let them in. Tosser and Capo carried buckets of paint brushes and large rolls of white polythene for protecting furniture from paint splatters.

Featherstone looked at the two dead Orientals with an approving eye. "Where's Allan?" he asked, and Riordan nodded towards the back deck. "How's he holding up?"

Riordan said, "I tried to convince him he'd be happier at the safe house for a few days but he decided to go off down south on his own. So it's one less thing to worry about." Capo and Tosser were starting to wrap the first body in the material. The blood showed up in stark contrast to the white sheets.

"What should we do with the knives, boss?" asked Capo.

"My prints are all over them," Riordan said. "Take them out and I'll toss them in the dishwasher. I don't think Allan will want to be using them again." Tosser, grunting with exertion, had to make a sawing motion with the knife to widen the cut and it suddenly came free with a loud sucking noise. Featherstone winced.

"Are you making any progress on the other side?" asked Featherstone.

Riordan nodded. "The guy contacted me last night and I have the package addressed and ready to go. It's a post office box in Santa Barbara, but that means he could be anywhere up or down the Pacific coast."

Featherstone said, "I did a bit of training down there with the SEALs. The area is pretty remote, especially in the hills north of Santa Barbara; lots of big ranches and movie stars who like their privacy. It would make sense that Slade would hole up somewhere like that. What do you want to do next?"

Riordan walked towards the kitchen. Capo and Tosser had completely wrapped the first body and secured the sheets in place with bands of silver duct tape. The oriental now looked like an oversized larvae.

Riordan said, "Let's have some coffee. I was going to wait and see if this guy likes the tape and contacts me again. The next time we could put a tracking device into the tape and follow the signal, but now I'm not so sure I want to wait that long. I've got to find Slade quickly 'cos he's got everything I hold dear under siege at the moment. To do that I think we should stake out the P.O. box in Santa Barbara and see who comes to get the tape."

Riordan took two large mugs out of the cupboard, opened the fridge and lifted out a carton of fresh cream, and then poured them both a generous helping of coffee. Featherstone's eyes sparkled in anticipation of action as he sipped his coffee. He said, "All we need to do is find where the P.O. box is located in Santa Barbara. We'll pay a quick visit to it overnight and leave one or two of our little gadgets in place. That way we can tell when the box is opened. If this guy is as twisted as you think he'll be in a hurry to get the tape."

He paused for a moment, calculating times in his head. "If we get to Seattle tomorrow morning and FedEx the parcel, it will be delivered sometime the following morning. There are lots of these places in the US where you can rent PO boxes; some are legit and some not. I imagine this would be one of the seedier ones, like a long-term cheap motel or something, and if that's the case the guy may have slipped the proprietor a few bucks to let him know when a package has arrived."

Riordan realized where Featherstone was going and interjected. "We can put a tap on the phone and listen in when the parcel gets delivered."

Featherstone had a shocked look on his face, and put his hand over his heart. "A phone tap. In a foreign country. But that's illegal, we'd be breaking the law." Riordan eyes cast a sideways glance at the body on the floor and Featherstone laughed out loud.

"You do have a point," he said.

CHAPTER 17

Mammy

The next morning, shortly after 4:00 a.m. and amidst much grumbling, the four set off on the trip to Santa Barbara, Riordan and Featherstone in the front in their Range Rover, Capo and Tosser bringing up the rear in a rented Ford Mustang Cobra. They made a quick stop at a postal outlet in Seattle to mail the package containing the video, then it was a straight drive down through the remainder of Washington, into Oregon, and on through into California. The temperature increased slowly from the cold, rainy day that was Vancouver to the searing heat of Sausalito and wine country and they were soon into San Francisco and speeding along the central coast highway.

They took turns driving, music blaring and coffees poured from two large thermos flasks they had filled before crossing the border and refilled at rest stops along the highway. Featherstone had brought a cooler containing sandwiches and fruit, refusing to spend any longer than necessary in the roadside restaurants which he caustically referred to as 'choke and pukes.' The other car with Capo and Tosser was never far from view and, from Riordan's perspective, the two seemed to be constantly arguing about something. There was even a high speed tug of war over what appeared to be a cassette which at one point went sailing out the window of the Mustang.

Riordan mentioned the incident to Featherstone who was lying back in his seat, eyes shut and his breathing shallow. He didn't bother to open his eyes but said, "If those two aren't constantly taking the piss out of each other then I worry. Otherwise, the world is good! Do you want me to spell you?"

"No thanks," Riordan replied, feeling quite content to focus on the road and the task ahead. Last evening had been a hard night. Sleep had eluded him for several hours and when he did eventually drift off, the slumber was restless, twisting and turning to avoid dark haunting images, omens of the past or perhaps the future. It was always the way.

When he had lived in Belfast, and especially after several killings, on the evening before going out to find the next target his rest would be ruined by specters of those who had gone before. He would awaken with the bedclothes in disarray and his sheets sweat-stained and damp and his being shaken to its very core. And here I go again, he thought to himself. Rubbing his tired eyes, he yawned loudly and stretched as much as possible, holding the steering wheel in place with his knee.

A few miles from the tiny town of Santa Maria, a place which Riordan had visited many times in his previous life as David Spence, he pointed out to Featherstone the large sign for a town called Buelton, world renowned for its split pea soup. Featherstone, rubbing his stomach, suggested that they stop for a bowl and a bit of a stretch. According to the map he held in his hand, Santa Barbara was less than 30 miles away so they could have a quick snack to satisfy the hunger pangs and then eat later. It would be dusk when they reached the city, and that would give them time to find the address of the PO box and allow Tosser and Capo to weave their magic tricks.

In the hilly area their cell phones kept breaking up, so Riordan allowed the Mustang to get close and then indicated that they were turning off at Buelton.

Their hunger somewhat sated, and following a competition in the parking lot between Capo and Tosser to see who could pass wind the loudest, they were soon back on the highway. Riordan knew the road well. He raced down the steep incline that cut through a high mountain pass before cresting a last grass-covered hill. At the top of the hill they could see a wide panoramic view of the pacific coast. Featherstone was in awe of the vista, but for Riordan it was old hat.

As they drove along the highway Featherstone put his binoculars to his eyes and focused on the ocean. "Magic," he exclaimed. "I thought that was a whale I saw, but there's a whole pod of them out there."

"They are impressive," Riordan replied, "and it never ceases to fill me with awe. When we get down closer to Santa Barbara, you can probably see a school of dolphins at play."

They came upon Santa Barbara quickly, and Riordan took the first exit off the highway, leading them on to Carillo, the street address of the PO box. Slowing for the volume of traffic, they crossed State Street into a quieter part of the town. Featherstone pointed at the numbers as they went past. Large trees lined the darkened street, and the houses had definitely seen better days. A couple of parked cars looked as if they had been in the same spot for several years.

"Fuck," Featherstone exclaimed, "there it is." Riordan looked over and saw the tiny variety store set on the corner of the block, and a display in the window advertising 'postal boxes for rent'. The owner was called Diego, attested to by a red neon sign above the store. The 'O' was broken, and flickered on and off from time to time like the tail on a firefly.

"What's the problem Feather?" Riordan asked, pulling over to the curb.

"Look behind the variety store." Riordan turned his head around and read the sign on the wall of a low-rise stuccoed building beside the variety store. The sign read, "Santa Barbara County Probation Department." Riordan's heart sank. At the same moment a police cruiser pulled out

from the side of the probation building and turned away
down Carillo.

"Ah well," sighed Featherstone. "Nobody said it was
going to be easy."

Tosser knocked on the side window of the Range
Rover and Riordan slid the window down. A waft of warm
night air stole into the car, cicadas clicked merrily in the
darkness and the scent of laurels filled their nostrils. Tosser
said, "I'll go in and buy some goodies and Capo can case
the place to see where we can get in or out. There's a
vacant apartment above the store for rent. Maybe we could
get a short term on it. This seems like the kind of area
where people would be transient."

"Good idea," said Featherstone. "But first, why don't
we go and book a couple of rooms at the motel back up the
road. You won't be able to do anything for a while,
especially with all those cops around so a hot shower and a
change of clothes would be appreciated. Then we can get a
bite to eat and get the gear ready."

"Look guys," said Tosser, turning his head around
towards the front of the Probation building. A tall, blonde-
haired lady wheeled a bicycle out through the front
entrance, locked the door with a key from her purse, then
lifted one leg and set off down the street, the blue skirt
riding up to show an expanse of thigh. "Good Christ,"
groaned Tosser, "that's a bit of all right. I wouldn't mind
sniffin' that saddle!"

"Jeez, Tosser," groaned Featherstone, "keep your fucking perversions to yourself, would you. I'm just about to have some grub."

Tosser grinned and threw a quick wink at Riordan.

Riordan said, "I know where there's a good Indian restaurant, if you fancy a curry that is." Two heads turned to look at him in anticipation of an explanation. When Riordan remained silent Featherstone grinned and said, "What was her name?"

"How did you know there was a she?" asked Riordan, scowling, annoyed with himself at letting Featherstone push his buttons.

"Written all over your face mate," laughed Tosser. "And I would love a chicken vindy. It's been a while since I've had a good one. You guys go on back to the motel and get us registered. Capo and I will be along later. I want to check out the area a bit more."

Following a leisurely dinner at the Indian restaurant, the men went back to the motel to make their preparations. Riordan was amazed at how much food Capo and Tosser could put away. The table had been littered with bowls of Curry, Vindaloo, Tikka Masala, and Tandoori chicken, an ample supply of basmati rice and a never-ending pile of Naan bread. Riordan was full after sampling several of the Samosa appetizers.

In the motel, guns, knives, and a variety of high-tech equipment lay on one of the beds and the men lounged in armchairs that were threadbare and stained. An air-conditioner struggled in the corner of the room. The TV was on, fed with a pile of quarters which Capo had gotten from the receptionist, and several couples were having sex with wild abandon on the screen.

Riordan tried hard to keep his face straight amidst the constant banter from Capo and Tosser which was much more entertaining than the movie, but failed miserably and burst into a loud guffaw of laughter. Behind him, on a small, formica covered table sat a model of the corner store and surrounding area. A hand drawn map sat beside the model. The plan had been made and the men were quite confident that the break and enter would be, in Capo's terms, 'A piece of piss'. Riordan believed them. He picked up and examined one of the tiny disks sitting snugly in a foam backed case, no bigger than a cigar carton.

"Neat little device that," commented Featherstone.

"Miniature flashbang?" Riordan said, thinking out loud, but on turning it over he could not see any sort of trigger mechanism. He treated the device with the utmost respect because he had seen some devices with liquid triggers that activated by breaking a thin glass tube inside a rubber coating.

"Nope, but pretty close," answered Featherstone. "You attach these to a target's tires with a dollop of crazy glue. It actually contains a radio-detonator and a small charge of Semtex. When detonated it will blow a hole in the tire and then fly off, which is a good way of incapacitating a vehicle without leaving any evidence. If the target shows up tomorrow, we'll put one on each tire, just in case we need to disable him that way. Sort of a backup plan should we lose him for any reason. Of course there will be a radio transmitter somewhere and all of us are pretty adept at surveillance, so we should have all the bases covered.

"As Capo says, 'A piece of piss.'"

It was a little past two o'clock in the morning when Tosser and Capo, dressed in black jogging outfits, slipped out of the motel room and set off on their "Mission". Featherstone received a one-fingered salute when he told them both to 'be careful,' and then there was the caustic 'yes mammy' from the pair. Riordan snorted from laughing so hard, especially at the indignant look on Featherstone's face as he closed the door behind them.

"You're right Feather," Riordan said, settling back down into his chair for a few hours of sleep. "If they're not taking the piss, there's something wrong. It's too bad that they have to take the piss out of you!"

Closing his eyes in an attempt to attract the sleep he knew would not come, Riordan rested his feet on the coffee table and pulled his jacket across his knees. Behind him he heard the bedsprings squeak as Feather lay down on top of the sheets. There was nothing more either of them could do except wait.

It seemed as if he been drowsing for only a few minutes when the door opened and Tosser and Capo slipped back in. Both men were quiet, and Riordan heard two quick hisses as beer can lids were popped, then there came a gut wrenching roar as Tosser farted loudly, and the two men fell into fits of giggles.

"Fuck me," groaned Tosser. "That chicken vindy is not sitting at all well. My poor old arse is so fucking hot you could light fags off of it!"

"Thanks for sharing mate," replied Capo, sarcastically, "but that's a little too much information, know wot I mean?"

The bed springs groaned again and Riordan heard Featherstone say "No problems?" and the reply "no bother at all boss, no bother at all." He closed his eyes again and the next thing he knew Featherstone was shaking him gently by the shoulder.

"Daniel, Daniel, it's time to get moving." Riordan cracked open his eyes and saw sunlight streaming into the room where Featherstone had pulled open the curtains. Featherstone said, "You went off into a deep sleep so I let you rest for a little while. The lads have planted the devices and all the gear is working just fine. The store opens at 9:00 a.m. so we should get over there in case the owner comes early. Tosser and Capo are going to go in and get us some coffee and bagels for breakfast."

Riordan blinked his eyes open and ran a tongue around parched, dry lips. "God, it's been a while since I slept like that," he offered. "Have I time for a shower?" he asked. Featherstone jacked a round into the chamber of one of the pistols.

"I'll shoot you if you don't," Featherstone said.

"Point taken," grinned Riordan and headed for the shower. Having showered, shaved and put on fresh clothes, Riordan felt totally refreshed. Rubbing his stomach, he said, "My stomach thinks my throat's been cut."

"Don't worry," replied Featherstone, grinning. "We'll get those fresh bagels and cream cheese shortly. Might even get some alfalfa sprouts on them as well to fill you up. After all, this is California!" Riordan frowned. "Whatever happened to a good Ulster fry? Alfalfa sprouts my ass!"

The equipment was working perfectly, and Riordan watched as Featherstone pointed out what each of the devices was being used for. After parking a few yards away from the store on the opposite side of the road, Featherstone used his cell-phone to place a quick call to the store, and Riordan listened in amazement at the clarity of the sound produced by the bug the men had planted in the owner's telephone unit. A digital read-out screen in the device would display out the digits of any number the storeowner called.

Tosser appeared in the doorway of the store carrying a brown bag and two Styrofoam cups, one precariously balanced on top of the other. He made his way over to the car and was about to go back and join Capo when the blonde lady from the previous evening rode up and parked her bicycle outside the store. She was wearing a white dress, which showed off her well-tanned body to perfection, and when she disappeared inside the store, Tosser set off after her. "Going for a better look," he said.

Featherstone shook his head in amazement. "Fucking incorrigible pussy hound, he is. I wouldn't be surprised if he asks her for a date."

Riordan laughed. "Jeez Feather, talk about the pot calling the kettle black!"

The coffee tasted delicious, and even the bagel went down well, Riordan totally surprised at how hungry he was. Featherstone offered him half of his bagel and Riordan gratefully accepted.

A few minutes later, a Federal Express van pulled up outside the store, and the delivery man carried one package into the store. "That's ours," commented Featherstone, putting a tiny pair of binoculars on the console between them. "Let's hope that we see some action soon."

When the deliveryman had left, Tosser came out the door of the store beside the blonde lady, they had a bit of discussion and Tosser wheeled her bicycle up to the front of the probation building. Riordan watched him receive a peck on the cheek and then a beaming Tosser walked back across the road and climbed in beside Capo.

"He's picking up the phone," said Featherstone, watching as digit after digit appeared on the tiny screen. "It's a local number." Riordan listened to the phone ring at the other end, and then a voice said, "Hello?" There was a suspicious tone to the voice.

"It's Julio, from the store. The courier just left a package in your box a few minutes ago."

"That's great," came the response. Riordan noted that the timbre had changed, from suspicion to excitement, almost anticipation. The caller continued, "I have to get some supplies so I'll come over the mountain tonight and pick it up. I should be there about nine o'clock."

Featherstone rolled his eyes towards heaven. "Such is the life of a soldier," he said. "Hours upon hours of fucking boredom punctuated by moments of incredibly intense action. A bit like my love life at the moment!"

Riordan grinned. "I thought you were doing rather well with the Ward Sister from the hospital that you met at the christening." Featherstone smacked his lips together.

"You're right there," he said, a wide smile lighting up his face. "Sharon." He closed his eyes, as if recalling a sweet memory. "What a body! And the things she could do with it as well! I remember..."

"Please," pleaded Riordan, squirming in his seat, "don't go there."

Featherstone wrote down the number on the digital readout, and then opened the door of the car. "I'll go and tell the lads that we can stand down for a while. Any idea what the caller meant about the 'over the mountain' statement?"

Riordan nodded. "There's a cutoff from highway 105 that takes you up over the mountain towards a little place called Solvang. It's a Norwegian community settled in the midst of the desert, and is a bit of a tourist trap. A lot of film stars have ranches up in that area."

Featherstone nodded sagely. "And you know this because..." An eyebrow lifted, his entire face waiting for an answer.

"Same lady as the Indian restaurant," replied Riordan somewhat sheepishly. "Look Feather, Nancy doesn't know about this one, okay?"

Featherstone shook his head. "You know me mate. Absolutely the soul of discretion. So what shall we do for the rest of the day? You seem to know this place pretty well."

"Well, for your hormonal friends back there I suggest we head for the beach," replied Riordan. "The University of Santa Barbara is just across the road from the shore, so I can imagine there will be plenty for them to play with. I'm only allowed to watch! We just have to go across to State Street, turn left and drive all the way to the bottom. If we had more time here I'd introduce you to the concept of the State Street crawl. When they reach the coast road, they turn right and keep going until they see the sign for USB. It's about two miles along the road."

After a long day at the beach, which consisted of Capo and Tosser chatting up every female in sight, especially those in skimpy bikinis, they had supper at the yacht club on the pier while watching a light mist roll in off the sea. The soldiers reveled in the fact that they had fresh seafood, and Riordan was amazed at their restraint in relation to alcohol. They ate pan-seared scallops, steaming bowls of shrimp and fresh crab, all cooked in vast amounts of garlic. He knew how much booze each of the men could pack away, but no one touched a drop of alcohol. Despite the merriment, they knew what lay ahead, and knew that there was a good possibility of some sort of confrontation later in the evening. Having run across Slade and his goons once before, they knew what faced them, and there was no way they would compromise any of their faculties.

Supper over, and the cars both reeking of garlic, they headed back to their original spots outside the probation department. Featherstone was his usual chatty self, not caring too much whether Riordan responded or not and the conversation, as always, was punctuated with many of his movie star impressions. Riordan's nerves were starting to fray, and even a quick call to Nancy was not sufficient to calm him down. At a few minutes after nine o'clock, a dark Toyota Land Cruiser pulled up outside the store and a man got out. Riordan recognized him immediately, especially with the missing right hand.

"That's him, Feather," he exclaimed, slamming a fist into the palm of his hand. "We've got the bastard."

A light on the console flashed. "He's just opened the box," said Feather by way of explanation. "The lads wired a tiny microswitch in there." Picking up the two-way radio he said, "Capo. Our target is in the store. He's driving the Toyota."

"Okay boss," came the reply, and Riordan saw Capo get out of his car and walk across the road to the Toyota. He paused for a moment by each of the side tires, attaching one of the little explosive devices Riordan had examined the previous evening, and then ran back to his own car.

Featherstone switched on another box, from which emanated a loud beep. "Tracking device just in case we lose visual on him," he explained. "Okay lads, stand to. He's coming out of the store now and is heading back towards State Street. He'll probably go on across and get on the highway at Dawson. You keep on his tail and we'll be right behind."

There was some traffic on the road, so Capo and Tosser kept a few cars behind, reporting back on any moves the Toyota made as it headed north. As Riordan had thought, the man cut off the highway and started northwards following the sign for Solvang. The road twisted and turned around the side of the mountain, each dangerous corner illuminated by rows and rows of posts covered with multi-colored luminous paint. One particularly well-decorated corner prompted Featherstone to comment, "Looks like a full friggin' mass with all those bleedin' lights. I'm surprised there aren't more accidents with all that shit on the road. Damn near blinded me."

Riordan felt his ears pop and soon they were at the top of the mountain and beginning their descent down the other side. In the distance Riordan saw the lights of the Toyota, and several car lengths behind Capo and Tosser were maintaining their distance.

At the intersection leading to Solvang, the man stopped and headed north, towards the town of Santa Maria. "It's pretty desolate up that way," commented Riordan. "You could lose an army out there."

"Seems the perfect place for Slade to set up shop again," replied Featherstone.

Riordan put the night-vision binoculars to his eyes and focused on the road ahead. At the same time the radio crackled into life. "Boss, boss, he's turning off the main road. We're going on past. It's pretty even country up here so we'll head up a bit and turn around. I suggest you pull over now."

Featherstone eased back on the accelerator, killed the lights and pulled over to the side of the road. Riordan focused on the dust trail thrown up by the jeep until it disappeared over a low rise. "This is it," he said. The beep from the tracking device faded by degrees, until it was almost inaudible, then it remained at the constant low level.

"He's stopped now," said Featherstone. "Probably about a mile beyond that ridge. And sure, isn't it a lovely night for a walk." A set of headlights appeared in the distance and grew larger and larger and soon Capo was pulling onto the shoulder at the other side of the road. It was pitch black outside when they killed their headlights, like extinguishing a candle in a closed room. Riordan waited a moment to allow his eyes to adjust, then climbed out of the car, as did Featherstone. The desert air was cool against his skin, and above him stars twinkled brightly in the clear air. The others were already waiting.

"So what's the plan, boss?" asked Capo, rubbing his hands together.

Featherstone said, "I propose we do a little recce, and then go in and pay Slade a visit. He'll likely have some guards, but there won't be any dogs running free here. He'll probably have some girls here like the place in Vancouver, but anyone else is fair game. And unless it's absolutely necessary for you to take him out, leave Slade for Riordan."

A smile creased Riordan's face when he heard the protestations from the others, but he knew it was good-natured.

Yes, he thought to himself.

Slade is mine.

It ends here and it ends tonight.

CHAPTER 18

Torment

The desert air was cool. Riordan was glad of the black hooded sweatshirt he had brought with him, and the thin, black leather gloves he wore afforded some protection for his fingers. The land beneath his feet was parched and crumbled with each footstep. After applying black greasepaint to each other's faces, each man had donned his night vision goggles, especially after Featherstone's warning that there could be rattlesnakes around. His comment that there were anti-venom syrettes in the first-aid kits did nothing to lessen their unease.

They walked single-file across the open land, ever vigilant of the small creeks and gullies that criss-crossed the terrain before them. Several times they had to scramble down crumbling banks of dried up streams, a precarious endeavor especially in the low light. Twice Riordan heard muffled curses from behind him as Capo and Tosser both lost their balance and tumbled down in the sandy bottoms.

When they reached the top of the rise, Featherstone lay down, as did the others, and Riordan followed. Even though it was dark they did not want to be silhouetted against the night sky in the event that there might be guards on patrol. Riordan saw the lights of the house about half a mile ahead the distance. By his estimation, it was a sprawling Hacienda, with a main two-story building and several others attached to it. Lights were on in several of the rooms and he could make out figures moving around inside. A large swimming pool was illuminated by a multitude of underwater lights, and there were several young females in the water, splashing about and generally having fun.

Off to one side a white-fenced corral surrounded a barn.

"Obviously the games haven't started yet," Riordan said, and Featherstone nodded.

"Don't see any dogs," said Featherstone, moving the night-vision binoculars slowly from building to building, "but there might be horses in the barn so we better stay away from there. There are two Orientals with guns sitting out on the back patio beside the pool, but they're just having a quick fag. There are some girls in the pool, and there's one large table with a canopy blocking my view. Looks like there might be some people sitting out there. Here, have a look."

Riordan took the proffered glasses and focused in on the house. Beside him, Capo and Tosser were doing their own survey, and muttering about what would be the best approach and covering arcs of fire and how evil it would be to be bitten on the dick by a snake. "That's when you find out how good your friends really are," said Tosser. "Somebody would have to suck out the poison."

"Well you better be careful tonight," replied Capo. "Cos' if you get bitten on the willie you're going to die!"

"Would you two shut the fuck up!" hissed Featherstone in an exasperated tone of voice. "I'm trying to think."

A sharp movement at the house caught Riordan's eye, and he moved the binoculars to the patio doors that had just opened. His breath caught in his throat. Slade and the man with one hand were there, and Slade was pointing over to one of the buildings beside the barn. As Riordan watched, Slade lit up a huge cigar and stared up into the hills directly at the position where he was lying. Riordan shivered. It was as if Slade knew where he was.

The man carried the package off towards the building, and Slade went and spoke quietly to the guards, then went over to the table that was hidden by the canopy. There were obviously people there because Riordan could see Slade grinning and looking over his shoulder back to the pool. The girls had clearly not been ill treated yet, as there was no trace of fear on any of their faces when Slade walked past. One of them even splashed him with water.

"I'd feel better if I knew how many guards there were," commented Featherstone. "I hate surprises."

"We have the element of surprise on our side," Riordan commented. "Besides, I'm going down there and anything that's not a young runaway is going to die. Those murdering bastards who have paid for the girls are every bit as bad as Slade so the world won't shed too many tears if one or two of them get wasted. If you have any problem with this just say so and I'll go down on my own."

"Okay, okay," said Featherstone, to the group. "This is what we'll do. Daniel and I will go around the right-hand side of the house and you two can go in the front door–it appears to be open. Then we can catch them in a crossfire. Switch on your comms units."

Following a quick check of the equipment, Capo and Tosser moved off into the night towards one side of the house, and Featherstone and Riordan went in the other direction. Riordan received a constant update from the others through the combined transmitter/receiver in his ear, and the house was soon looming in front of them. It was much, much larger than he had estimated when they got up close, and he moved into the side wall where there was no light, merging with the shadows. The silenced MP5K was up and ready, the fire selector switch set to three round bursts and his finger tightened on the trigger.

He felt the flashbang grenades bounce against his chest.

His heart hammered.

"In position boss," came the message.

"Go," whispered Featherstone, and motioned for Riordan to move around the side of the house.

Riordan took two steps and suddenly there was a deafening roar from inside the house as the Semtex charges lobbed by Tosser and Capo exploded, shattering windows and hurling jagged pieces of glass like daggers across the patio. The girls in the pool screamed in fright and Riordan stepped around the corner of the house followed by Featherstone.

The two Orientals reacted quickly and were on their feet, had their guns out and were already moving towards the house. Riordan cut the two guards down in a flash by firing a three round burst into the back of each man, then stepped out on to the patio and fired burst after burst at the group of men sitting on the bench. The MP5K was surprisingly quiet, the only sound coming from the shell casings rattling on the patio stones. The bolt locked back when the magazine ran dry. Riordan ejected the magazine, slammed in a fresh one, pulled back the cocking arm and continued firing.

Featherstone was across the patio in an instant, kicking away the guns from the guards, and firing a round into each head for good measure. There was little motion from the other side of the pool and Featherstone efficiently dispatched any survivors from Riordan's original assault.

Riordan, hot on his heels, quickly surveyed the carnage and just as quickly realized that Slade was not amongst the shattered bodies. The girls in the pool were huddled together like frightened animals. "We've come to get you out," said Riordan. "Stay where you are until we come back!"

Shots erupted from inside the house, there were two more explosions and suddenly the entire house was pitched into darkness. The reports at first came from small arms, and then Riordan heard the ugly crack of an AK47 on full auto. Things were escalating, and not in their favour. Curtains at the front entrance caught on fire, and the smoke alarms went off with an ear-piercing wail. Given that Capo and Tosser had silenced weapons, Riordan realized that there were more guards who had not yet been eliminated.

"Sitrep," called Featherstone, sliding his night vision goggles back up on to his head. Riordan did the same.

"Found a couple more guards inside watching television," replied Capo, breathlessly. "They went nighty-night. There are three more upstairs and they've got us pinned down at the moment. No sign of Slade."

"Fuck!" Riordan exclaimed. "Don't take too long. If this place is anything like the house on the island he'll have wired it to explode too."

An upstairs window shattered and the barrel of an AK47 appeared. Before the man could fire, Featherstone loosed off a burst, there was a scream and the weapon fell to the ground. Unpinning one of his fragmentation grenades, Featherstone stepped back and lobbed it through the shattered window. A heartbeat later there came a huge explosion and the firing from upstairs ceased.

"Good work boss," came Capo's voice. "You've got them all. We're checking the rooms now."

Featherstone stepped into the main house and fired a round into the fire alarm. "I hate those fucking things," he said. "I wonder where Slade went."

"If it's anything like the last time he's probably bolted," Riordan said, his voice hard. He could feel the frustration building. They had been so close, so close. "I'm going to go over this place inch by inch, but I think the bastard's gotten away again. He doesn't strike me as the type to stand and fight, but just in case, I'm going to go over to check the building beside the barn."

Featherstone nodded and said, "I'll go and help the lads clear the house."

Riordan ran out of the house and across to the other building beside the stables. The girls still cowered in fear in the pool. The horses in the stables had been spooked by the explosions, and skittered restlessly in their stalls. Riordan opened the door to the building and stepped inside. The room had a greenish hue through the night-vision goggles, but he could see that it had been outfitted with the same type of computer equipment as Slade's previous house on the island.

The equipment was all up and working with a variety of pornographic screen-savers running on the monitors. Riordan guessed that the room probably had an alternate power source or a UPS that was not connected to the mains. He pulled down the PNV's and scanned the interior. In one corner of the room a tiny 14-inch TV/VCR combination unit was on and the videotape which Riordan had put in the mail was playing. An armchair sat in front of the television.

Riordan slipped off one of his gloves and placed the back of his hand on the seat. It was warm. He slipped the glove back on, ever wary of leaving fingerprints. A bottle of baby-oil lying on the floor leaked slowly an ever-increasing puddle. On the television a pre-pubescent girl dressed in a school uniform and wearing her hair in pigtails was on her knees on front of a much older man. Riordan fired a round into the television, causing the picture tube to explode in a shower of sparks. At the same time a noise came from one corner of the room. Riordan spun around and walked over to a large sofa, pulled it away from the wall and cowering behind it was Dickson, completely naked. He immediately started whimpering.

"Please, please don't hurt me," Dickson said, one hand covering his genitals and his stump protecting his head. His hand was shiny with baby-oil.

Riordan, the image of the young girl fresh in his mind, switched the fire-selector switch to full auto and emptied the remains of the magazine into the man's head. "All clear here," came a voice through the earpiece.

"Clear here too," said Riordan, replacing the magazine with a full one. He opened a door at the side of the computer room and stepped through into a large bedroom with a king-size bed sitting on a dais in the center. He shivered. This was the killing room. He flipped a switch and the lights came on, bright glaring lights for the video-cameras mounted high in the four corners and the others mounted on free-standing tripods. He closed his eyes for a moment, thankful they had gotten here before the room could be used.

Hearing a noise behind him, he raised his pistol and turned to see Featherstone step through into the room, smoke curling from the silencer on his weapon. Featherstone shook his head at the sight. "Jesus, too bad we missed the bastard again. On the positive side though, all the law enforcement agencies in the United States will be after him now as well as those in Canada. They'll get him eventually."

"That's not much comfort to me, and anyway I'm not so sure," Riordan replied grimly. "Having a fuckin' psychopath on the loose who wants to kill me and my family doesn't exactly hold a lot of appeal. He is one slippery bastard as he has proven once or twice already. But enough of the chat, we better get out of here just in case it's wired for explosives. We can call the police when we're on our way back up north, and if we go up through Santa Maria like you suggested, we can get off this greasepaint and re-pack our weapons." Featherstone nodded in agreement.

"You might want to call the safe-house and let Jean-Marc know what has happened," Riordan said, putting the empty magazine back into his pocket. "I realize it's a bit of a long shot but with this bastard Slade you never know. But don't say anything to Nancy yet. I don't want her to worry."

"Don't worry, Daniel," Featherstone said reassuringly, flipping on the safety catch on his weapon. "There's no way that Slade can get to the safe house. Besides, it's not in Vancouver."

"No?" said Riordan. "I thought it was."

Featherstone shook his head. "It's a summer cottage up on Lake Joseph. I bought it in my mother's maiden name so that there's no connection back to me or the firm. She visits several times during the year and when I need it she goes off down to Florida for a few days, to another condominium she sort of owns down there. There are only ten cottages on the lake and the neighbors, some of Vancouver's rich and famous, really like their privacy. Only a few people know about the place, and I'm quite sure Nancy has no idea where she is."

In the basement of the house, which was now smoldering as Capo and Tosser had used extinguishers to put out the flames, Slade watched and listened to Riordan and Featherstone on a video monitor. The room had been built as a secret extension to the rec room, and was well concealed behind a wall of bookshelves. None of the others knew about its existence. He had been fortunate to escape the carnage above by going down to his 'office' to retrieve some of the CD-ROM's from Dickson who was preparing a presentation for one of his new 'clients'.

At the sound of the first explosion, he had switched on the outside surveillance cameras and watched the black-clad, black-faced men execute his guards and clients. They were obviously pros, given the rate at which they had dispatched the guards, but it was not until he heard the voices from the bedroom that he realized that it was Riordan and Featherstone who had carried out the assault.

Grating his teeth together in fury, he could easily have destroyed the building that Riordan and Featherstone were standing in, but when he heard their discussion an evil grin split his face and his eyes glimmered with madness.

Riordan would die, but not yet.

Slade was going to kill his family first, and in front of him. Let him feel the heart-rending torment of seeing his children die, one by one, and then his wife.

And then Riordan.

Or perhaps not.

Perhaps he would let Riordan live for a little while with those images, let him be haunted to the point of madness and despair. Yes, that was a much better plan. Cut the bastard's eyes out so that the last images he had were those of his dead wife and children.

Slade opened a side passage that led up to the back of the garage. He opened his safe and emptied the contents, mostly high-denomination used bills, into a backpack. Then, taking his favorite katana, he slipped a pistol into the back of his pants and ran quietly up the stairs to the back of the garage where, behind the Toyota landcruisers, sat three dirt-bikes. Using the katana he slashed the tires of two of the bikes, rending pursuit impossible. Strapping on a crash helmet and a pair of night-vision goggles, he opened a door at the back of the garage and wheeled the remaining bike out into a gully running parallel to the left-hand side of the house.

He had already tested this route on several occasions to ensure that he could flee if necessary. In his chosen profession contingency plans were an obsession, which was how he had managed to keep one step ahead of his rivals. When he was far enough away from the building and well concealed behind a low rise of hills that would baffle the sound of the engine, he kicked the motorcycle into life and set off along a dirt trail, which several hundred yards ahead would bring him to the main road. In three hours he would be in San Francisco and once there he had access to a car and papers to get him back across the border into Vancouver.

CHAPTER 19

Styx

Slade crept along through the darkened trees, his footfalls masked by the spongy earth under his feet. It was like walking on a thick pile carpet. When he was about a hundred yards away from the cottage, he found a good vantage point and lay down. Mosquitoes whined past his ears but he ignored them. Even though it was almost midnight, the air was muggy and beads of perspiration trickled down his brow. A slow movement of his hand to wipe them away.

Light from the cottage spilled into the surrounding area. He put the tiny night vision binoculars to his eyes and focused on the large glass windows. Inside the building he could see Nancy Riordan, dressed in a pair of shorts and a baggy sweatshirt, sitting talking to a man who was probably a minder. A wry smile crossed Slade's face and his fingers reached back and touched the razor sharp Katana strapped to his back. His tongue flicked out like that of a snake and moistened his lips, an involuntary motion, anticipation of what was to come. He had never felt more alive.

Nancy Riordan did not pose a threat, so Slade focused his attention on the man. He was short and stocky, with a closely cropped military style haircut and as Slade watched, the man stood up slowly, one hand touching his left side as if it hurt him to move. In the back waistband of the man's jeans was a pistol, which looked like a beretta. Twelve shots, thought Slade. He moved his attention around the room to see if there were any more weapons in sight, but there was nothing visible. Good, that meant that they were not expecting any trouble, which indicated that there had to be guards somewhere in the woods.

Focusing the binoculars on the edge of the cottage, Slade began a slow arc into the woods, the darkness transformed into a greenish day by the image intensifier as he searched for the guards. From one clump of trees to the next he moved, pausing for a few seconds and then moving on. He was between one stand and another when suddenly there was a sharp motion that made him move the glasses back. Slade grinned. The guard was almost concealed in the bracken behind two large pine trees but was flicking his hand against his neck to kill a mosquito, the movement betraying his position. As Slade watched, the man moved a few inches and he saw the silenced machine pistol cradled in the man's arms.

Slade moved the binoculars again. There had to be at least on more guard–there was always one more somewhere. Featherstone was a pro, and would not leave a safehouse protected by only one guard. No, there would be at least one more, if not two. It took him only a few more minutes to identify the other guard, this one resting back against a tree, his head cradled by a forked branch. Through the binoculars Slade saw the man's head droop and then jerk back up as if startled. The man was falling asleep.

Slade watched the man fall asleep, waited a few minutes until he was certain that there would be no wakeups, then crept forward, slowly unsheathing the Katana. He could just as easily have used his pistol, which had a silencer, but the blade was much more personal. The ground under his feet was soft, silent and the sleeping guard did not hear him approach.

Taking a deep breath to focus himself, Slade swung the blade as hard as he could and felt a momentary resistance before the blade bit deep into the tree behind the guard. The man's head bounced on the ground and rolled away, blood pumping in great dark gouts from his neck. The torso remained erect for a few seconds and pitched forward but Slade had already crept off into the woods, and was circling around behind the other guard.

This guard was much more vigilant than the first, but continually slapped at mosquitoes that buzzed around his head. At each attack by the miniature pests the guard was momentarily distracted and Slade used the opportunity to creep forward to within a few feet of the man, all the while keeping a clump of trees partially blocking his view. In the darkness, even with his night vision, Slade had difficulty making out the man's presence. The man cursed under his breath, set down his rifle and walked behind the trees and unzipped his fly–obviously he did not want to stink out his observation post.

Slade could hardly believe his luck. A long stream hissed off into the darkness and splashed against the tree, and Slade stepped forward and thrust hard with the blade, penetrating the man's back and tearing through his heart and out through his chest. The man gave a sigh, like air escaping from a balloon, and his legs started to buckle. Slade ripped the blade back out in one fluid motion and waited until the man collapsed before wiping the Katana on the man's sweatshirt.

Lifting his head, he looked up towards the cottage and put the binoculars to his eyes. The couple inside were sitting down by the empty fireplace, the man reading a magazine while Nancy Riordan sewed the hem on a pair of pants. The television in the corner was turned off, but a faint melody reached Slade's ears.

Putting away the binoculars, he crept off into the trees and was immediately swallowed up by the darkness. The porch light was on, casting a yellowish glow across the steps leading to the door, but immediately beyond there was no light, only blackness. Slade stood outside the perimeter and peered into the room through large double-glazed windows. At the side of the house an air-conditioner clicked on and commenced a low hum, silencing the crickets for a brief moment. The couple had not moved, but were engaged in some amusing and animated conversation, the man throwing back his head and laughing loudly. Faint echoes of voices reached Slade's ear and he could tell that the man was French, probably one of the ex-commandos hired by Featherstone. Slade made it his business to know about his adversaries.

Slipping the Katana from its sheath, he crept across the moat of light and approached the steps, testing each one before putting his whole weight on the riser, like the movement of a cat. Adrenaline flowed, powered by the knowledge that he was close to getting his revenge on Riordan. First Riordan's wife, then his children, their heads lined up like trophies on the table to greet him. And Slade would be there to see the expression on the bastard's face before Riordan too was dispatched.

Easing the handle on the front door, Slade cracked it open a fraction, released the handle and raised the blade. A deep breath and the door was kicked in. The man was rising from the couch but Slade was across the few feet in a heartbeat, the blade slicing downwards across the man's torso. The man said 'Merde,' his hands touched the bright red slash appearing diagonally on his shirt, and his legs buckled and he collapsed. Continuing the movement, Slade swung the heavy blade around toward Nancy Riordan, slapping her across the forehead with the flat of the blade. Her eyes rolled up into her head and she tumbled backwards into the chair, unconscious.

Slade ran for the stairs, taking them two at a time, kicking open each of the bedrooms, looking for the children, but the rooms were empty. Frowning, he walked back downstairs, blood dripping from the Katana. A huge red stain pooled on the carpet around the Frenchman, and Nancy Riordan was still unconscious. Slade snarled, a primitive feral noise, the hunter deprived of its prey. Then the phone rang, distracting him.

On instinct, more than anything else, he picked it up and said 'Oui?' A voice on the other end said, "Jean-Marc, it's Daniel. I've just put the teapot on. Come on over when you can. I'll put the dock light on." Slade hung up the phone, his mind racing, and he ran over to the windows facing the lake. A few lights were dotted here and there in the darkness, but then a row of lights came on in the distance, illuminating a small dock. A wide grin split Slade's face and he lifted the Katana and ran his tongue along the blade, savoring the blood of his enemy. Riordan was on the other side of the lake, and the children were probably there as well. Featherstone was trying to be too clever but he had been outsmarted.

Slade went over and pulled Nancy Riordan up so that her head was leaning over the back of the sofa with her throat exposed. He raised the blade once more.

A few minutes later he was sitting in a tiny aluminum boat which had been docked at the back of the cottage, the engine chugging as it powered the craft across a dark, glassy lake, like the ferryman from the river Styx. In front of him sat a bloody head, glassy eyes staring out across the water. A present for Daniel Riordan.

One cottage down from the illuminated dock, Slade cut the engine a few feet from shore and glided into a dock. He got out, grabbed a handful of hair, and crept across a bed of pine needles to the other cottage. This time he had the pistol out; he did not want Riordan to die first. He wanted Riordan to see his children die before his eyes before Slade administered the coup de gras, probably with the katana. He waited by the tree line for a moment and saw Daniel Riordan step out through open patio doors on to the deck. Riordan peered out into the lake for a moment, swatted away some mosquitoes, and went back into the house. When Riordan's back was turned, Slade sprinted across the clearing, up the steps and into the cottage. Riordan started to turn on hearing the footsteps.

"Don't fucking move," hissed Slade, pointing his gun directly at Riordan's chest, and swung his other arm, tossing the head on to the floor at Riordan's feet. Riordan's face went white, and his eyes narrowed with anger.

"You fucking animal," Riordan spat, and Slade grinned.

To the left of both men a door swung open, and Nancy Riordan backed into the room holding a tray on which there was a pot of tea and several mugs.

"Was that Jean-Marc I heard?" she said, and turned around, saw Slade, saw the head and recoiled in horror, dropping the tray onto the floor.

China shattered.

Riordan felt a cold fury inside at the sight of Christine's head. Such an indignity to cause to another human being, but he realized the mistake Slade had made, one which he himself had made only a few weeks earlier and wondered if it had been a deliberate ploy on Featherstone's part. The safe house had actually turned out to be two houses, a mis-statement by Featherstone. He felt the pressure from his Browning in the small of his back but there was no time to draw the gun, even though Slade had been distracted by Nancy.

He had one chance.

Flexing his wrist, he felt the ceramic blade slide down into his hand and he whipped his arm up, the blade flying across the room like a projectile. Slade saw the motion and immediately started to swing the pistol back around, but the knife found its mark, embedding itself deeply in Slade's wrist. Slade screamed, the pistol dropped to the floor and Riordan had his weapon drawn in a heartbeat, the barrel wavering in Slade's direction. Slade tore the knife from his shattered wrist and tossed it aside angrily.

Nancy Riordan turned to her husband, fury blazing from her eyes, and said, "Kill him Daniel, kill the bastard. He wanted my children dead."

Riordan's expression did not change. Inside he felt calm, at peace, the adrenaline rush having abated as the situation came under his control. The gun still pointed casually in Slade's direction and Riordan could see the man sizing up his situation. In Slade's position, Riordan knew he would be doing exactly the same. Spots of blood seeped through Slade's fingers where he had a tight grip of his injured wrist. The man exuded menace, like a large jungle cat forced into a corner. A sneer crossed Slade's face.

"Yes, Daniel," Slade spat, mimicking Nancy's words. "Why don't you shoot me? Or don't you have the balls for it? Those other guys wouldn't give it a second thought but you, you're different. You're not one of them."

"That's true," Riordan said, raising the pistol.

Two shots rang out, blurring into one another, and two cartridges danced a brief staccato beat on the wooden floor of the cottage. Gunpowder fumes filled the air, smoke twisting lazily up from the gun barrel like a cigarette burning in an ashtray.

"I'm much worse," said the Raven.

ISBN 141201610-X